RUFF'D UP

RUFF'D UP

A Melanie Bass Mystery

CHRISTINE FALCONE

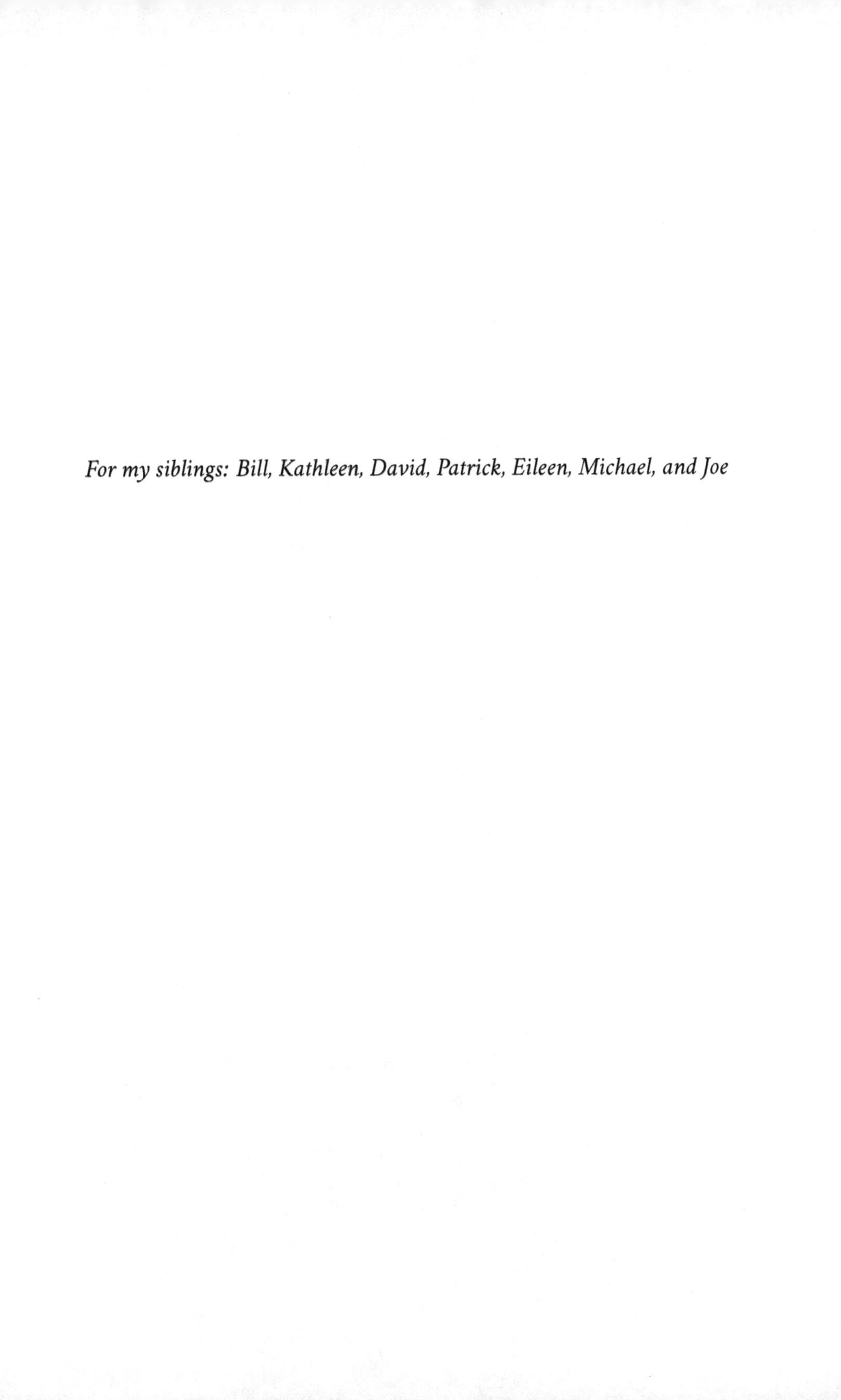

For my siblings: Bill, Kathleen, David, Patrick, Eileen, Michael, and Joe

Praise for Ruff'd Up

"Fast-paced, emotionally charged, and packed with heart, *Ruff'd Up* delivers a twisty mystery with a fearless heroine you'll root for to the last page."—**Lucy Burdette**, *USA Today* bestselling author

Chapter One

I was alarmed when my first patient after lunchtime, Kelly Monet, answered the door. She was flushed, and I could see that she was trembling. My first thought was that she was reacting to the meds she was taking after her kidney transplant, or that she had an infection. It had been an unusually warm June in Connecticut, but I could feel the cool air wafting out from the air conditioning in her house, so I was confident she wasn't just affected by the hot day.

"Are you feeling all right, Mrs. Monet? We should have a seat so I can take your vital signs," I said.

"I'm not okay, but it has nothing to do with my health." I could see the tears starting to pool in her eyes. "It's Corky. She's gone."

I searched my memory, trying to remember if I ever knew the names of her children.

She motioned me into her living room and collapsed on her sofa. I took a seat opposite her. "Corky is—"

"Corky is our puppy. I took her out to do her business. She was taking a long time, sniffing every blade of grass. I left my phone inside, and I was expecting a call from my son's teacher about whether he needs to attend summer school, so I went back in to get it. I was only gone for a couple of minutes, and when I came back outside, Corky was gone! The gate was open a crack. I must have forgotten to pull it all the way closed this morning; the latch sticks sometimes."

I could understand her panic. If my dog, Bruno, had wandered off, I'd be equally upset. "When did this happen? She might be just sniffing around your neighbor's yard. I can help you look for her. What does she look like?"

"She's a golden retriever, six months old." She shook her head. "I've already called all my neighbors, but no one has seen her." She started to tear up again. "What will I tell the kids? We got Corky to help them cope with my being so sick before I got my kidney. What will Hank say—we paid the breeder a huge amount for her."

I couldn't bear to ask her if she had checked the roadsides in her neighborhood—that would be the worst thing I could imagine. "Let me check your surgical site and take your vital signs, and then we can think of what we need to do next to find Corky." I made a note that Kelly was upset at the time I took her blood pressure to explain its slight elevation.

I stayed with Kelly while she called the police and the dog pound to report her missing puppy.

When she ended the call, she said, "The officer I spoke to was sympathetic, and he said they would keep an eye out for her, but I could hear a lot of noise in the background, like there was something going on. He sounded a little rushed." She put her phone down on the table beside her. The dejected look on her face told me she didn't have a lot of hope the police would have much time to look for her dog.

I had to leave to make it to my next appointment, but before I did, I suggested she post a lost dog notice on social media. "There's a possibility she wandered farther than you thought, and someone has seen her. In the meantime, please try to stay calm, and remember you need to rest and recover from your own health issues." I felt terrible leaving her. I had had an episode where my dog, Bruno, was missing and could remember how frantic I was to get him back.

As I drove slowly down her road toward the home of Mrs. Paine, who was next on my patient list, I searched for any sight of a spunky blonde ball of fur. I thought of the fact that I had noticed quite a few postings on Facebook lately of missing pets in the surrounding towns. It seemed as if either people were not being as mindful of the local leash laws as they should have been, or they underestimated the ability of their pets to break free of their yards and follow their natural inclination to explore. I'd have to ask my boyfriend,

Justin, if he thought of having his veterinary practice start a campaign to encourage pet owners to get their pets microchipped.

I also wondered what was going on that caused the police station to be in an apparent uproar when Kelly Monet called to report her missing dog.

For the first time since I had known her, Mrs. Paine was hesitant to open her front door when I rang her bell. She pulled it open a crack, leaving the security chain in place as she peered out at me as if to make sure I really was who I said I was.

"Oh, hello, Melanie. Let me take off the chain." She briefly closed the door, then opened it again and motioned me to quickly step inside. She was lacking her usual smile and looked more tired than usual.

"Are you feeling all right, Mrs. Paine? You look a bit shaky." Despite her eighty-four years, Katherine Paine was one of the most cheerful and lively of my patients. She had a history of congestive heart failure but had been doing very well for the past several months.

She did smile then, but it was more rueful than happy. "Well, I am feeling a bit shaky." She held up a hand as if to restrain me as I reached for her to steady her. "No, I'm okay on my feet, it's just…you heard about what happened to Ada Watkins two days ago? How some gang of hooligans broke into her house in the middle of the day, held a gun on her, robbed her, and beat her up?" Mrs. Paine sat on the edge of one of the easy chairs in her living room and motioned for me to also take a seat.

"Yes. I did hear about that incident. It was horrible. It happened in Branford, right?"

Mrs. Paine nodded. "Ava is a friend of mine. I play bridge with her once a week." She shook her head, "She lives alone. Like me. The same thing happened to a man in Cheshire a month ago. I read about it in the paper. He was in his late eighties. I didn't sleep a wink last night thinking about it."

I could see why Mrs. Paine was upset. "I think it's a good idea that you're being cautious about who you let in, Mrs. Paine. I'm very sorry that happened to your friend and that these awful incidents are upsetting you."

She sighed, "I always prided myself on being pretty fearless, but now… I don't know." She straightened up then, and said, "I'll tell you one thing, though, I think I would put up a pretty good fight if they tried to get in here. Did I ever tell you I skated roller derby when I was younger? Only for two years, but my name was Kat-tastrophy. You know, because my name is Katherine."

"No. I never knew that! I thought you were a teacher." Mrs. Paine's stories of her younger years never failed to amaze me.

"Oh, I was, but first I was a Derby Queen. I even had a reputation, you know. Then I met Thomas, my husband, and that was the end of my skating career. My priorities changed." She smiled as if thinking of something, then said, "Maybe I'll tell you the whole story another time."

Despite her history, the very thought of her trying to fight off intruders alarmed me. "I believe you, Mrs. Paine, but I think the best tactic is to continue to be cautious. Call the police right away if you think that someone is lurking around."

"I will."

"Promise?"

She nodded, and I said, "Okay. Let me check your blood pressure, and you tell me how you're feeling, other than angry and nervous."

"I feel fine, really. After you check me out, let me get you some tea and cookies. I just finished baking before you got here."

I was glad that Mrs. Paine did turn out to be doing fine, but I had to get to my next appointment and had to decline her offer of tea and cookies. "Remember, keep the door locked, and check who is there before you answer, just as you have been. I'm sure the police will catch whoever is responsible for these break-ins soon."

I really hoped they would. A good number of my patients were elderly, and so far, it seemed they were the age group being targeted by these thugs. I made a mental note to check with Sunny Cody; I was sure her department was working to help the other local police departments in solving the crimes. I began to wonder if the commotion at the department this morning had anything to do with the home invasions.

Chapter Two

When I got home, I thought about Kelly Monet and her missing dog again, and I gave Bruno some extra hugs and kisses. I decided to call her and see if her puppy had been found yet.

My heart sank when she answered the phone. I could hear someone crying in the background. "I was thinking about you and wondered if you found Corky yet."

"No, not yet. I posted on Facebook like you suggested, and a few people responded, but the dog they saw wasn't Corky. My husband is taking the kids to drive around the neighborhood again and see if they can spot her." She paused for a few seconds, then lowered her voice, "A few of the people who commented on my post said they were missing their pets also, one of them swears there was no way her dog could get out of her yard. One person said she captured something on her ring camera where it looked like someone was calling her dog over to them, but whoever it was wasn't on camera."

I had a sinking feeling that I knew what she was thinking. I heard her say goodbye to her husband and children as they left to look for Corky, then she said to me, "Do you think someone may have taken Corky?"

"I'm afraid that is one possibility. When you called the police did the officer mention that they have had multiple reports of missing dogs?"

"As I told you this morning, he didn't say much; he seemed busy and just said they would notify me if anyone reported finding a puppy." I could hear the strain in her voice. "If someone did take her, do you think there's any chance that we could get her back?"

"I'm sure it is possible." I didn't go into the story of how I had gone through a similar situation. My circumstances didn't involve a random dognapping.

I heard her sigh. "Thank you for checking on us. I'll let you know if we find her."

As soon as our call ended, I googled "stolen dogs," but what I found out did not prove comforting. While some dogs were recovered, many were never found again. A cute puppy like Corky could easily be sold online. I refused to think about the other possibilities, such as sale to an unregistered breeder or a dog-fighting ring.

My thoughts were interrupted by Bruno running to the front door, his tail wagging madly. There was a quick knock, and then my friend, Lynn, walked in. After greeting Bruno, she said, "I took a chance you would be home now. I'm going out for wine and cheese with a few of the women who work at High Life Derm. I haven't seen them in a couple of months, and the office manager, Bethany, called me to see if I wanted to join them. I was hoping you might want to come along."

I felt a night out with the girls might lighten my mood after worrying about lost dogs and home invasions. "Sure. Justin is working late tonight, so I don't have any plans. Just let me feed and walk Bruno first."

"Good. I'll walk with you."

I grabbed Bruno's leash, and we set off. "Speaking of High Life, have you spoken with Alex lately?" Lynn had called off her wedding to one of the physicians at High Life Dermatology after a particularly serious disruption in their relationship. However, they did still stay in touch.

"I've talked to him a couple of times, but I think now we both realize that it was good we cancelled the wedding. Not only because of everything surrounding what happened, but also because we weren't as suited to each other as we first thought." She smiled ruefully, "I'm just glad I stopped working as a receptionist at High Life Dermatology when I did."

"Yes, that would be an uncomfortable situation," I said. "You've kept in touch with some of the other receptionists, though, I see."

She shook her head, "Not really. I suspect that this outing might be about pumping me for info on whether Alex and I are really through, and maybe to share a little gossip." She looked at me, "So once again, I am glad you'll be along for emotional support."

Lynn was right about what the theme of the evening would be. She made it clear early on that she and Alex were not getting back together, though. Talk soon turned to what was going on with the other partners in the practice. I knew them all, as my now deceased ex-husband, Artie Krapaneck, was one of the founding partners. I was glad to hear that Rachel Harwood was back full-time after a family emergency, and that Bobby Wang and his wife would be welcoming a new addition to the family in the fall.

My ears perked up when Bethany said, "Speaking of additions to the family, can you believe Malcolm Devlin got a dog!"

"Malcolm got a dog?" I put the wine glass I had just picked up back down on the table. "I never pictured him being responsible for another living thing. Well, other than his patients."

She laughed, "Yes, he got a very sweet bulldog. He is totally smitten. He got her from a friend of a friend. Supposedly, the guy he bought her from knows someone who breeds bulldogs."

Perhaps because of what had happened this morning, my antenna immediately went up. "Did Malcolm get paperwork with her and everything?"

Bethany shrugged, "I don't know. I don't think he cares if she is AKC registered or not, he calls her 'his girl.'"

Sandy piped in, "He told me to be on the lookout for her papers. He said the seller is supposed to mail the documents to the office." With that, the talk turned to how good the wine was and what everyone was reading at the moment.

I told myself that there was no reason to suspect anything unethical about where Malcolm got his dog, but after the research I'd done earlier, I found I kept thinking about unscrupulous breeders and couldn't concentrate on the conversation any longer. I decided that I would call Malcolm and ask if he minded if I came to meet this new dog of his.

Neither Lynn nor I had eaten dinner, so after we said goodbye to Sandy and Bethany, we stopped at a diner to get something more substantial than cheese and crackers to eat before heading home. I thought it would also give us a chance to dissect the conversation of the evening. I could tell there was something on Lynn's mind. "Thank you for inviting me to come along. I don't know Sandy and Bethany well, but they seemed very nice."

Lynn snorted and turned to look at me. "Do you think I made it plain enough that Alex is now definitely back on the market?"

"Yes, I have to say that they seemed pleased to learn that. Does that bother you?"

"No." She laughed, "Well, maybe, but only a little. I always knew that at least two other women in the office had designs on him. I have no right now to care if he moves on."

"Still, it's natural for it to sting a little," I said.

We waited while our waitress put our pancakes down in front of us and made sure we didn't need anything else, then as she walked away, Lynn said, "I know I made the right decision, but I admit I do feel a bit of jealousy at the thought of Alex dating other women now." She paused a moment, then smiled ruefully at me, "But I've been through similar situations before, and I got over it."

I knew she was referring to her second husband, Doug, who immediately found someone else after they separated. I didn't even want to dwell on the fact she had been married to my ex, Artie, before he married me. "Well, I'm always willing to listen whenever you want to vent your feelings."

"The same goes for you. How are things going with Justin? He seems to be working late a lot of evenings recently."

She hit a nerve with that. I was discouraged that Justin had to put in so many hours at the veterinary practice of late. "I know. Dr. Reddy is cutting back his hours even more in preparation for retirement. They're looking for someone to take his place in the practice, but so far no one seems to be the right fit."

"Well, I hope they hire someone soon. Much as I love spending time with you, you need to see more of your man."

I laughed. "Really, we're fine. We agreed last fall that we would take things slow, that we wanted to be sure that our relationship would last. We both have busy lives, and..."

Lynn leaned across the table toward me. "Blah, blah, blah. That sounds like a lot of good relationship advice, and I know I'm not one to talk, but if you love the man, pin him down!"

"I do love Justin, and I know you're just looking out for my happiness, but I don't feel right pressuring him. I want him to commit of his own free will."

Lynn leaned back against the booth we were sitting in. "Why do you think he is so hesitant? You never mentioned if he was engaged or married before."

"He wasn't. I think he was close to getting engaged in graduate school, but the woman was killed." I didn't want to go into the whole story that Justin told me about how she had been shot when mistaken for someone else.

Lynn's eyes widened, "Okay, that is pretty traumatic. Still, I would think that gives him even more reason he would want to make sure he didn't lose you, too."

"I know——"

"All right. I'll drop the subject for now. But if you need me to give him a nudge, just let me know."

We had been talking for quite a while when I looked at my watch and realized how late it was. "This was just what I needed tonight, but I can hardly keep my eyes open now. Maybe it's time we headed home."

Lynn stifled a yawn. "I think you're right. At least I don't have an art class to teach until noon tomorrow. I hope you don't have an early patient, though."

"Lucky for me, I'm off," I said.

As she drove me to my house, we both expressed disbelief that Malcolm Devlin would become so devoted to a dog. This led to me telling her about the Monets' missing puppy.

"Poor thing, I hope she's found soon," she said. "You said Mrs. Monet thinks the puppy escaped through the open gate?"

"That's what she thought at first, but—wait. Slow down." We were only a few houses from mine by now. "Did you see that? It looked like someone walking around toward the back of the Feldmans' house." While not totally secluded, the road I live on is well off the main road.

Lynn slowed to a stop. "No. Are you sure you saw something? It's late, but could it be their son coming to check on them?" Lynn knew the Feldmans from when she was my housemate, and we would walk Bruno. They're an elderly couple, and Ernie Feldman had a stroke several years earlier, leaving him with mobility issues. Lana always waved to us as she tended to her front garden.

"Their son usually comes on Wednesdays, and it is awfully late. I know I'm tired, but I'm sure I saw someone," I said.

"Let's see if we can get a better look," Lynn said. We were just past their house, but she put the car in reverse and then pulled into the Feldmans' driveway. The house itself was dark, as if Lana and Ernie had already gone to bed. The headlights on her car illuminated the front and one side of their house. "I don't see anything," she said.

"I don't either, but maybe we'd better call the police to come and check the property." I had just pulled out my phone to call when a huge buck came barreling around from the other side of the house, causing both of us to yelp in surprise.

"He scared the devil out of me," Lynn said, her hand to her heart.

"Me too!" I laughed.

"That must be what you saw," Lynn said.

"I don't know. It didn't look like a deer. I could have sworn it was a man."

"It's late, and we're both tired. Are you sure?"

I hesitated before answering. "I don't know. I was talking with a patient this morning about the recent home invasions that are in the news. I guess I could still have that on my mind. We'd better go before we wake the Feldmans."

When we pulled into my driveway, Lynn waited for me to go inside before she left. Normally, I would have told her she didn't have to. I could hear Bruno's bark signaling all was secure, but this time, I was glad she'd waited.

Chapter Three

The following morning, as I was eating breakfast I heard the approach of sirens. I wasn't sure at first, but it sounded like the sirens stopped somewhere on my road. I peeked out my front window but couldn't see where they went. After I finished eating, I grabbed Bruno's leash in preparation to take him for his morning walk. We started toward where I'd heard the sirens earlier, and I realized they had stopped at the Feldmans' house. Three police cars were parked in front, and an ambulance was just pulling away. The Feldmans' son, Roger, was out in front of his parents' house, talking to a police officer. He looked distraught.

Bruno and I rushed over to where he was speaking with Officer Bridges. "Roger, is everything all right?"

"Someone broke into my parents' house last night. I came early this morning to check on mom and dad, and I found them. They—" he paused as if to gain control of himself, "my mother is all bruised; they hit her and tied her up. She told me my dad tried to fight back with one of his canes. He's in pretty bad shape."

I felt a sinking in my stomach. "I was driving by with my friend last evening, and I thought I saw someone or something go toward the backyard. We pulled in to get a better look, and a deer came around the house. I thought that was what I saw." I had to fight now to get the words past the lump in my throat. "I wish now I had gotten out of the car to investigate further."

I could see a flash of anguish cross Roger's face. "Why…"

Officer Bridges interrupted him, "No, it's better you didn't. You could have been accosted by the perpetrators and injured also." He took a pen and pad out of his pocket and said, "What time did you drive by? Could you give me a description of exactly what you saw?"

"It was a little before midnight. It looked like a man, large and dressed in dark clothes. But it was dark, and I was tired. When the deer came running from the back of the house, I thought I was mistaken, and what I saw wasn't a man."

"All right. Well, if you remember any other details at all, let me know." I could see the disappointment on his face. He turned to Roger, "I need to check with the rest of the officers and see if they were able to find anything inside to help identify who could have done this." He strode toward the Feldmans' front door, then turned and said to me, "You know, we're glad to check on any suspicious activity; you can always feel free to call. Even if you think it could just be an animal."

I knew he had meant well, but what Officer Bridges said added to my self-reproach. When I thought about it, that deer was acting as if it was frightened by something. In spite of what Officer Bridges said, if I'd gone around to the back of their house, I might have been able to scare the intruders away, or if they had already done their damage, I could have gone into the house and done something to help Lana and Ernie. Roger interrupted my thoughts.

"My mother said it was around midnight when they broke in, so that is consistent with what you saw. They jimmied the lock on the slider in back. My mother said she had just gotten up to use the bathroom and thought she heard a noise coming from the kitchen. She thought it was the cat up on the counter again, and she went to check." I could hear the strain in his voice. "When she turned on the light, the intruders were already inside."

"Was she able to give the police a description of them?"

Roger shook his head, "Not much. She said they were wearing face coverings and blue surgical gloves. She said there were three people. Two were big, over six feet, and burly. She said one of them looked to be not as large and seemed to be hanging back at first." He paused for a moment, then said, "She said one had a baseball bat and another a knife. They tied her up and threw her onto the sofa. They told her if she screamed, they'd kill her. My dad must have heard the commotion and shuffled out using his walker and brandishing his cane. One of the big ones hit him, knocking him down." He paused again, drawing a deep breath, "Mom said while one of them started grabbing valuables, the other was holding some kind of cloth bag and kept looking under and around furniture like he was looking for something specific."

"She didn't know what it was?"

He shook his head. "There was some sort of ruckus when the cat jumped out from behind the sofa, and one of them stepped on it. The one with the knife seemed angry with him, and finally said, 'Never mind that, just grab her purse and whatever else you found and let's get out of here.' Then he told Mom she better give them their ATM password or he would 'finish' the old man. They gagged my mother before they left. She could barely breathe when I found her this morning. My dad was on the floor. He—" Roger shook his head, "I don't know why my dad didn't just call 911 when he heard the noise." I could see tears in his eyes now.

"Would you like to come and sit for a few minutes at my house? Maybe have a cup of coffee?" I asked.

He shook his head, "No, thank you. If the police are done with me, I need to get to the hospital and check on my parents."

"Of course. Let me know if there is anything I can do."

Just then, a police officer came out of the house. "I'm sorry, Mr. Feldman, no luck finding her. She's probably scared and just hiding. We can check again later."

Roger said, "Yes, please! My mother will be devastated if her cat isn't found on top of what they went through last night. She loves that cat. My dad bought it for her for their fiftieth wedding anniversary. It's a pure-bred Russian Blue."

I remembered Mrs. Feldman once mentioning that they had a cat, though I had never seen it. I knew how much a pet can be a comfort during stressful times, and I felt even worse for Mrs. Feldman that she didn't have hers to console her. "As the officer said, I'm sure your mother's cat is just scared. She'll come out later when all the commotion in the house has settled down."

Up until now, Bruno had been very patient, sitting at my feet while I spoke to Roger Feldman, but he had begun to get restless, eager to get on our way. "Please let me know if you need help with anything, and give my best to your parents."

Roger nodded, "Thanks. I will."

Bruno and I finished our walk, but the whole way I vacillated between anger at the criminals who had done such a thing, and regret that I hadn't investigated further what I thought I saw the previous night.

As Bruno and I neared our house, I could see my next-door neighbor, Karen, out in her front yard. She called me over. "You see what was going on down the street? It looked like it might have been at the Feldmans' house. Ernie all right?"

I told her what had happened and watched as a look of horror, then anger spread over her face. "I knew it! I saw a strange van driving down the road the other day, going slow like they were looking for something. I bet they were scoping out who lives where. You know Lana is always out in her garden. I'm sure they pegged her for an easy mark!"

She had obviously jumped to conclusions, but what she said did seem like it could be true. "Did you see who was driving the suspicious van?"

She shook her head. "No. It was a panel van, and the sun was reflecting off the windshield when it passed my house. So, I couldn't see who was driving."

That was too bad, even if it turned out the driver of the van was not involved in the home invasion, it would have given the police a place to start. "What kind of van was it?"

"White, there was no writing on the side. I wish I'd gotten the license plate number."

The previous night, I hadn't noticed any unusual vehicles parked on the road or in the Feldmans' driveway, so there probably was no way to connect the van Karen saw to one belonging to whoever was responsible for the break-in.

"Do you think I should call the police and tell them what I saw?" Karen asked.

My feelings of guilt over not doing that very thing the previous night weighed on me. I was in no mood to dismiss anything anyone saw that was unusual. "Yes, it might turn out to be helpful."

She nodded, "Okay. Make sure you keep your doors locked. I'm going to do the same. It's just terrible that you aren't safe in your own home these days."

I took Bruno back into the house and called Lynn to let her know what happened.

She was as sickened by the attack on the Feldmans as I had been. "So, you really did see someone last night. Those poor people!"

"If only I had called the police like I planned to or gotten out of the car to check."

"No. I agree with the police. You could have been another victim. Even if I had gone with you, we would have been overpowered. If anyone should feel guilty it's me. You said you thought it was a man, and I questioned that. I'm sorry."

"I've been in enough tight situations in the past year to trust my instincts. I should have reported what I thought I saw, no matter what."

"Let's just hope the Feldmans recover and they catch whoever did this." Lynn sighed and then said, "I need to leave to teach an art class now. Let me know if you hear how Lana and Ernie are doing, or if you hear anything more about the break-in."

After I talked to Lynn, I called the hospital and learned that Lana was in stable condition, but Ernie was in the ICU in guarded condition.

I knew he might be busy, but I took a chance that I could catch Justin between patients and called the vet practice. I was in luck.

"What happened? I can tell by the tone of your voice that something is bothering you," he said.

I told him about the break-in at the Feldmans', and how I had thought I saw someone lurking there last evening. "I should have gone with my gut instinct. I should've called the police. Now Lana and Ernie are in the hospital, and there's a gang of criminals somewhere who got away with it." I took a deep breath, "I feel terrible."

Justin's voice was calm as he answered, "It was not your fault; the blame lies squarely on the creeps who did this. I'm really glad you didn't try to investigate what you saw; you could have been seriously hurt. I'm also worried. Like you said, who knows where these crooks are now and if they will circle back to your neighborhood. You need—"

"I know. I need to be extra careful. I will, don't worry."

"Okay. Well…I can hear my next patient raising a racket in the waiting room. I need to go, but I'll call you later."

After I ended my call with Justin, I stepped outside to look up the road toward the Feldmans' house and saw that all the police cars had gone. It was a gorgeous early summer day, but I found I wasn't able to enjoy it now. Just as Karen said, our quiet neighborhood didn't seem safe anymore.

Chapter Four

I spent the rest of the morning on a series of necessary, but mundane tasks: grocery store, hardware store for screws to repair the loose handle on a kitchen cabinet, and a birthday card for my co-worker Debbie. I tried to concentrate on each task, but I had to struggle to put what happened to the Feldmans out of my mind. I kept trying to remember exactly what I saw, but as I told Officer Bridges, I had only the impression of a hulking man-shaped form at the side of their house, nothing specific.

Once I was home, I spent the afternoon outside in the yard weeding my garden and playing with Bruno. I thought about what Karen said about the intruders scoping out potential victims, and I felt a chill. Was it mostly the elderly they targeted, or were they also looking for women who lived alone? I shook off that thought quickly. Bruno ran up to me with his ball in his mouth.

"You'll protect me, won't you?" I reached down to scratch under his chin, then threw the ball and watched his little furry form as he retrieved it. He was small, but ferocious when he felt I was being threatened. That made me remember what Bethany said about Malcolm Devlin getting a dog. I was curious to see him with her, and thought paying them a visit might help me stop thinking about the previous night's break-in.

I called Malcolm to see if I could come to his house after he got home from the office.

"Melanie! How have you been?" He seemed surprised but pleased to hear from me.

We exchanged pleasantries for a few minutes, then I said, "What's this I hear about you getting a dog? I'd love to meet her."

"She's an angel! I never thought of myself as a dog person, but I dated a woman for a few months who had this little poodle mix. We broke up, but I found I still missed the dog." He laughed. "I'm free later this afternoon. If you want to stop over, we can catch up, and you can meet Daphne."

"That sounds great!" My spirits had already begun to lift. I felt a bit guilty leaving Bruno behind, but since I was meeting Malcolm's dog for the first time, I didn't want to presume she would be comfortable around other dogs.

Malcolm Devlin was one of the founding members of High Life Dermatology, along with Bobby Wang and my ex-husband Artie Krapaneck. Malcolm had been marginally involved in the illegal use of an anti-aging drug Artie was prescribing to his patients. It was a money-making practice that led to Artie's murder. Malcolm had tried to protect me from the fallout when he learned Artie had left clues to what the killers were after in my unknowing possession. He had to face some charges himself after the incident, but his legal problems were mostly behind him now. Ever since I'd known him, Malcolm had been a womanizer and a heavy drinker, but underneath it all, I believed him to be a good guy.

A chunky brown and white form greeted me when Malcolm answered his door. I bent down to pet her, "Hi! You are a little sweetheart, aren't you?"

"Here, Daphne, let her in." Malcolm guided the dog back into the house and reached out to give me a quick hug. "So glad you called. It's been a while. Come on in. You drink tea, right?" He led me toward the kitchen, Daphne waddling behind us.

I sat at his kitchen island as he made coffee and tea for us. "She really is adorable. How old is she? Where did you get her?"

"She's just over two years old. When I decided I missed having a dog around, I figured I'd go down to the shelter and pick up some mutt. But then a patient said he knew of a friend of a friend who had a bulldog he was selling. The guy was moving overseas or something and couldn't take the dog with him. My patient said I'd be doing the guy a big favor by taking the dog."

"So, he was willing to give the dog to you? That's wonderful." Daphne was sitting watching us as if she knew we were talking about her.

Malcolm set my tea down in front of me. "Well…he didn't exactly give her away. He did charge me a lot less than he said he paid for her, though." Malcolm looked down at his dog, and I could see the love in his eyes. "Once I saw her, how could I say no?"

I knew what he meant. "Anyway, I'm so glad you found each other." As if on cue, Daphne ran over to pick up a little stuffed rabbit and dropped it at Malcolm's feet.

After he tossed it for her, he said, "I have an appointment with that veterinarian boyfriend of yours in a couple of days to get her checked out. I want to also get her microchipped."

I thought about the Monets' missing puppy, Corky, and said, "That's a great idea. I know I'm biased, but you're going to really like Justin. He's wonderful with all his animal clients and always willing to answer any questions you may have. His partner, Dr. Reddy, is amazing, too."

Malcolm bent to pet Daphne. "That makes us feel better, doesn't it, girl?"

I spent another hour chatting with Malcolm and playing with Daphne, then realized it was time to head home to feed and walk my own dog. "Maybe sometime we could get Bruno and Daphne together for a play date," I said as Malcolm walked me to the door.

"That would be great. Give me a call, and we can set it up."

I felt much lighter as I drove home. It was good to see the soft side of Malcolm Devlin, and Daphne clearly adored him, which said a lot.

* * *

The next day, I had an appointment to do a health check on Justin's grandfather, Charlie Duggan. Charlie had mellowed a bit from when I first started following him for his type II diabetes, but he still intimidated most home health care providers. Since I was the only one he didn't give a hard time; his insurance agreed that I should be the one to do his yearly health and welfare assessment.

I didn't even get a chance to say hello when Charlie opened the door. "I heard on my scanner about that home invasion two days ago. That was right by you, wasn't it?"

He motioned for me to follow him into his living room.

"Yes. It was a neighbor's house." I hesitated before I continued, "Lynn and I were driving by right before it happened. I thought I might have seen someone lurking around there, but then we thought it was just a deer. I feel terrible about not having done something at the time."

Charlie had worked for over thirty years as a security guard and had a keen interest in law enforcement. I waited for him to chide me for not immediately reporting what I saw that night.

Instead, he said, "When I had been on the job for a year or so, I heard a clamor like a garbage can or something tipping over in the alley on the side of Wegley Manufacturing. I was working security there at the time. I went to look. Sure enough, there was a garbage can tipped over, and some rebar stacked against the building had been knocked down. Two tom cats darted out from behind some empty boxes and started hissing and clawing at each other. I figured it was them that knocked things over. Never even noticed then that a side window was open a crack. Turns out someone had broken in and stolen two thousand dollars' worth of equipment and supplies." He stopped and looked hard at me, "You see what I'm saying? It's easy to dismiss things when you find an easy explanation. I missed something big, and it was my job to see it!"

I felt like a weight had been lifted from my shoulders. "Thanks, Charlie."

"Now, let's get on with this health interview you gotta do so we can talk about how things are going with that grandson of mine. Any new developments?" He raised his eyebrows at me.

"Things are just fine the way they are for now. Never mind that, how are things going between you and Loretta?" Charlie had started seeing a widow he met at a senior citizen's function a few months prior. I had never met her, but from what Justin told me, she gave his rather cantankerous grandfather a run for his money.

He grinned. "Like you said, just fine. She got a connection over at the college in West Haven, wangled us an invite to sit in on one of the classes at the Henry Lee College of Criminal Justice and Forensics." He looked very pleased with himself. "It's just the one time, but that Loretta is a gem."

"Wow! Let me know what you learn. It sounds like Loretta has almost as many contacts as you do!"

"Yeah, well…"

After I filled out my assessment for Charlie's insurance, I said, "So what do you make of these home invasions lately? My neighbor seems to think that whoever it is sends out someone ahead of time to look for potential victims."

Charlie nodded, "Could be she's right. I always kept a lookout for people who 'accidentally' entered the business when I was working. I remember one guy in particular. He said he was looking for somewhere else, but I could see him scoping the place out while he kept asking me all kinds of questions. Things like how long my hours were. Gee, did I get bored just standing around all day? Did they ever let me take a break? He was obviously trying to see how tight security was. I sent him on his way pretty quick."

"So, I guess you'd notice anybody who seemed out of place in this neighborhood?" I was trying not to be obvious in my concerns.

"Before you turned in my driveway, you stopped to let a squirrel run across the road, a red Toyota was coming the other way and just missed it. Don't worry, I still got it."

I chuckled. "Okay, I'm sorry I doubted you. I'm just on edge after what happened to my neighbors. I would never want anything to happen to you."

"I…"

"I know you were going to say you can take care of yourself, but these crooks sound vicious."

"I was going to say I know to look out for who is at the door, and to lock up. As far as taking care of myself, I might only have one good leg, but I still know a trick or two," he said. "Not that I plan to have to use them."

"Well, good. I need to get to my next patient, but I'm counting on you to remain cautious. Lock up after I leave."

"Go! I told ya I can take care of myself!' He made a motion as if to shoo me out.

I turned before I left and said, "Be sure to say 'hello' to Loretta for me."

Chapter Five

I noticed Roger Feldman's car in his parents' driveway as I was coming home after work. Roger was hunched over, inching his way along the front of the house, parting the lower branches of a rhododendron bush as if searching for something. I pulled into the driveway behind his car.

"Roger? Is everything all right? Can I help you?" I said.

He grabbed his lower back and groaned as he straightened up and turned toward me. "Hi Melanie. The police never found Nika in the house, so I promised my mother I'd have a look myself. I checked inside again and couldn't see her anywhere. I'm afraid she may have gotten out during the break-in."

"I assume Nika is your mother's cat."

He took a handkerchief from his pocket and wiped the perspiration from his forehead. "Yes. My mother is going to be released from the hospital soon. I'm trying to convince her to stay with Darlene and me for a few days afterward, but she said she wants to be here, and she wants Nika with her. I thought if I found the cat and brought it to our house, she'd agree to come, also."

I could understand how Mrs. Feldman felt. I would have reacted the same way if Bruno was missing. In fact, I had, in one very frightening incident several months ago. "Glad to hear your mother is doing better. Poor woman, she certainly went through an awful experience. How is your father doing?"

He pressed his lips together and shook his head. "Not well, I'm afraid. As a result of the run-in with those criminals, it looks like he's had another stroke." He paused a minute, looking across the street toward the marshlands, "This one was really bad."

I felt horrible for him, for his whole family. I reached out to touch his arm. "I'm sorry."

"When he comes home, if he comes home, I don't know how my mother is going to be able to manage." He took a deep breath. "We'll figure that out later, I guess. Meanwhile, if you have a couple of minutes, I could use some help looking for that darn cat."

"She's gray, right? Any other markings?" Not that there were many cats wandering the neighborhood. Most people kept their cats indoors.

"No markings. She's all gray—actually a sort of blue gray. She is a beautiful cat, a purebred Russian. My mom showed her at a CFA show in New York last fall and she took second place in her breed category." He laughed, "My mom was so proud of her. She even let a guy who was making a YouTube video of the champions film Nika."

"Nika is in a YouTube video?"

He nodded. "You wouldn't believe the number of views it has gotten."

"Actually, if we don't find her today, maybe you could post the video on Facebook. Get more people looking for her."

He nodded. "That's not a bad idea." He bent again to continue his search.

I combed the backyard while Roger finished canvassing the front. Neither of us had any luck finding his mother's cat. The day had gotten much warmer, and after our search, we both were sweaty and smudged with dirt.

I met Roger in the front yard. He said, "We've looked everywhere I can think of where she might be hiding. I'll post that video, and maybe you could spread the word in the neighborhood in case someone sees her." He gave me a wan smile. "Thank you for helping me. I really wanted to find Nika. I hoped to at least set my mom's mind at ease that her cat is safe. She has enough on her plate right now."

"Have you heard if the police have made any progress in finding the criminals who broke into their house?"

He shook his head, "They did get a video taken at a local ATM shortly after the break-in, but the person kept their face turned away from the camera. Right after the break-in they took out the maximum daily amount allowed, but haven't tried using the card since. I put a hold on my parents' account the day after the break-in, anyway."

"I'll put the word out about Nika. It's possible someone will see her soon," I said.

I was planning on Justin coming over for dinner that night, so I fed Bruno and rushed to clean myself up before starting to cook. When I got out of the shower, however, I could see that Justin had called and left a message.

"Hi! Never mind making dinner, we're going out to celebrate! See you soon." He sounded excited.

I was curious what we were celebrating, but glad for any bit of good news after the discouraging update about Ernie Feldman.

When Justin arrived, he was grinning ear to ear. He kissed me and handed me a bottle of wine. "This is for later."

Bruno rushed up to greet him, and as Justin bent to pet him, I said, "What is it we are celebrating?"

"Us getting to spend more time together. We found someone who I think will fit in nicely in the practice." He smiled at me expectantly.

"Oh."

Justin's smile faded just a bit. "That's good news, isn't it?"

"Yes, of course. That's wonderful!" When he first mentioned we were celebrating something, my thoughts immediately went to what Lynn had hinted at a few nights before about us getting engaged. I wasn't sure if I felt relieved or disappointed that his surprise wasn't that he wanted to propose. I threw my arms around him and gave him another kiss. "Come on, tell me about him." I went to sit on the sofa. Bruno hopped up on one side of me, and I motioned to Justin to sit on the other.

"Her name is Stella Antonio. She just left a practice in the northeast corner of Connecticut."

"Oh. Does she have a lot of experience in small animal medicine?" I hoped it wasn't obvious that I was trying to gauge how old she was. "Why did she leave her previous practice?"

"As far as her experience, not a lot, two years. She wasn't specific about why she left her last position; she said it had something to do with a difficulty with one of the staff members. I find that hard to believe. She seemed very easy to get along with and is certainly the most enthusiastic candidate we've interviewed."

I was unsettled by the small tweak of jealousy I felt when I found out his new partner would be a woman. Justin worked with all female vet techs and receptionists. This was no different, I thought. "So, what else do you know about her? Does she have a family? Is she moving to the area, or does she already live nearby? What does Dr. Reddy think about her?"

He laughed. "I should have had you interview her. Dr. Reddy thinks she is a good choice, also. She said she is in the process of moving to Durham, I think. As far as family, I did ask if she had children only because that could be a consideration in making out the work schedule. No children, and she mentioned being divorced, so no husband's schedule to consider either." He put his arm around me. "Does that answer your questions?"

"Yes. For now." I gave him a quick kiss. I didn't like the fact that she was unattached, but I realized I was being ridiculous to feel any jealousy. "I'm glad you finally found someone to share the workload when Dr. Reddy cuts back his hours. When does she start?"

"She's coming in to get a feel of the day-to-day operation of the practice tomorrow. I hope she can start seeing patients by the end of the week."

"How soon can she be on call after the practice closes for the day?" It would be wonderful if Justin didn't have to be available for emergencies so many evenings.

"Dr. Reddy is willing to be on call two nights a month for now, and Dr. Antonio and I will alternate the rest of the time. So, we should have a few more uninterrupted evenings soon."

"Good. I'm looking forward to that." I turned to Justin, giving him a kiss that told him just how much I liked that idea. Suddenly, Bruno jumped up from where he had been sitting by my side and leapt over me and began to lick Justin's ear.

"Stop that, Bruno!" Justin gently pushed him away, but we both had dissolved into giggles at this point.

I managed to choke out, "I don't know who he is jealous of, you or me!"

I got up and grabbed one of Bruno's favorite toys, and holding it out for him, said, "Come on, play with your hedgehog." He obliged, but our intimate moment was disrupted for the time being.

Justin looked at his watch, "Come on. I promised you dinner out to celebrate finding a new partner."

As we drove toward the restaurant, Justin said, "You're happy we hired Stella, aren't you?" He glanced over at me. "I got a feeling that you were less than enthusiastic when I told you."

I was too embarrassed to tell him what my first thought was when he said we would celebrate. We had agreed last fall to take our relationship slow. I knew it was the right decision. "No. I mean, yes, I'm very happy you found someone to work at the practice. I'm sorry if I didn't come off as pleased at first. Anything that lets us spend more time together makes me happy." I smiled at him.

"Okay. Good." I could tell he knew I wasn't being completely honest about my reaction, but was willing to let it go for the moment.

Chapter Six

The following day, I had an appointment to see my friend Detective Sunny Cody's father, Jim Moran. He had suffered a heart attack a few months previously, and while in the hospital, he had been diagnosed with type II diabetes. I planned to check his blood pressure, make sure he was following his prescribed diet, as well as checking his blood sugar and taking his medication. Pauline Moran answered the door when I rang the bell.

"Hi Melanie. Come in. Jimmy is in the kitchen. He's checking his blood sugar right now." She had raised her voice as she said that last part.

"Good, I'm glad to see he is following his physician's orders."

She snorted. "Not really, but he knew you were coming today, and he wanted to be able to tell you what it was when you asked. I try to get him to eat properly, remind him to take his medication, but he accuses me of nagging him."

Mr. Moran came into the living room where his wife and I were. "You ratting me out, Pauline?" He laughed.

"I told you I was going to tell her if you didn't follow your diet and take your pills." She shook her head at her husband. "You and your daughter are so alike—stubborn, don't like to be told what to do."

I had to agree with her description of their daughter, Sunny Cody. I had taken care of her after a hit-and-run had caused her severe injuries. I put my work bag down on the coffee table. "Well, what is the verdict? How was your sugar?"

Mr. Moran put his hands up in a surrender gesture, "Not good, but I promise to do better." He looked from me to his wife, who stood with arms crossed.

"Do I need to give you the lecture about taking care of yourself so you don't end up in the hospital again? Or worse? What will Katie do without her Poppa?" I knew Jim and Pauline took care of Sunny's daughter while Sunny was on duty.

"Okay. I get it. Don't tell Sunny." He extended his left arm so I could wrap a blood pressure cuff around it.

His blood pressure was good at least. "That checks out all right. But when I come for my next visit, I want to hear a good report, understand?"

Pauline walked over to gently rub her husband's back. "You will. Right, Jimmy?"

"Sure. But I draw the line at eating that kale salad you made the other day again."

The rest of my visits that day were post-surgical checks, and all my patients were healing as expected. After I finished my charting, I headed home. I couldn't help but wonder how Justin's day had gone with the new vet, Stella. I decided that after I changed my clothes and took care of Bruno, I'd call him and ask. I'd be sure to stress how glad I was that he and Dr. Reddy now had more help.

As soon as I pulled into my driveway, my fifteen-year-old neighbor, Jenny, came to meet me. "I think I saw the Feldmans' cat in back of our house, but before I could catch her, she ran away in the direction of your yard."

"How long ago was this?"

"Only about ten minutes ago, I was searching your yard for her when I heard your car pull in."

"Okay, let me just put my work things inside, and we can look together. You stay here and watch to see if she appears again."

Bruno was highly insulted when I left him inside while I followed Jenny into my backyard. "Did you see where she ran?"

"No. I—" Just then, a grey streak ran from behind my house toward the bushes lining the west side of my driveway.

"There. In the hedge," Jenny said.

Both of us inched toward the hedges, approaching the grey shape, softly calling out "kitty, kitty," and making smooching noises. The cat waited until we were within a few feet, then bolted out from under the bushes and across the neighboring front yard.

Jenny and I ran in hot pursuit, and the entire time I was willing Nika to keep to the grassy areas and out of the road. When we got to the Feldmans', she was curled up on the doorstep, meowing loudly. I quickly scooped her up, "It's okay, girl, we have you now. We'll call your mamma."

She was a gorgeous cat. Soft blue/gray with the most striking bright green eyes. I turned to Jenny, "I'm going to call the Feldmans' son, Roger, to let him know we have her. In the meantime, do you think you could keep Nika at your house? She isn't acquainted with Bruno yet, and I'm not sure how their meeting would go."

Jenny's face lit up, "Of course. I know my mom won't mind—not too much anyway. I have been nagging her about getting a kitten, and I think she is very close to giving in." She took Nika from my arms and cradled her as the cat began to purr loudly. "Good," she said to Nika, "when I show you to my mom, keep doing that!"

When I got back into the house, I grabbed my phone to let Roger know I at least had a little good news for him. I saw that I'd missed a call while I was outside chasing Nika. I was surprised to see it was from my sister, Meredith. It wasn't that my sister and I didn't get along, but to be honest, we were just never close. Meredith is thirteen years older than I am. My mother said I was definitely a late-in-life surprise for them, though she always was quick to add that she and my father were delighted. Our parents are both dead now, and Meredith moved to England years ago and still lives there with her British husband and two sons. We speak a few times a year, mostly around the holidays and our birthdays, but otherwise usually only when something happens—good or bad. I found myself holding my breath as I checked my voicemail.

"Hello, Mellie! Just calling with some news. I guess I'll call back tomorrow and hope to catch you then. It's quite late here now, so we will speak tomorrow, okay? Bye!"

Her voice was neutral, so it was hard to gauge whether her news was good or bad. Of course, now I was going to be wondering what it was she wanted to tell me. I knew it was late where she was, but I was tempted to call her right back. However, experience had taught me that Meredith liked to be in control of most things, so I reluctantly decided it might be best if I waited for her to call me back.

Bruno came over to me and sniffed my pants and shoes thoroughly. "I know. You smell Nika." I reached down to scratch between his ears. "Don't worry, she's going back to be with her own family." I entered Roger Feldman's number, and he answered after only two rings.

"Yes?"

"Roger, I wanted to let you know my neighbor Jenny and I found Nika. Jenny took her to her house."

"Okay. Good. That will be some comfort to my mother at least." His voice shook a bit as he continued, "I'm afraid my father didn't make it."

"Oh! I'm so sorry. Please let me know if there is anything I can do for you or your mother."

"You have been a big help already by finding Nika. My mother insists she wants to return to her own house. She says she needs some time alone to adjust to my father's death. I know she wants Nika there, though. I'll pick up her cat when I drive her home tomorrow."

"All right. I'll tell my neighbors to expect you." I hesitated to ask, but said, "Have the police found out any more about who was responsible for the break-in?"

"No. But I was contacted by a Detective Cody. She said they're considering the break-in a more serious crime now that my father's death can be linked to it."

Good. Sunny Cody was involved now. "I know Detective Cody. She'll do everything possible to catch whoever was involved." I told myself there was no reason to get mixed up in solving the crime this time; I had every confidence in Sunny.

"Thanks for letting me know about the cat, Melanie. I'm sure once she has had some time to deal with her grief, my mother will want to thank you also.

I'm sorry, but we're still making arrangements for the service. I need to go now."

I felt a fresh wave of sorrow for the Feldman family after my call with Roger ended. I would check with Lana in a day or so, make sure she was doing all right on her own.

I checked the time. I wanted to find out how the new veterinarian was working out at Reddy Vet, the practice where Justin worked. Justin told me he planned to go to his mother's after work to help her put up some new bookshelves. I hoped to catch him before he got too deep into the project.

He sounded very upbeat when he answered my call. "Hi. I was going to call you later. I have some news that may be of interest to you."

I could hear his mother's voice in the background yelling, "Tell Melanie I said hello!"

I chuckled. "Tell your mother I said hello back. Is she feeding you before she puts you to work?"

"I just finished eating. Pot roast. She's having me bring the leftovers to my grandfather later. Do you want her to save some for you?"

That certainly explained his good mood. "No. I love pot roast, but let Charlie have it," I said. "I wanted to see how today went with your new vet. How did she do?"

"I think she's going to be great. She already saw a couple of cases on her own and seems comfortable with the office routine."

"Good." I paused for a few seconds, then said, "What was it you wanted to tell me?"

"Oh." He suddenly sounded considerably less cheerful. "I saw your friend Malcolm Devlin's dog, Daphne, today. He wanted her chipped after I updated her vaccinations. But to both our surprise, she already has a microchip."

"No!" I remembered that Malcolm said he had purchased the dog from a friend of a patient. "The previous owner must have forgotten to tell Malcolm about it."

"That's what I thought at first, but I checked the company's registry, and the ID number on the chip was registered to someone in Massachusetts. Malcolm said that it wasn't the man he bought the dog from."

"What does that mean?" I had a sinking feeling in my stomach.

"It's possible that the breeder had the litter chipped before he sold them, but I think that is unlikely. Unfortunately, it could mean that the guy who sold Malcolm the dog was not the owner."

"You mean that Daphne might have been stolen."

"I'm afraid so."

That was the thought I was trying to squash. "Poor Malcolm! He loves that dog. What will happen now?"

"That's a problem. Usually, it's up to the veterinary practice where the chip was scanned to notify the person the dog is registered to. If the person in possession of the dog agrees that the dog needs to be returned, there is no issue. But I could see that Malcolm was crushed by the possibility of losing Daphne. I haven't done anything yet. I wanted to give Malcolm a bit of time to get used to the idea."

I felt a mix of rage and sadness. Angry at whoever would steal someone's pet, and sad for both the original owners and Malcolm. "There's no way around what you have to do, is there?" Even as I said it, I knew the answer.

"No. I do have a responsibility to protect Malcolm's privacy as he is a client of mine, so you could argue that since Malcolm bought Daphne ignorant of the fact that she didn't belong to the seller, I could just not report it. But I also know how I'd feel if Jasper was missing and the vet who found him failed to notify me."

"What about the man who sold the dog to Malcolm? Shouldn't he be reported to the police?"

I could hear wood being dropped down. "Malcolm was in a bit of shock as he left the office. I left it up to him whether he wanted to notify the police that he was sold a stolen dog. I told him that while it was deplorable, I wasn't sure what they would be able to do to follow up on it."

"I just feel so badly for Malcolm." It was too late to call him then, and I realized he might need some time to deal with what he found out. I resolved I would contact him the next day, though, and see if there was anything I could do to help. "I'll let you get back to your project. Thanks for letting me know about Daphne."

"Sorry I had such bad news," he said.

"Unfortunately, it's been a day for bad news, I'm afraid." I told him about Ernie Feldman. "The one small consolation I could offer Lana is that we found her Russian Blue cat. Ernie bought it for her as a gift. The cat must have escaped during the break-in at their house."

"I saw Nika for her yearly checkup last year. She is beautiful. And quite valuable," he said.

I could hear someone calling to Justin. "I better get to work; my task master is coming upstairs to see how I am doing with this bookshelf. I'll call you tomorrow."

I really hoped when my sister called back the next day, it would be with good news. As if he was able to read my mood, Bruno came to sit on the sofa next to me, and I spent some time just stroking him. The weight of his head on my thigh felt comforting.

Chapter Seven

I jolted awake to the sound of my cell phone at 5:30 the next morning. My heart was racing as I answered the call. "Hello?" The word had come out as more of a croak than a question as I tried to clear my throat. "Oh, did I wake you? I thought you might be up already, it's…oh. Sorry."

"Meredith?"

"It is early there, isn't it? I can call back in an hour or so if that would be better for you."

I swung my feet onto the floor, searching for my slippers. "No, that's okay, I'm awake now. How are you? Is everything all right?" Bruno had jumped up from where he was sleeping by my feet when I fumbled for my phone, but he settled back down now near the foot of the bed.

"Yes, we're all fine here. I called because I have good news. Phillip has been tapped to do some consultation work on a project regarding financial institutions involved in climate change. They are sending him to New York. Of course, it makes perfect sense for me to come with him. The boys are both in university now and fine on their own for the time being, so no issues there. I thought since we'll be so close by, perhaps you and I could spend some time together."

A mix of emotions raced through me. I hadn't seen Meredith since our mother's funeral six years before. I felt joy at the thought of seeing my sister again, but also apprehension. She was a little controlling. And opinionated. But we also found we had a lot of laughs when we were together. "That's wonderful! When will you be coming to New York?"

"Four days from now. Phillip's company is putting us up at a place in the city while we are there, but it will be boring just hanging around every day while he is at work. I'll call you after we are settled in."

New York, boring? I didn't know where to begin to remind her of the things there would be to do there. "That sounds great."

"All right. Bye for now."

She ended the call abruptly, and I realized she hadn't even asked if I was doing all right. Four days! I had a lot of questions: did she plan on staying with me for a while when Phillip was busy? I'd better get Lynn's old room prepared. How long were they going to be in the country? Meredith had opened a small bookstore in the Bloomsbury section of London a few years ago; was it doing well enough for her to take time away? Was there something else going on that she wasn't saying?

"Bruno, your Aunt Meredith is coming!" He looked up at me and wagged his tail, but then put his head down on his paws and went back to sleep. He obviously didn't feel this was as momentous an occasion as I did. I suddenly felt like I was five years old again. Would she like Justin? How about Lynn? Would they get along? What if I couldn't take a stretch of time off from work? Would she expect me to? It was happy news, but I could already feel the tension building in the back of my neck.

I took a deep breath, telling myself that she's my sister, I am a grown-up. It will be fine. Just as I was getting my anxiety under control, I thought of her reaction to my ex-husband, Artie. She had only met him once before our wedding and had strongly advised me not to marry him. She didn't hold back with her "I told you so" when I informed her we were getting a divorce. I knew I shouldn't let any opinions she had on my life affect me, but I had always found myself trying to get the approval of my big sister.

I figured I might as well shower and get ready for work since I was up already. To take my mind off Meredith's impending visit, I tried to think of a way I could help Malcolm or at least help him deal with the probability of having to return Daphne to her rightful owners.

Once I was showered and dressed, I checked the time to make sure my neighbors would be awake. I hadn't had a chance the previous evening to call Jenny and Karen to let them know that Roger and his mother would be stopping by to get her cat. Jenny answered the phone, and while she sounded a bit disappointed at first that Nika was going home so soon, she whispered at the end, "It worked! Mom and I are going to the shelter on the weekend."

I couldn't help but feel happy that one pet was being returned to her owner, but so very sad at the prospect of another also being handed over to hers.

My first visit of the morning was to Mrs. Paine. I noticed she had a new doorbell camera installed, but I identified myself anyway as soon as I rang the bell. I could hear her removing the security lock and was glad to see she was still taking good precautions.

"Come on in." She chuckled as she admitted me. "My grandson came over the other day and insisted he was going to install a Ring camera for me, so I saw you as you came up the walk."

"I'm glad to see you have extra security now," I said.

"I was really frightened after what happened to Ada. Then I decided I had gone through quite a lot in my life, and I wasn't going to end it like a scared rabbit. So, I'm still taking good precautions, but no more letting fear of some ruffians stop me from living out the time I have left, and from doing what I want."

I noticed she had her purse and a sweater sitting on one of the easy chairs in her living room, and there was the unmistakable fragrance of fresh baking coming from the kitchen.

She looked at her watch. "After you check me over, Greta Knowles is picking me up. We are going to Ada's to play Bridge." She smiled at me, "I just baked some cinnamon muffins, would you like one?"

I usually was able to resist the temptation of the treats she offered, but I felt my stomach growl in anticipation. "I would love one!"

When she returned with the muffin on a delicate blue china plate, I said, "How is Mrs. Watkins?"

"Still frightened after what happened to her, but Greta and I are working on her, trying to get her confidence back up. I think she will do all right given time."

"That's good." After I finished what turned out to be one of the most delicious muffins I'd ever tasted, I checked Mrs. Paine's vital signs and went through my list of questions related to her congestive heart failure—no shortness of breath or increased fatigue, her oxygen saturations were good, and all her vital signs stable. "I'm glad to say that you passed with flying colors today, good work. So please go and have a wonderful time."

My visit to Mrs. Paine left me feeling uplifted. I knew just what she meant about going on with her life. After a few nearly disastrous events in my own life, I'd had to carry on. But then, I was a great deal younger than her. I hoped I would still have the courage she has once I reached her age. I found myself smiling as I headed to my next appointment.

* * *

I called Malcolm after I finished with my last patient of the day to let him know I was going to stop over, but he didn't even ask me why. When he answered the door, Malcolm looked like he had just lost his best friend, or was about to. Daphne still greeted me joyfully, jumping around and wiggling her body.

"Come on, let Melanie in." Malcolm gently guided her out of the doorway so I could enter. I couldn't help but notice her new bejeweled collar.

"I'd ask how you are, but I can see for myself. I'm so sorry, Malcolm." I gave him a quick hug. "Justin said he contacted the people who first had Daphne, and you are supposed to meet at the vet office this weekend."

He nodded. "Yes. That's right. As a matter of fact, I wonder if you could be there too? When I meet them, I want someone else I trust to be there also to assess them, make sure they look dependable. I mean, they lost her once, will they be more careful now?" He reached down to pet Daphne, "I know it's the right thing to do, but it's...hard."

I cursed the person or persons who had led to this situation. Also, Malcolm had a point. I wondered how Daphne had been taken, assuming she hadn't just wandered off and then been found by the man who later sold her. "I would be glad to meet them with you. I'm also curious as to what happened; how the man you bought her from got her."

He led me into the kitchen while he put on water for tea and coffee. "I tried calling the patient who gave me the name of the guy I bought Daphne from. He hemmed and hawed a bit but finally admitted it was someone he met at the dog park, and he really didn't know him well. I called the number I had for the creep who sold me Daphne, but the number was no longer working. I'm pretty sure the name the guy gave me wasn't real either. I feel like a fool."

"Did you contact the police? That man must be guilty of something; fraud, maybe," I said.

"I talked to Detective Cody, but she said they couldn't do much since I had no idea who the guy was, or that he was the one who took Daphne. Even if they could find him, he could claim that he bought her in good faith from someone else."

I had a thought. "Do you have a receipt, or a canceled check, or anything we could use to trace the person you bought her from?"

He looked embarrassed, "The guy insisted on cash—the whole about to leave the country excuse; he said he'd already closed his bank account. He gave me a written receipt, but the name is so scribbled I can't read it, and, like I said, I doubt he used his real name anyway." He sighed, "I don't even know what good it would do to track him down. All that matters to me now is that I need to hand Daphne over to someone else."

I could understand his feelings. But I couldn't help but think of the Monet family and their missing dog, Corky. I told him what happened to her, and that it was possible she was grabbed by someone also. "If there is some kind of pattern, maybe the police will be able to get more involved," I said.

"Maybe." Malcolm was letting his coffee cool untouched.

I suddenly remembered Roger Feldman saying that the intruders at his parents' house seemed to be looking for something besides the obvious valuables, and Justin saying that the Feldmans' cat, Nika, was quite valuable. "What if these people are involved in more than just pet theft?" I said. I knew she would think I was crazy at first, but I decided to speak to Sunny Cody and share the suspicions I was beginning to have.

Daphne eventually got tired of the toy she was playing with and came to nuzzle Malcolm's legs. He reached down to scratch behind her ears, and when he looked at me again, his expression had hardened. "All I know is I'd like to get my hands on the guy who is responsible for this mess."

We talked for a few minutes more as Malcolm updated me on what was going on with the other doctors I knew at High Life Dermatology. He told me how much he liked Justin, even though his visit to the vet office resulted in discovering Daphne belonged to someone else. "I can't blame him. He seemed almost as shaken by the discovery as I was." He smiled at me. "You deserve to have a good guy like him in your life."

I returned Malcolm's smile. "Thank you. He does make me very happy."

Malcolm walked me to the door. "I appreciate you being there on Saturday when I meet the people who originally had Daphne. I value your opinion, and I want to make sure they'll take good care of her. This time."

"I'll be glad to buy you lunch afterward if you want to sit and talk," I said.

Malcolm hesitated. "That's very nice of you, but we'll see how things go. I have a feeling I won't have much of an appetite."

Chapter Eight

Lynn called me the next day and suggested we meet for a cup of tea after I was through seeing my patients. She was already seated at the Dunkin' Donuts when I arrived and waved to me as I entered. I could see she was excited about something.

I barely had a chance to sit down before she gushed, "Guess what! I've been invited to do a showing of my paintings at the Branford Arts and Cultural Alliance. There will be a reception on Tuesday evening and everything. Not only will it be a good opportunity to sell some paintings, but with any luck, I could get more patrons and pick up a few requests for private lessons."

"That's terrific! Congratulations!" I quickly did the calculations in my head and realized my sister Meredith would probably arrive in New York on Monday or Tuesday. It would take a bit of time for her to settle in, so maybe she wouldn't be planning on coming to see me until later in the week. I should be able to make it to Lynn's showing. "I'll be there." But what if Meredith did arrive on Monday and planned to come to Connecticut on Tuesday? She would want my full attention. Although, she did appreciate art, so maybe—.

Something in my expression made Lynn say, "What's bothering you? Is it what happened with the Feldmans? Because you—"

"No." I felt a little guilty for a second. My problem was minor compared to Lana Feldman's. "My sister is coming to visit next week, and I'm not sure what day she is going to arrive."

Lynn sat up straighter in her chair, "You have a sister? You never mentioned that! Where is she?"

I realized that in spite of all we had been through together, there was still a lot Lynn and I didn't know about each other. "Sorry. Yes, Meredith is quite a bit older than me, and we were never very close. She moved out of the country when I was fifteen. I always looked up to her, though, and I guess I still feel a bit intimidated by her." I took a sip of my tea.

"Why feel intimidated? She doesn't bite, does she?"

"Not with her actual teeth, no." We both burst out laughing. "I do have scars from some of her comments, though," I added.

"I'm an only child, so I'm no expert on family dynamics, but it seems to me that since you are both grown women now, you should have quite a bit more in common. Why did she decide to come for a visit now? Did something happen?"

"Her husband is consulting on something at one of the think tanks in New York, so she decided to come along. Their children are older and away at school, so she doesn't need to stay in London while he's here," I said.

"Well, if she comes before Tuesday and you can't make the showing, I understand."

"No. I'll be there. I'll just tell Meredith I'm busy until Wednesday." I realized I was being ridiculous to be nervous about telling my sister what I wanted. In the past, I'd stood up to people who had guns and planned to do me serious harm.

We ordered second cups of tea, and I told Lynn about what had happened with Malcolm's dog, Daphne. "I promised to be there with him when he has to hand over Daphne to her previous owners. It's going to be difficult. Especially for him."

"If he's lucky, maybe the people just won't show up," Lynn said. "It's good of you to be there to support him if they do."

"I have to admit my only motive isn't just to support Malcolm, I'm curious to hear what happened, how she was taken." I recounted for her the story of Corky's disappearance and Mrs. Monet's fear that she could have been stolen.

"What kind of lowlife steals someone's pet?" Lynn made a disgusted sound before taking another sip of tea.

I drank a sip of my own tea, then said, "Did I tell you the night the Feldmans' house was broken into Mrs. Feldman's cat escaped? She loves that cat, not to mention Ernie bought it as a special gift for her. Roger said he paid a small fortune for her, too." I raised my eyebrows at her.

"Okay, that's…oh!"

"Roger told me that his mother said the thieves seemed to be looking in odd places, as if they expected to find something other than the usual money and valuables. I know it sounds crazy, but I think they may have known she had a cat who was worth a lot of money."

"But how would they find that out?"

I explained that someone had taken a video that featured Nika after she won a prize at a competition, and Mrs. Feldman had posted it on Facebook. "I'm sure she was just so proud and didn't think how some people might use information gained on social media."

"Your theory is a bit of a stretch, but I agree it is possible. After all, the authorities wouldn't be looking for someone trying to sell a cat." She was quiet for a moment as if she was thinking about it, then, "How much would we be talking about?"

"Justin said Nika would likely be worth four figures. If the thieves planned on taking her and selling her, it would be hard to trace them, too. Unless the person who bought her was someone in the show cat world who knew most of the breeders, they might not know to check on the person who had her for sale," I said.

"But the intruders didn't take her, right?"

"No. Like I said, she must have somehow slipped past them as they were entering or leaving the house. Jenny and I found her wandering in the neighborhood a couple of days later."

"Good." Lynn looked relieved. "I think low life is too mild a word for these people! What made you realize the intruders may have wanted to take Mrs. Feldman's cat?"

"Malcolm said he paid quite a bit for Daphne, so the man who sold her to him made an easy profit by stealing then selling her. The same could be true for the Feldmans' cat. I will admit, though, that breaking into someone's house to get her is a bit extreme," I said.

"Obviously. Even if they were initially after her, they were also intent on robbing the Feldmans. Have you heard if there are any leads on who these criminals are?" Lynn said.

"No. I plan to speak to Sunny Cody and let her know my suspicions about them wanting to steal Nika. I know she'll at least hear me out, though I don't know if she'll think my theory is too wild. I'll ask her then if they are making any progress with finding who broke into the Feldmans' house and assaulted Ernie and Lana."

Lynn looked at her watch. "I need to get ready for the adult ed class I'm doing at the high school, so I better go now. Let me know if you find out anything when you talk to Detective Cody." As we both stood to leave, she said, "You *are* going to introduce me to your sister when she gets here, aren't you?"

"Of course. But I don't think she needs to know all about our past escapades, okay?" I cringed at the thought of Meredith hearing all about our crime-solving exploits.

"What if how we came to know each other comes up in conversation? I might just need to tell her about it." She must have seen the look of alarm on my face; she grinned and added, "Don't worry, I promise to omit a lot of the details of what has happened since then!" Lynn grabbed her purse and hurried off.

Chapter Nine

I went to speak to Sunny Cody the following morning. She listened quietly while I explained to her the possible connection I'd drawn between Malcolm being sold a stolen dog and the intruders intending to steal Mrs. Feldman's cat, Nika. "I know it's a bit far-fetched, but I think there might be a link between the two." I waited for her reply.

"I've learned not to dismiss your theories off-hand, but I don't know in this case. These are two different sorts of crimes. The Feldman home invasion was violent, and in the case of Dr. Devlin's dog, there is no proof the dog was stolen. It could have been a case of the seller finding the dog and then not being honest enough to try to find the owners."

"That's true, but I'm just asking you to keep the possibility the two are connected in mind." I paused, "I heard that you're now amending the charges in the break-in to include a homicide charge since the assault on Ernie led to his death."

"Yes. We're still reviewing the facts and talking to Mr. Feldman's physicians to determine exactly what charges to bring. But first, we need to apprehend the perpetrators."

"Any closer to finding who did it?"

She shook her head and said, "You know I can't tell you that. Have you by any chance been able to remember more about what you saw the night of the break-in?"

My shoulders slumped. "No. I just remember thinking I saw a figure going around the house. I'm not sure of anything else. I can't even be sure if any memories I have now are influenced by what I know happened."

"All right. Thank you for admitting that. I'll keep what you suggested in mind."

Before I left, I asked, "How are Katie and her dog, Beanie, doing?"

She smiled, "Katie is getting bigger every day, and much smarter than I think a five-year-old should be. She loves that big oaf of a dog, and I have to say Beanie has kind of grown on me, too."

As I was driving home past Mrs. Feldmans house, I saw her out in her front yard tending to her flowers. As I had admitted to Sunny, I could no longer form a good picture in my head of what I saw before the break-in. I only caught a glimpse of one of the intruders. Mrs. Feldman, unfortunately, had a much closer look. Maybe she had some memories that she didn't feel were important, but could help find the criminals.

I pulled into her driveway. "Hello, Lana. I wanted to stop and see how you're doing. Is there anything I can do for you?"

She looked up at me, then extended a gloved hand for me to help her up. "No, but thank you for asking. I'm getting on all right, taking it day by day." She took a deep breath and reached down and gently stroked a dark pink blossom on one of her plants.

"Your flowers are gorgeous. I don't think I've ever seen peonies so large!"

"Thank you. They are one of my favorites. I only wish their bloom lasted longer." She paused to remove her gardening gloves and put one hand on my forearm. "I never got a chance to thank you for finding Nika. My mind has been very scattered since…well, you know what happened."

"I'm so sorry. Especially about what happened to Ernie."

She nodded sadly, then smiled. "Poor Ernie, he never really adjusted to his limitations after his first stroke. He always tried to act as if he was thirty years younger than he was."

"I know your memories of that night are still very raw. I'm sorry to ask, but have you remembered anything else about the intruders? Anything that could help the police find them?" I rushed to add, "My friend and I were going by your house around the time of the break-in and I thought I saw someone in your side yard. Then I convinced myself I was mistaken. I feel terrible that I didn't just call the police to check out your property." I waited for her angry reaction, and I wouldn't blame her.

She put her hand on my arm again, "Roger told me. Don't blame yourself. I wish I'd done things differently that night, too. I should have just screamed for Ernie to call 911, and I wish I'd fought them harder, but I froze when I saw those figures in my kitchen."

"Was there anything about them that stood out to you?" I was sure the police had asked her this, but sometimes things noticed in a traumatic moment come back later.

She shook her head. "No. Not much. Just as I told the police, there were three of them. Two large men and one shorter one. They were all dressed in black with balaclavas pulled over their faces. One of the biggest ones grabbed me right away and pulled my arms behind my back and faced me away from them and marched me toward the living room." She paused for a moment, rubbing her forearms. "The ties he used were tight. They were those plastic ones and cut into my wrists."

Mrs. Feldman's breathing had become slightly faster, and I was afraid it was upsetting her too much to talk about it. "I'm sorry. It might be better if you didn't think about it again right now. We—"

She shook her head. "No. I want to tell it again. I'm angry, is all." She paused for a moment, then continued, "As I told the police, one of them had a knife and threatened me with it. He said I was to sit on the sofa and not make a sound. My shoulders hurt from my arms being pulled back by the ties, and I asked if he could loosen them. He didn't answer. He was tying my ankles together when I heard Ernie coming to see what was going on. He had his cane and was swinging it at the one who approached him. I heard the sound when that one hit him with some kind of club or something he pulled from his belt." She looked hard at me. "He hit him more than once. I could tell Ernie was really hurt. I cried out and tried to get up to go to him, but the one with the knife pushed me back down and shoved one of the napkins from the sideboard into my mouth so I couldn't speak." She stopped and looked toward her house as if she was envisioning what happened all over again.

"Do you want to sit for a moment?" I led her toward the two Adirondack chairs positioned several feet away.

She sat, then turned to me. "I just remembered something. His voice. One of the intruders was making strange noises every so often, like a soft hiss or shushing sound. I thought he had a speech impediment, but later I realized it might have been words in another language. It sounded Slavic or Scandinavian."

"That's good. It could be helpful once they identify possible suspects." I had another thought, however. "This is going to sound like an odd question, but Roger said you told him one of them seemed to be looking in strange places, like under a chair, and behind furniture as if he was looking for something specific. Was it the one making the odd sounds?"

She nodded. "Yes, I think so."

"I just wonder if he was looking for Nika. I understand she is quite valuable."

She seemed startled. "That's...well...I suppose he could have been. He might have had some kind of bag with him, I don't remember. I know the others were grabbing whatever valuables they could find and shoving them into sacks." She paused. "The big one with the knife made me give him my bank code, then seemed annoyed with the others and told them they had enough, they had to go, to forget looking for 'it.' I didn't know what 'it' was."

"What did his voice sound like? Would you remember it if you heard it again?"

She shook her head. "No. I think he was trying to disguise his normal voice. When he said they needed to leave before they were discovered, the one making the odd noises started to argue with him, but the one who had the knife told him to shut up and shoved him, saying, 'Just go!'"

I was pretty sure my theory was right now. "I think the sounds you heard the intruder making were meant to coax your cat from hiding."

Mrs. Feldman sat up straighter in her chair. "I never would have thought that someone would want to steal my Nika, but it could be you're right! She did come out of hiding to see what the commotion was. The shorter one said, 'grab her,' but when one of the larger ones did, she put up quite a fight, scratching and biting and hissing." Mrs. Feldman smiled. "I think she got him good! He yelped and dropped her, and then she fled. I was so worried when Roger couldn't find her afterward, though." She pushed herself up out of her chair. "I need a glass of lemonade. Won't you come in and join me?" She grabbed her pruning shears and gardening gloves and led me into the house.

She got me settled in a lovely little sun-drenched room that faced the back yard and went to get our lemonade.

As we sipped our drinks, Mrs. Feldman talked about her garden, then how she and Ernie had met, and how happy they were when they were able to buy a house in Madison. "Of course, it was different all those years ago. But then all things change, don't they?" It seemed to help her to talk about her husband and all the happy times they had together, so I let her reminisce. Finally, Mrs. Feldman said, "Oh, dear, I've been going on quite a bit. Sorry to have kept you."

"Not at all. And be sure to let me know if you think of anything I can do to help you."

Just as we were about to get up out of our chairs, Nika scampered into the room and began to rub her face against Mrs. Feldman's legs. "Hello, my brave girl. I know, we are invading your space, aren't we?"

Mrs. Feldman pulled the cat up into her lap. "It used to be rather dark in here, but ever since we had the two new windows installed, this is where I can find Nika sunning herself for most of the day. She has claimed this room as her own!"

"I can see why." I remembered Karen mentioning a white van driving around the neighborhood. "When did you have the windows put in?" I had a vague memory of hearing some construction being done in the neighborhood recently. I hadn't really been paying attention to where at the time.

"I'd say it was a month or so ago. Why do you ask?"

"It's just a thought, but wouldn't the men who installed them have been inside your house to complete the work?" I could see she understood why I was asking.

"No. Frank Eastman is a friend of Roger's. He owns the company. I'm sure he—" she paused for a few seconds. "One of the workers was smitten with

Nika; he asked Ernie where he had purchased her, but seemed flabbergasted when Ernie told him what he paid." She shook her head. "No. He seemed like a very nice young man. Both men seemed nice. They wouldn't…" She let her voice trail off.

"You're probably right, but I think the police might want to talk to them. I think at this point they're examining every avenue. Do you have the name of the company?"

She got up wordlessly and went to get a receipt for the work done. "I'm certain neither of those men had anything to do with the break-in, but I suppose it wouldn't hurt to give the officer working on the case this information."

"Would you mind if I took a picture of the name of the construction company?"

Mrs. Feldman hesitated briefly, then said, "No, I guess not."

I took out my phone and was careful to only include the name and address of "Rockwell Construction" in the photo. I could see that she was upset at the thought that someone they had allowed into their home had been responsible for what happened to Ernie. "You're doing the right thing by notifying the police."

"I suppose so." She smiled weakly at me.

I stood up to leave, and Mrs. Feldman walked to the door with me. "Thank you for stopping by, dear. As I said, I will do as you suggested and notify the police, though I truly hope the men from Frank's company had nothing to do with what happened."

Even though the police were handling the investigation, I felt a twinge of excitement at this new information and tucked it away.

Chapter Ten

Justin told me he had arranged for Daphne's original owners to meet Malcolm at Reddy Vet on Saturday at two p.m. I took Bruno for a walk and gave him a hug before I left. I could feel my hands sweating and my heart rate sped up as I headed there. I planned to arrive a bit early, just in case the Wright family arrived before the appointed time. Even though I was only there for support and an assessment of the people who said Daphne was theirs, I felt as nervous as if someone had claimed Bruno. I knew on one hand it would be a joyful scene: I was sure Daphne would be thrilled to see these people, but any pleasure at seeing a pet reunited with her owner would be overshadowed by the grief I knew Malcolm would feel at losing her.

When I opened the door to Reddy Vet, I could hear angry voices. Someone was haranguing Traci, one of the receptionists. I approached the desk, where Justin was trying to calm the man down, his voice even and reasonable-sounding. It didn't appear to be doing much good. Another gentleman and I watched as the angry man slammed his hand down on the counter and said, "Why don't you people get your act together!" He then turned and stormed out, pushing by me without another word.

I worried that the first man's anger might have something to do with Malcolm and Daphne, and the exchange set to take place shortly. "What was that about?" I asked Justin.

Justin shook his head. "A dissatisfied client. He was arguing about his bill and getting verbally abusive with Traci. My stepping in to explain the charges didn't seem to help."

Traci said, "Thanks, Justin, but he is always nasty to deal with. In spite of his complaints, he'll be back when his cat needs his meds again." She turned to the other man who had been watching the whole exchange. "I'll let Dr. Antonio know you want to speak to her."

Justin motioned me to follow him toward the exam rooms in the back. "It's very kindhearted of you to come to support Malcolm Devlin. I know he really appreciates it, but are you sure you're up for it, because I know I'm dreading it." When I nodded, he put an arm around me and guided me to an exam room in the back. "I thought it might be best if we did the exchange in private. Malcolm should be here soon, also. He said he wanted to arrive a little early so he could already be in the room when I showed the Wrights in."

I took a seat on the wooden bench provided for pet parents to sit on while they waited. "I think I would have chosen to do it this way, also." I looked up and gave him a weak smile, "I'm glad you'll be here." I reached for his hand.

"Always." Justin leaned down to kiss me. Suddenly, the door burst open, and a very attractive dark-haired woman started to enter. "Oh, sorry, I didn't know you were… uhhm…using this room."

Justin bolted upright and, turning to the woman, said, "Oh, hi Stella. I'd like you to meet Melanie. Melanie, this is Stella Antonio, our new vet."

I stood up and as Stella came over to shake my hand, I said, "So nice to meet you, Dr. Antonio. Justin has told me you're settling in nicely." I tried not to make it obvious I was giving her the once-over. She looked to be in her early thirties, like me, and about my height, but as far as I could see, that was where our resemblance ended. She had sleek dark hair pulled back into a neat bun instead of the light brown, almost-auburn curls I had, and I could tell even though she was wearing scrubs, she had way more curves than me.

She gave Justin a knowing smile and then turned back to me and said, "I heard a lot about you also. So glad to finally meet you." She did seem genuinely pleased to meet me, and I felt guilty over the jolt of jealousy I'd felt when I first saw her. Then, she edged closer to Justin and placed her hand on the back of his neck and said, "When you are through here, I want to discuss a patient with you." The look in her warm brown eyes as she spoke to Justin told me my first reaction was the right one.

Justin seemed not to have noticed the intimate nature of her gesture. At least it was a considerably more cozy touch than I thought appropriate for new colleagues. Nor did he seem to sense my reaction to it.

After she left the room, and before I could say anything about what had just happened, Justin gave me a quick kiss again and said, "I better check out front for Malcolm Devlin."

Malcolm's expression was stoic as he led Daphne into the room. As they came in, Daphne wagged her entire back end and pulled on the leash to reach me to say hello. After I pet her, I patted the bench next to me, and Malcolm took a seat.

"It's taking all the courage I have to not just go back out that door and take her home," he said. I could see the tears glistening in his eyes.

"I understand. Have you thought of asking these people if you could check on Daphne occasionally, and maybe visit?" I silently said a prayer that the Wrights would not show up to claim Daphne.

"No. That might be harder for me, and for her also." I noticed he hadn't taken his hand from her head since he sat down. He continued to rub her ears gently.

I could hear Justin speaking to someone as he came down the hall. When he opened the door, he ushered in a man, a woman, and a boy of eight or nine.

Daphne looked up but did not seem to react at first.

The woman knelt in front of her, reaching out a hand to pet her. "Hi, Pudgy, we missed you!" Daphne's stubby tail did a few quick wags, and she let the woman pet her but did not leave her position wedged against Malcolm's knee.

The woman stood and, putting out a hand to Malcolm, said, "I'm Amanda Wright, and this is my husband George and son Noah. Thank you so much for finding Pudgy. We didn't think we would ever get her back." Malcolm stood and silently shook her hand.

I stood also, and extending a hand, said, "I'm Melanie. How did you happen to lose Dap... your dog?"

She didn't seem to question why I was involved, so I guess she assumed Malcolm and I were together. I didn't correct her. George spoke up. "I had Pudge at the dog park, and some of the other guys and I got to talking about the Sox's chances this season, and I guess I lost sight of her. The park is fenced in, so I didn't think anything could happen to her. Then, when I looked for her to go home, she was gone. One of the women there said she thought she saw a dog that looked like Pudgy being led out of the gate with somebody else."

"Did she say what the person looked like?" I said.

He shook his head. "I asked, and she only remembered they were slightly built, wearing a ball cap and maybe a blue or green shirt. It was a few months ago, and there were a lot of people there that day. I didn't recognize most of them, and I can't picture who the woman might have seen."

Malcolm had been silent after greeting the Wrights, but he said then, "You have to watch your dog, you know, even when they're in a fenced-in park."

Mrs. Wright's eyes cut to her husband, who had tensed a little at Malcolm's words. Then she smiled at her son. "Noah, come say hello to Pudgy. She's missed you."

Up until then, Noah had been examining the otoscope on the counter and the posters of dog anatomy on the wall. He dutifully came over and gave Daphne/Pudgy a few pats. She wagged her tail briefly again, but there was no spark of recognition in her eyes. He said to his mother, "Can we still get a pet rat? You promised!" He turned to me. "Rats are cool, my friend Andy has one, and he taught it to do tricks."

Amanda put her hand on his shoulder. "We'll talk about that later. We have Pudgy back now, and we're so happy, right?"

"Yeah." He nodded and went back to playing with the otoscope.

Malcolm spoke again. "Don't feel you have to take her back. I'd love to keep her if you aren't sure. I'd be glad to buy her from you."

The Wrights looked at each other. Mr. Wright spoke. "No, we're thrilled to get Pudgy back. Her full name is Graph Manner's Pudgy Princess. Her sire was a runner-up in Best of Breed at Westminster two years ago. We aren't into the whole show routine, but we are planning on breeding her." His eyebrows shot up in alarm. "You didn't have her spayed, did you?"

Justin answered, "No, she hasn't been spayed. It's hard to say what happened when she was with the man Dr. Devlin bought her from. But Malcolm has been sure she is kept in the best of health and updated on her vaccines."

Amanda smiled at Malcolm. "Thank you. I'm so glad that Pudge ended up with someone like you. We'd be glad to reimburse you for her care if you like." When Malcolm didn't respond, she looked at her watch. "I'm afraid we have a long ride and need to get on the road soon."

George Wright reached for Daphne's leash, and I saw Malcolm hesitate, then lean down and whisper something and kiss her head before he handed her over. Daphne went with George Wright but turned her head to watch Malcolm as the Wrights filed out of the room.

I turned away for a minute to wipe my eyes.

After the Wrights left, I said a quick goodbye to Justin, promising to call him later, and walked out with Malcolm. He was silent as we headed to our cars, then shook his head and said, "Who the hell gives a beauty like her a name like Pudgy?"

I was glad that Malcolm declined my offer to go out for coffee and a bite to eat because I had lost my appetite also.

When I got home, I decided to take Bruno for a walk on the bike path at Hammonasset Beach State Park. I needed to unwind after the events at Reddy Vet earlier, and a long walk would help with that, and help me sort out my thoughts about it.

It was a warm weekend at the beginning of summer, and the beach and the bike path itself were packed. Bruno walked jauntily along as we dodged bikes and other walkers. A lot of the people we passed were also walking their dogs, and without fail, each dog seemed to be periodically looking up at their people, checking in, checking they were still there. I noticed Daphne, I could only still think of her as Daphne, had not seemed that enthused to see the Wrights again. In all fairness, it had been a while since she had been with them, so maybe it would take a little time to re-bond with them. They seemed like good people. I was sure they would take good care of her. But when Daphne was with Malcolm—. The term "heart dog" seemed to apply to both of them. I was starting to tear up again, and we were coming to a section of the path that was not as heavily trafficked. I said, "Come on, Bruno! Let's run for a bit." And my own dog of my heart and I began to sprint.

After hearing George Wright's explanation that Daphne had been snatched at the dog park when he had only taken his eyes off her for a few minutes—at least he made it sound like a few minutes—I was extra vigilant when I had Bruno out in the yard. He was not a full breed; the shelter where we found him guessed he was a mix of Yorkshire Terrier and either Cairn Terrier or Jack Russell. They said the couple that brought him in seemed to like the idea of a dog better than the actual day-to-day care of one. How anyone could have ever given him up is impossible for me to imagine. Full breed or not, though, I could certainly see some despicable person thinking he would be worth stealing.

Chapter Eleven

I had just walked through the door after work on Monday when my sister, Meredith, called.

"I wanted to let you know we have arrived. Our flight came into JFK shortly after noon your time. I'm only just calling now because I needed to settle into the rental and take a nap before I could do anything else. I found the flight exhausting!"

I felt a twinge of elation at the thought of seeing my sister again after so long, mixed with apprehension about how our visit would go. "Well, I'm so glad you're here. How was the flight, other than exhausting? What is the apartment where you're staying like?"

I heard a long sigh. "The flight was a bit bumpy, and the flight attendants not as accommodating as I might have hoped. But we made it here in one piece, so I suppose that's the most important thing. The apartment is nice enough, not as nice as ones we've stayed at in Rome or Barcelona, but then I don't like to complain."

I was glad she couldn't see the look on my face as I tried to stifle a laugh. In my opinion, Meredith had perfected the art of complaining. "What are your plans over the next few days? I wasn't sure when you were going to be coming to see me, so I wasn't sure when to ask for time off."

"No worries. I need to take a day or two to re-acclimate to being back in the States, and Phillip has some sort of dinner meeting we both need to attend tomorrow. I hoped to do a bit of shopping on Wednesday. I thought I would take the train into New Haven on Thursday. I'll let you know what time to pick me up after I check the schedule."

"All right. I'll wait for your call." I hadn't been completely honest with Meredith. I had already arranged to take some time off from work. I had rightly guessed that my sister would expect me to drop everything and be available at her beck and call. Luckily, I had a lot of vacation days accrued. The fact that she wasn't coming until Thursday worked out perfectly. This way, I could relax when I attended Lynn's art show on Tuesday. I knew that no matter how many times I told myself that my sister's opinion shouldn't matter, any negative comments, whether directed at me or someone I cared about, would still have the power to sting.

* * *

Justin picked me up a little after six p.m. on Tuesday. Lynn's event at the Branford Arts and Cultural Alliance was scheduled to start at 6:30, and I wanted to be there early so I could offer her some emotional support in case she was nervous. Also, I planned to take a few photos of her with her work before the gallery became too crowded. I was thrilled to see that several people were already there when we arrived, and Lynn was chatting with them as they looked to be admiring her paintings.

As soon as she saw us walk in, Lynn excused herself and came over to greet us, a huge smile plastered on her face. "You aren't going to believe it! See that gentleman in the yellow print shirt standing by my painting of the Grass Island Shack in Guilford? He wants to buy it! *And* he offered me considerably more than I planned to ask for it."

I looked over to see a very handsome man in a yellow shirt standing by her painting. Just then, the woman in charge of the event placed a small card with the word "sold" under the painting. I hugged Lynn. "Congratulations!"

Justin gave her a hug, also. "Don't forget us little people when you're famous!"

The gallery began to fill up as more and more people came in. "Why don't you go and mingle with all your admirers. Justin and I will look around on our own and catch up with you in a little while," I said to Lynn.

As we walked around the room admiring Lynn's paintings, I realized that while I'd seen many of them before as she worked on them, several were new to me. Seeing them all displayed together as they were gave me a new appreciation of just how talented she was. I overheard several comments from people who seemed to agree with me.

We were standing and admiring a seascape Lynn had done, when I heard a voice call out, "Justin! Good to see you."

It turned out to be one of Justin's soft ball cronies, Ryan Peters, and after a quick greeting, they got into a blow-by-blow rehash of the game they had played the previous Thursday. Lucky for me, I saw Malcolm Devlin come in just then, and I excused myself so I could go talk to him.

"Malcolm! Lynn will be so happy to see you here. How are you doing?"

He shrugged. "I'm okay, I guess. Who ever thought I'd find my soul mate in a dog?" He chuckled, but I could see the hurt in his eyes. "Anyway, I couldn't miss Lynn's big event. I've heard a lot about how good an artist she is." He glanced around the room. "Bobby and Susan Wang said they were going to come also, have you seen them?"

Lynn had worked for several months as a receptionist at High Life Dermatology, and during that time had gotten to know the doctors, as well as the other staff. "No, I haven't seen Bobby or Susan yet." I had a sudden thought, "Do you know if Alex planned to come also?" I wasn't sure how Lynn would feel about her ex-fiancé attending her big event.

"No. I think he realized it might be awkward."

Justin still was in conversation with Ryan, so I walked with Malcolm as he studied the paintings Lynn had on display. "I've been thinking of updating the décor in my office. I really like this one of the lake showing the reflection of the autumn leaves. What do you think?"

I was about to tell him I thought it was an excellent choice and would look great on the wall beside his desk, when a woman who appeared to be in her early fifties rushed up to us.

"Dr. Devlin! Abby Long." She put her hand to her chest. "You treated my psoriasis? I just want to say that you are a miracle worker! I'd suffered for years until I came to you! I saw other doctors in the past, but no one helped me the way you did." Even though the room didn't seem crowded enough to warrant it, she had inched her way forward until her generous bosom was now pressed right against Malcolm's arm.

"Thank you. I'm glad to hear the treatment worked." He took a tiny step away from her, but she came right along with him.

"I'm such a patron of the arts! I'm so pleased to see that you are also!" I swear she actually batted her eyes at him.

I looked over to see Justin wave to me. He was standing by the refreshment table now, and he was holding up a glass of wine. "Excuse me, I'm wanted across the room. I'll talk to you later, Malcolm."

He gave me a plaintive look, and I did feel a twinge of guilt at abandoning him to Ms. Long, but I had every confidence he'd gracefully extricate himself soon.

As I made my way toward Justin, I heard someone say, "The painting they took was worth thousands."

The voice sounded male and seemed to be coming from a small group gathered in the middle of the room. I stopped near them and pretended to be looking for something in my purse.

A woman said, "I heard they followed her into the house as she was carrying in her groceries. It was the middle of the day! So brazen!"

"I know. These kinds of crimes are getting completely out of hand! The police—"

Justin came up beside me. "What's wrong? Did you lose something?"

The group I was listening to started to move away. I closed my purse. "No. I was just…okay, I was eavesdropping. I think those people were talking about a break-in. It sounded like the one that happened to Mrs. Paine's friend. I just wanted to hear if they had any more information on what happened. I wondered if it was the same creeps who broke into the Feldmans'."

Justin put his arm around me and guided me toward the refreshment table. "I know how upset you are about what happened to your neighbors, but please, let the police handle these crimes. If they are connected, this is a very dangerous group of people. It sounds like they could be professionals, and if that's the case, the police have the best resources to find them." He planted a kiss near my temple. "Not that I doubt your sleuthing abilities."

I knew he was right. The best course of action was to let the police conduct their investigation, but I also didn't see the harm in paying attention to any information I happened to come upon. "Okay. But there's no reason I can't still be interested in how that investigation is going." I didn't give him a chance to respond. I picked up two glasses of wine and said, "I'm sure Lynn can use a little refreshment by now. Why don't we go and find her?"

Lynn was standing with Malcolm by the painting he had picked out earlier. I could see that it now had a sold sign also.

I handed Lynn one of the glasses of wine. "Things really seem to be going well tonight!"

She smiled. "Much better than I ever expected." She turned to Malcolm. "To top it off, I'm to be displayed in the office of one of the shoreline's most famous dermatologists!"

Malcolm raised his own glass. "I'm honored to have one of your paintings."

Just then, we were joined by Bobby Wang, one of Malcolm's partners, and Bobby's wife, Susan. Both were impressed by Lynn's work, and Susan asked her about buying one of her paintings she thought would look wonderful in Bobby's home office. We chatted for a while about how lovely the gallery was; Susan talked about how excited they were to finally be pregnant and her fears about being an "elderly primipara" at forty-three. I reassured her that in spite of her age, I was sure she would do fine and told her how thrilled I was for them.

By now, the crowd had started to thin, and I could see Justin trying to hide a yawn. I said, "It looks like Lynn has everything under control here. I think we can probably leave now if you like." I looked for Lynn to say goodbye and saw her standing by the refreshment table, smiling and talking to the man in the yellow shirt. He looked to be thoroughly engrossed in their conversation. She happened to glance my way, and I waved and gave her a quick thumbs-up.

Chapter Twelve

I planned to take a week off while my sister was in the country, although I had no idea how long she and my brother-in-law, Phillip, were planning on staying. Though I suspected it would be longer than a week since his company had rented them an apartment.

I worked half a day on Wednesday, seeing only three patients in the morning. I wanted to do a final straightening up of Lynn's former room in the afternoon in preparation for my sister's arrival on Thursday. Justin was very eager to meet Meredith and had offered to take us both out to dinner that evening, but I felt it would be better if Meredith and I spent the night in, catching up on our lives. I promised him the three of us could go out the following night.

Kelly Monet was my final patient of the morning. She had developed a urinary tract infection due to the immunosuppressives she was on, and her physician wanted a follow-up visit to be sure her temperature and blood pressure were back to normal. She looked a bit tired, but otherwise healthy as she answered the door.

"I told Dr. Wayne I was doing much better; he probably didn't need to request your agency do a visit." She led me into her living room. "Not that I'm not happy to see you. You were so kind to help us try to find our puppy."

"I was glad to help. Have you had any luck in finding her?"

She shook her head. "No. The kids put up posters all around town, but no luck. My son misses her a lot. He had been after us for a while to get a dog, and he and my daughter were so good about taking care of her. I told him we would wait a little longer, then if we still couldn't find Corky, we could go to the animal shelter and he and his sister could pick out another dog." She paused a moment, then said, "I realize that sounds harsh, and I hope whatever happened to Corky, she is being well taken care of, but, honestly, I don't have high hopes of ever getting her back."

I felt a sharp pang remembering what had happened with Malcolm and Daphne. "That's a good plan. Getting a dog from the shelter would be a wonderful experience for both your children and the lucky pup."

Kelly did, indeed, check out perfectly. I told her to call her physician immediately if she started to experience any more symptoms of infection or rejection. I drove back to the office to chart and then headed home.

Justin called shortly after I got back from walking Bruno.

"Hi. I thought we could go to Lenny and Joe's and grab something to eat tonight since you're planning a girls-only night tomorrow."

Bruno was sitting by my feet, looking up intently at me as I spoke to Justin. "How about you get takeout from Lenny and Joe's and come here. Bruno is giving me that 'please don't leave again' look."

Justin laughed. "Okay. Deal."

I spent the afternoon playing with Bruno and puttering around in my back yard. Even though I'm not anywhere near the gardener Mrs. Feldman is, I was proud of how lovely the roses on my bushes had bloomed this year. I picked a small bouquet of yellow and pale pink roses. I thought they would look good in the spare bedroom. I hoped Meredith would agree. I had just gotten the flowers arranged in the vase when I heard Justin's car in the driveway.

While I got out plates and utensils, Justin unpacked the food. "I got an interesting call today," he said. "A vet from Dudley, Massachusetts called me to ask if I could send him the records that I had of vaccinations and blood work for the Wrights' dog, Pudgy."

I turned and gave him an anguished look. "She'll always be Daphne to me. Anyway, I suppose we should be glad they are at least planning on caring for her properly."

"Yes. He did mention that they were particularly concerned that she is in good health as they plan on breeding her."

I sighed. "I guess that is their right." Mr. Wright had mentioned Daphne's father being a champion, but I still felt a bit uncomfortable at the thought of poor Daphne being pressured to preserve the bloodline. I had a sudden thought. "I wonder if Malcolm would be interested in one of her puppies. How many do they usually have in a litter?"

"She could have three or four. Breeding Bulldogs can be a bit tricky, though. It sometimes may require a C-section to deliver the puppies because of the size of their heads. I checked on Dr. Foley, the vet who contacted me, and he has a good reputation, so hopefully it will go well." Justin dove into his fish and chips.

I offered Bruno one of my French fries. I wouldn't mention the whole breeding Daphne saga to Malcolm until we found out she actually had had puppies and that everything had gone well.

Justin took a sip of iced tea. "So tell me more about your sister. I know you're nervous about her coming here. What are you afraid of?"

"It's not that I'm afraid of her. It's more that I've always tried to get her approval. Our parents were always so proud of her; I felt like they were holding her up as an example for me. She graduated with honors from Yale and then got a job at a major publishing house in New York. That's where she met her husband, Phillip. Not only did they move back to his native England, but besides their home in London, his family has a 'holiday' home somewhere in Cornwall."

"So. You've been very successful in your own career. You may not have two homes, but you have been instrumental in saving lives both in your work and in your involvement in solving more than a few crimes. Though that last one scares me."

I smiled. "Okay. Thanks for trying to make me feel better. It's just that when I was young, Meredith was like a second mother to me. But once I got to my teens, it seemed she was much more disapproving of my choices in life, even if that disapproval was relayed by phone or through my mother. She didn't like that I went to a state school; she wanted me to go to an Ivy League college like her. Never mind that my choice was a lot more affordable and that I would get an excellent education. She didn't like my choice of nursing as a career—why not a doctor? I thought she might be happy when I married a doctor, but even after only meeting him once, she really didn't like Artie—I have to give her credit for her insight there."

Justin stopped eating and, looking at me, said, "Is that what it is? Are you afraid she won't like me?"

"No!" I went around the table to plant a kiss on his lips. The thought that I might make him think that stung more than anything Meredith could say. "I don't care whether she likes you or not. I love you." I realized now that there was no need to be nervous about getting her approval, since what she thought could never change how I felt about Justin, or Lynn, or a good deal of the other things in my life. I could feel some of the anxiety I felt about my sister's arrival slipping away.

Chapter Thirteen

Meredith called Wednesday evening to say she would get the 9:35 a.m. train from Grand Central Station the next day, and she would arrive in New Haven at 11:40. I promised to be there early since she made it clear she was uncomfortable with the thought of having to wait to be picked up. Whether it was nerves or excitement, or even just being used to getting up for work, I was up and dressed by six a.m. I took Bruno for a walk on Windy Reed Road after breakfast and then decided to surprise Justin and take coffee and bagels to Reddy Vet. I still had plenty of time before Meredith's train arrived, and I knew that seeing him would be a lovely way to start the day. I was sure he would have the right words to calm any final nerves over my sister's impending visit.

The clinic wouldn't be open yet, but I figured if I knocked on the door, the receptionist, Traci, would let me in, especially since I was bearing gifts. Even before I reached the parking lot, however, I could see blue and red lights flashing through the trees surrounding the office. When I pulled into the parking lot, there were two police cars there, as well as a fire engine and ambulance. One more police car screeched in behind me as I parked. I abandoned the bagels and coffee in the car and raced to the entrance.

Traci was talking to a police officer at the front desk as I entered. Her face was pale and tear-stained. "Traci, what happened?" Even before she answered, I started toward the back exam rooms to look for Justin.

A police officer I didn't recognize stepped in front of me. "I'm sorry miss, the vet office is closed for now. You'll need to leave." She gently took my arm.

Traci spoke up. "No. It's okay. She's Dr. McKenzie's...fiancée."

As the officer released my arm, Traci said, "Oh, Melanie! I'm so sorry! The paramedics are taking care of him now."

"Paramedics?" I felt a chill. "Justin? Is he all right?" I didn't wait for her answer; I rushed to the back of the clinic toward the sound of voices.

The sight that greeted me made me stop short. I'd seen many grisly scenes in my time as a nurse, including friends injured, and my first husband's body shortly after he was murdered. Nothing had ever made me feel so devastated as what I was witnessing then. Justin was being strapped onto a stretcher, blood covering his head and chest. He had an oxygen mask strapped to his face, and his color was ghastly. I called out his name, and he didn't move or open his eyes. But it was the fact that the paramedics ignored me and were moving so fast to get him out to their vehicle that scared me the most. My brain unfroze. They were moving fast, so that was good; they thought there was still something to be done for him, I thought. I croaked, "He's alive?"

One of the paramedics turned before he followed the others. "So far."

My first instinct was to race after the ambulance, but as I started for the door, I felt someone grab my arm again. "Give them time to get him to the hospital. I think you need to take a minute or two to calm down a bit before you try to drive." It was the female officer who had initially tried to stop me when I came in.

I knew she was right. My hands were now shaking. I had been in that same position myself, where I had to advise a patient's loved ones not to try to keep up with the ambulance, to drive safely to the hospital. I nodded, "Okay."

I still had no idea what had happened or how Justin came to be injured. I finally looked around the back room where he had been found. It was a mess. Instrument trays were overturned, the otoscope base pulled from where it was plugged into the wall, drawers hung open, and supplies were thrown around. I noticed strips of adhesive tape lying scattered on the floor and a puddle of blood where Justin must have been. I felt a wave of nausea. It looked like whoever did this to him restrained him using the tape. I could hear voices from across the hall, where there was a room with some crates and kennels for patients who had to remain at the clinic for a short time. I followed the voices.

The vet newest to the practice, Stella Antonio, was talking to two police officers. Her face was almost as white as Justin's had been. "I locked the back before I left last night. I'm sure of it. They must have broken in." Her voice shook, but she repeated, "I know the door was locked when I left."

I saw that the doors to two of the crates were dangling open.

"What time did you leave the office last night?" Officer Bridges was the one questioning her.

"It was a little before seven. We didn't have any more patients scheduled. I was on call, but I didn't get any messages about patients needing to come in urgently. I have no idea why Justin was here so early." She seemed upset, but her voice was almost angry now instead of frightened.

I could hear the rumble of Dr. Reddy's voice as he approached us. When he walked through the door, I ran into his arms.

He rubbed my back and said, "It will be all right. Justin'll be all right, he's a fighter." I released him and stepped back, wiping my eyes. He cleared his throat and said to Officer Bridges, "The alarm system has been giving us trouble lately. I put in a call to the company yesterday, and they said someone would be out today or tomorrow."

"What is the name of the company that handles the system?" Officer Bridges asked.

"Apex Alarms."

Officer Bridges made a note on his pad. "Are you able to tell what was stolen?"

"I can give you a list of the narcotics they stole from the cabinet. Other than that, it is a small amount of cash from a locked drawer, the two dogs, and some dog food and pet supplies."

"When did they break-in? How did Justin get hurt?" I looked from Stella to Dr. Reddy.

Officer Bridges answered me. "We estimate it must have been sometime very early this morning. It looks as if Dr. McKenzie surprised whoever it was who broke in. From what we can piece together, he was restrained and beaten."

I was startled when someone put their hand on my shoulder. "I'm sorry, Melanie, we'll find who did this."

I turned to find Sunny Cody standing next to me. I looked at her, bewildered. "I don't understand. Who did this? Why? What were they after?"

Sunny's voice was matter-of-fact. "My guess was they were mainly looking for drugs. The cabinet where the narcotics are stored has been broken into. They also took two dogs that were being boarded here overnight. Whether that was part of the plan or just opportunistic, it's hard to say."

"Why was Justin here?" I turned to Stella. "You said you were on call. Why was he notified if there was an emergency call from a client? Where was the client during the break-in?"

Stella gave me a startled look. "I...don't know. Do you think if he was meeting a client they might have seen who did this?"

"That's a good point," Sunny said. She turned to look at Dr. Reddy. "Is there any way to tell who might have called with an animal they needed to be seen emergently?"

Dr. Reddy said, "I'll call our answering service. If Justin got an emergency call, it would have gone through them. I'll ask why he was called instead of Dr. Antonio and get the name of the client." He looked at Stella. "You're right, maybe whoever the client was, they saw something out of the ordinary when they got here." He let out a deep sigh. "After that, I need to call the owners of the two animals that were taken." He shook his head. "Horrible, horrible situation."

As he left the room to make his calls, Sunny turned to Stella again. "Dr. Antonio, I want to ask you again about what you saw when you came in this morning. Could we...."

I wanted to know what happened, also, but more than anything, I wanted to be sure Justin was all right. It seemed like an hour had passed since I'd walked into the veterinary clinic to see them rushing Justin away, but it had probably only been ten to fifteen minutes.

The drive to the emergency department at the hospital seemed to take forever, and when I arrived, I saw that the waiting room was nearly full. I rushed up to the admission desk and, trying to keep my voice calm, said, "I'm here to see Justin McKenzie. He was brought in by ambulance a short while ago. He's been badly beaten." My voice caught on the last part.

The receptionist punched in Justin's name. "Are you a relative?"

"No. But—"

"I can see Mr. McKenzie was admitted, but I can't give you any more information unless you are a family member. Sorry."

I suddenly remembered what Traci had said when I ran into Reddy Vet that morning. "I'm his fiancée." I placed my right hand over my left to hide my naked ring finger. "Please?"

She hesitated, then said, "I'll see if one of the nurses is free to speak to you."

I stood awkwardly off to the side near the desk until I saw a nurse I recognized come out from the triage area. "Hi. I'm Melanie. I used to work in med-surg. My fiancé, Justin McKenzie, has been brought in, and I need to see him." I hesitated, "Or at least know how he is doing."

"I remember you." She smiled and held out her badge so I could see it, "Dani. I'm not working in trauma today, but I'll try to find out what I can." She peeked into a small conference room to be sure it was empty, and then said, "Wait here. I'll talk to Beth. I think he's her patient. I'll see what she can tell me."

I hoped it was one of the Beths that I knew from when I had worked at the hospital. I sat stiffly in one of the hardback chairs in the room; there was no way I could relax enough to sit on the low sofa. Dani was back in ten minutes, and with her was Beth Rogers. Beth and I had worked together in Med- Surg for two years before she transferred to the ED. She came and sat across from me. "They took Dr. McKenzie to surgery. I understand he is your fiancé." She looked at my left hand, but continued, "He has a subdural hematoma, three broken ribs, and a lot of nasty-looking lacerations and contusions. Whoever hit him did a job on him."

I felt my stomach clench. The subdural was a serious head injury; with quick treatment, he should survive, but there could be residual damage. I fought back the tears that came to my eyes. "Did he regain consciousness at all?"

"He did try to open his eyes briefly, but no, he never fully regained consciousness." She reached over to rub my arm. "It's going to be a while, but if you want, you can wait upstairs in the waiting room outside the neuro ICU."

I suddenly felt adrift. I had spent years working in this hospital, but now I felt frightened and out of place. I was in the position where I was the one waiting for news on a loved one, instead of the one offering information and support.

I took the visitor elevator up to the Neurosurgical Intensive Care Unit, where he would go after surgery. I used the intercom to let the unit secretary know I was waiting to see Justin McKenzie once he was admitted to the floor and able to get visitors. I didn't even wait for her question this time. I said I was his fiancée. She directed me to the waiting room and said someone would be out to update me once they had any news.

I sat in one of the chairs nearest the door and glanced around the room. There were four other people: two women hunched together in a chair by the window, and another woman and a man, who I assumed was her husband, seated across from me. The man was staring at the floor, while the woman with him sat crying quietly. She suddenly took a deep shuddering breath, and the man reached over and took her hand. A nurse entered the room, and we all looked up at her in anticipation. I knew it hadn't been long enough for Justin to be out of surgery, at least not if there was a good result. I gripped the arm of the chair, ready to jump up if there was any news for me.

The nurse gave the couple seated across from me a sympathetic look, and walking over to them, sat next to the woman. "The doctor is finished examining your mother now. You can come in to see her if you'd like. Dr. Gibbons will be right in to update you."

The woman gathered her things, and the couple followed the nurse out of the room.

Mrs. McKenzie! I hadn't even thought about someone needing to notify Justin's mother. My phone suddenly vibrated with a call. I'd somehow had the presence of mind to mute the ring when I got to the hospital. It was from

Charlie, Justin's grandfather. I stepped out into the hall to take the call.

"Melanie? Are you with him? How is he? What's going on?" Charlie sounded flustered for the first time since I'd known him.

I fought to keep my voice from breaking. "He's in surgery now. I'm waiting for news." I went on to tell him what I knew about what had happened at Reddy Vet this morning, that the police thought the break-in had happened in the early morning. I shuddered to think it could have been in the middle of the night, and Justin had been lying there until someone came in to open up.

I thought I heard Charlie swear. "Rita is away on a cruise—Alaska, of all places. I spoke to her, and she's going to catch the next flight out of Anchorage."

Now I remembered Justin saying his mother was going to be away for ten days.

Charlie continued, "I called my lady friend, Loretta, she's giving me a ride to the hospital."

I felt a small bit of comfort at the thought of him being there with me.

I went back into the waiting room once I'd ended the call with Charlie, and I heard the younger-looking of the two women by the window say, "I'm going to get us coffee." As she passed me, she said, "Can I get you a coffee also?"

I smiled at her. "No, thank you." The mention of coffee reminded me of the Box of Joe I'd intended to bring to the staff at Reddy Vet, and which was now cooling in my car. I flashed back to the whole scene of police, seeing Justin gravely injured, the wrecked exam room, and the open crates in the recovery/boarding room. Mostly, I couldn't forget the sight of Justin's bloody form as he was placed onto that stretcher. He was constantly worried about me getting into a situation where my life was in danger, and yet he was the one now fighting for his life. I felt my eyes tear up again. I tried to focus on what I'd seen and heard this morning at Reddy Vet to occupy my mind and to do something besides worry about Justin.

Justin was most likely there to see a patient who needed emergency care and somehow interrupted the break-in. But where was the pet's owner who called? Did they see anything? I thought of the night I'd seen something at the Feldmans'. Or failed to see anything specific. Another similarity to the Feldmans' occurred to me—it looked like Justin had been restrained, similar to what happened to Mrs. Feldman. Dr. Reddy said two dogs were taken, as well as any drugs that were on the premises. That seemed odd, and given that I had heard of several missing or stolen pets recently, a little alarm went off in my mind. Sunny Cody would probably say I was drawing some pretty shaky connecting lines, but I felt sure that there was some link between everything that had happened.

I noticed that the waiting room was now filling up with more people. The women who had been sitting by the window were gone; either I hadn't noticed anyone come in to get them, or they had gone to get something to eat. My stomach growled, and I realized it had been a long time since breakfast. I checked my watch. It was 11:30. Meredith! There was no way I could leave the hospital to pick her up. Not until I saw for myself that Justin was all right. My thoughts raced as I punched in Lynn's number to ask her to pick up my sister at the train station.

"I don't have a lot of time to explain." I gave her the briefest details about what had happened. "So, can you pick up Meredith for me? I'll text her to expect you."

Lynn didn't hesitate, "Sure. I got a news alert on my phone about the break-in at the vet. Is Justin all right?"

"I don't know."

"I'll get your sister settled at your house. I can get the key from Karen next door. Call me later when you have news." She ended the call.

I texted Meredith that there had been an emergency. That I couldn't be there to pick her up, and she was to expect my friend Lynn. I told her I'd explain later. I had just sent the text when someone else entered the waiting room. Stella Antonio.

I blurted out, "What are you doing here? How did you even get them to let you up here?"

She came over to sit by me. "I lied and said I was Justin's sister."

I could feel every muscle in my body stiffen.

She seemed not to have noticed my reaction and continued, "I wanted to make sure Justin was all right. I feel terrible that he interrupted the break-in. I should have been the one to be called; I don't know why he was notified instead."

"What good would that have done? Then you would have been the one attacked!" I felt guilty because, truthfully, at that moment, I would have preferred it had been her rather than Justin.

She ignored the fact that I was pointing out what she said made no sense. "Any news? Has he regained consciousness yet?"

"No. He's still in surgery." I looked over at her. "Don't you need to be at Reddy Vet, helping Dr. Reddy?" I realized my tone was a bit sharp, but the very fact of her being there irritated me. She was just Justin's co-worker, I felt only those closest to him should be with him when he was in such a vulnerable state. I flashed on the familiar way she touched him the other day.

"I told Dr. Reddy I needed a couple of hours to pull myself together." She looked at me with tears in her eyes, "It was a shock to walk in this morning and see what had happened. To see Justin like that."

I suddenly felt a twinge of sympathy for her. "Were you the one who found him?"

She took a moment to reply, as if she was trying to get the picture out of her mind. "Yes. Traci came into the clinic almost the same time as I did. We could see right away that something was wrong. The door to the practice's pharmacy was open. When I saw Justin on the floor in one of the rooms, I yelled for Traci to call 911."

I shuddered. "How did they get in? Did you notice anything that would help the police find who did this?"

"It looked like the back door was forced open. I've already told the police all I know. I'm not sure how much help it will be, though. As I told them, I was pretty upset by what happened."

I had really hoped she could at least offer some information that would help find who was responsible for the break-in. It made me think again of my lack of information on who was responsible for breaking into the Feldmans' house, though.

"Maybe when Justin recovers, he'll be able to remember something to help find who did this," I said. "Although, I'll be happy if he regains consciousness without any residual effects from his head injury." My voice caught as I said the last part.

Stella reached over to pat my hand briefly. "Of course. That is the most important thing."

I heard the ping of a text coming from her purse. "Sorry. I forgot to silence my phone." She checked her messages. "That was Dr. Reddy. I better get back to the clinic."

I felt relieved when she left. I knew I shouldn't be so territorial. She was just being a concerned friend, and Justin would need all the support he could get from his friends and family as he recovered. I looked at my watch, hoping that there would be news soon.

I jumped a few minutes later when I heard my name called. The surgeon came over to sit next to me in the seat Stella had vacated. He was not someone I recognized, but he had a very kind look, and he smiled briefly as he sat down. "I'm Dr. Lewis. I understand you're Dr. McKenzie's fianceé?"

"Yes." I didn't even hesitate. When everything calmed down, I was going to have to think about the fact it seemed so easy for me to say that.

"Luckily, his head injury wasn't as bad as we first thought. He did well with the surgery to relieve the pressure on his brain, and while he is really banged up, the only fractures were to his ribs. Those will be painful but heal with time. The nurses are getting him settled in now, but someone will be out shortly to get you so you can see him."

I felt some of the tension release from my shoulders. "Thank you."

Chapter Fourteen

I thought all my experience as a nurse would prepare me for what I would see when I entered Justin's room, but my breath caught at the sight of him. He looked so helpless. I winced at the bruises around his eyes, on his arms, and on his forehead. Parts of his scalp were shaved where they had had to enter to remove the clot pressing on his brain. I softly touched the remaining dark curls I loved so much. I knew that when he was stronger, he probably would want to shave the rest of his head to match where it had already been shorn.

One of the nurses came to stand beside me. "Hi. I'm Betsy. I'll be his nurse today. He's stable so far, but he may not wake up for a little while." She pulled a chair over to the side of his bed so I could sit. "I'll be right outside. Press the call button if you need anything."

I nodded and took Justin's hand. I sat that way for several minutes, just glad that he had survived the first hurdle after his injury. The steady sound of the cardiac monitor was comforting.

After about twenty minutes or so, Betsy came back into the room again and said, "There's another visitor for Dr. McKenzie. It's his grandfather. Do you want me to ask him to wait?"

"No. I'll be out in a minute." I gently squeezed Justin's hand and whispered, "I love you." I was sure I felt his fingers move in response.

When I went back out to the waiting room, I saw Charlie was seated next to a pleasant looking gray-haired woman. When I approached them, they both stood, and the woman offered me her hand. "Hello, I'm Loretta Wilson." Her eyes were a warm brown, and her handshake was not so much firm as reassuring.

"So, what's the news? He okay? What did the doctor say?" I could see Charlie was trying to hide how worried he was, but the strain was obvious on his face.

I motioned for them to sit again and took the seat next to Charlie. "Dr. Lewis said the surgery went well." I could see Charlie start to relax. "He is stable but still hasn't woken up from anesthesia." I didn't add that I hoped that he *was* still just under the effects of anesthesia and would regain consciousness soon. I pushed away the thought that he had sustained enough of an injury to cause his lack of responsiveness.

"But what do *you* think? He look okay to you?" Charlie said.

"He looks like he took a beating, but looking at his vital signs on the monitor, I agree that he seems stable." I swallowed the lump that was rising in my throat. "I trust the doctors and nurses here. I trust how tough Justin is…a lot like his grandfather."

Loretta gave a quick smile and took Charlie's hand.

"I want to see him." Charlie had already started to get up from his chair again.

"Okay, I already told the nurse I was going to send you in." I walked with him to show him where to press the intercom to ask to be admitted, and I went back to the waiting room to sit with Loretta.

She turned out to be the perfect distraction. She told me how she met Charlie at a community center program titled "How Not to Be a Victim," and that she had been a widow for twenty years. She said her husband had been a firefighter who loved his bacon a bit too much and died of a heart attack at fifty-two. She loved her job as a 911 operator in New Haven and had just retired two years previously. "It was both our interests in law enforcement and helping people that drew Charlie and me together. When I heard he had a police scanner, I knew I had found a soulmate." She laughed.

I shared a bit about how I met Justin and my surprise at finding out about his relationship to one of my favorite patients.

She laughed again. "One of your favorites? Don't tell Charlie that! He's sure he has no competition as your very favorite!"

For the first time that day, I laughed also.

Charlie came back into the waiting room after about ten minutes. "They had to do something with him, change his position or something, so I said I'd step out for a little while." He lowered himself into the seat by Loretta. "They better catch whoever did that to him." His voice was steely. "You able to get any information from your cop friend about what the police know so far?"

"Only that they think it happened in the early morning hours, and it looks like the back door was forced. From what they can tell so far, Justin was there to meet a client with a pet emergency. Doctor Reddy is trying to find out who that was and if they saw anything unusual." Just then, my phone vibrated with a text. It was from Lynn.

"Meredith safely at your house. Bruno not sure what to make of her! Love to Justin. Call me later."

"My sister is visiting from England. That was Lynn letting me know she's arrived at my house." Never in my life had I wanted more to be in two places at once than at that moment.

"First I heard of her, so I'm guessing it's been a while since you've seen her," Charlie said. He looked at Loretta. "We'll stay here. You go see to your sister. I'll give you a call if anything changes or we get an update."

"I don't know…I don't want to leave him."

Loretta said, "You need to take a break. Go home and see your sister. At least let her know what's happened."

I knew she was right. "All right. But I'll be back later. Call me right away if Justin regains consciousness."

* * *

On the drive home, I felt drained by all the morning's events. I struggled to muster the energy I was going to need to explain all that had happened to my sister, and to ask for her understanding. I was sure she had been expecting my full attention during her visit.

When I got home, Bruno ran over to greet me, jumping up and licking my hands. What I really needed was the comfort it would offer to sit and cuddle with him, but I could hear Meredith coming from the spare bedroom.

"There you are! I'm so sorry! Your friend told me a little bit about what happened." She hesitated for a moment, then pulled me into a quick hug.

I was surprised that after all my worry about it, how good it felt to see her again. "I'm sorry I wasn't at the train station to meet you. Did you have to wait long for Lynn?"

"It seemed long, I'm afraid, since I was worried about what the emergency was that you texted me about." She sighed. "At least it was easy for us to find one another since the station had emptied out considerably between departures and arrivals."

I couldn't really blame her for her implied criticism. I hadn't elaborated on what had happened. "I could really use a cup of tea right now. How about you?" I headed toward the kitchen.

Meredith followed. "Your friend made me tea already, but I'll have another cup if you're making yourself one."

"I see Lynn also showed you to your room. Good." I knew I could count on Lynn to take care of my sister until I could get home.

"Yes. She was lovely. She knew right where you kept everything. She even walked the dog after we got here. She must be a close friend."

"She is. We were housemates for a while." I didn't have the energy at that moment to go into how exactly we became friends. I tried to redirect the conversation instead. "Lynn is an artist, and her career is really starting to take off." I poured the water for our tea and sat down opposite Meredith. I knew she was into the arts and hoped to get her talking about all the museums and galleries I knew she would have visited in Europe.

"That's lovely. But never mind that for now." She scooped sugar into her tea. "Lynn said you were at the hospital. She tells me you have been seeing this veterinarian fellow for a while. Is he badly injured?"

"Yes." I took a deep breath to steady myself. "There was a break-in at his practice, and either he interrupted it, or they didn't know he was there when they broke in. Whoever did it beat him badly. He suffered a head injury. He's had surgery but is still unconscious."

She leaned back in her chair. "How awful! As I said, I'm sorry to hear that."

"Please forgive me if I seem distracted. I had planned on spending the evening with you, catching up, but if you don't mind, I need to go back to see Justin in a little while."

"It sounds as if your relationship with him is serious. Please just be careful this time, be sure this is what you want. After Artie—"

All the anger I felt at what had happened to Justin boiled up. I snapped back, "Justin is nothing like Artie! He is kind and honest, and I—"

"All right." Meredith put up her hands. "I'm just trying to look out for you. I would hate to see you hurt again. I assume he does know about your previous marriage and what happened after your divorce?"

"Yes, of course."

"Was he ever married? Children?"

"No. Neither of those." I glared at her, daring her to ask about his sexual orientation.

"What has happened to him is horrible, but you also do need to think about how this injury might affect him. He could be…different afterward. I know you're a nurse—but—well you see where I'm going with this."

I couldn't even respond to her. My anger was choking me now. "I need to take Bruno for a walk." Bruno trotted after me as I practically ran to the door, grabbing his leash on the way. I needed fresh air, and I needed it immediately.

Bruno and I started off at a much brisker pace than usual. I told myself that my sister had always been lacking in the tact department, and I knew she really was concerned about my welfare, but her words were so out of line as to be unbelievable.

The way I felt must have been obvious from the look on my face as I passed Mrs. Feldman, who was out watering her flowers. She called out, "Are you all right, dear?" and hurried toward me.

I slowed my pace. I hesitated at first to tell her what had happened; she had just undergone a similar trauma. I was pretty sure the burglary at Reddy Vet would be on the news, however. "I'm afraid there has been another break-in." I told her what I knew.

She shook her head. "I can't believe this happened again. Do you think it's the same criminals who broke into my house?"

"Probably." The violence of the break-in and the fact Justin had been beaten, as had Ernie Feldman, made them similar in my mind.

She was quiet for a moment, then patted my arm, "Dr. McKenzie is such a lovely young man, and very strong. I have every confidence he will recover. With any luck, he'll remember something to help the police catch these horrible people."

"I really hope so." Though more than anything, I wanted him to make a full recovery. My sister's words were still fresh in my mind. I knew any residual damage wouldn't change how I felt about him, but I knew he would need time to adjust to it.

Mrs. Feldman looked thoughtful for a moment. "You said whoever did this took two dogs also? I remember you thought whoever broke into our house wanted to take Nika. That is a strange coincidence, isn't it?"

"Yes. I wonder if it is a coincidence, though."

"As you pointed out, Nika is a valuable animal. Do you know anything about the dogs that were taken?"

"Not yet." I desperately wanted to talk to Sunny Cody and find out if they had caught anyone yet or spoken to whoever called the answering service with the emergency.

Mrs. Feldman gave my arm a final pat and said, "I'll let you get on with your walk. I'll keep Dr. McKenzie in my thoughts, and you give him my best when you see him."

Bruno and I set out at a slightly slower pace, and I felt some of my anger dissolve after talking to Lana Feldman. I tried to concentrate on the feel of the sun on my skin, listening to the birdsong, and taking deep, calming breaths as we continued our walk.

Suddenly, another thought popped into my mind. Justin's Golden Retriever, Jasper, and his Maine Coon cat, Miss Scarlett, needed to be taken care of. I knew he had someone come in to walk Jasper midday, but his animals would need someone who could care for them full-time until he could do it himself. Jasper was much spunkier than Justin's grandfather's dog, Rex, and I feared a bit too much for Charlie.

"Bruno, how would you like your buddy Jasper to stay with us for a while?" The two dogs knew each other well since Justin and I walked them together, and we would bring one or the other with us when we went to each other's house. Miss Scarlett was another story. She tolerated her housemate, Jasper, but wanted no part of poor Bruno.

Maybe Justin's mother could take the cat when she got home from Alaska, but until then, I'd have to come up with a different solution. As we neared home, my neighbor, Karen, popped out of her house.

"I hope it's okay that I gave the key to your friend Lynn. She said your sister is visiting and she needed the key to let her into your house. She said you were at the hospital. Is everything all right?"

"Yes, thank you. I'm afraid Justin was injured, and I went to the hospital to be with him."

"Is he going to be okay? What happened?"

I gave her a brief summary of what had occurred at Reddy Vet and watched as her concern turned to anger.

"See. I knew it! They need to catch these thugs. First the Feldmans', now this." She looked around as if expecting that we would be ambushed as we stood there and talked. "Anyway, I'll be praying for Dr. McKenzie. Let me know if there is anything I can do."

I had a thought. "Has Jenny gotten a kitten yet?"

Karen looked confused, but said, "No. Her friend Jada's cat is pregnant, and she promised her one of that litter. Why?"

"You both were so helpful by taking in Mrs. Feldman's cat. I was wondering if you would be willing to take Justin's cat for a day or two. His mother is away, but will take care of her once she gets home." I looked down at Bruno. "I am going to watch his dog, but I'm afraid Miss Scarlett is not Bruno's biggest fan."

Karen nodded, "I'm sure Jenny would love to do it."

I was relieved that one problem was solved. "Thank you." I only hoped getting to know Miss Scarlett wouldn't change their mind about getting a kitten.

By the time we got back home, my anger at my sister had started to subside. Even though she had only been looking out for my welfare, I was not an inexperienced twenty-one-year-old anymore. Plus, I realized I hadn't told her anything about Justin before this, so she had no idea what he was really like.

Meredith was sitting in the living room reading when I came in. She immediately stood up and said, "I'm sorry. I didn't mean to upset you."

I bent to unhook Bruno's leash. "Once you get to know Justin, you'll see how lucky I am to have him in my life. Besides, don't you think I'm capable of making my own choices, no matter what the outcome?" I marched toward the kitchen without making eye contact with her.

"I admit I might have overstepped my bounds. It's just...I'm worried about someone else, and maybe that influenced how I acted toward you."

I was taking things from the refrigerator and cupboards to start making dinner for us, but stopped. "Who is it that has you worried?" It was no excuse for how she acted, but I could see how that could happen.

She sat at the table. "It's Timothy, my eldest."

I tried to calculate how old Timothy was now, twenty? Twenty-two? I went to sit opposite her. "What's happened with him?"

"He's fine, but he's been seeing a young woman for a year now. She's quite a bit older than him, almost ten years. She's not very focused on her career and seems to flit from one position to the next. She gets upset when he goes out to spend time with his friends, and I get the impression she thinks he is too close to his father, brother, and me. On more than one occasion, she has lured him away from spending time with us when we had plans. I tried inviting her to join us, but she made a face and said she'd already made plans for the two of them. When she does come along, she quickly acts bored and wants Timothy to take her home early."

"I can see why you're worried. It doesn't seem like a good situation," I said.

"I'm afraid he's about to propose to her, and I think marrying her is a big mistake."

I had planned to make a home cooked meal, but my heart wasn't in it, and it seemed more important that I spend time talking with my sister, anyway. I got up to put everything back in the cupboard and refrigerator and sat down again. "Why don't we order in a pizza for dinner?"

"What is this woman's name? How did he meet her?"

"Her name is Lena, and he met her when she was a teaching assistant at his university. He is employed at a brokerage firm in London now, and she's left her previous position to work at a café near his office. Both Phillip and I had a talk with Timothy, asking him to slow down and really consider whether this was a relationship that would last. He told us to butt out of his life." She began to shred her tea bag onto her napkin.

"So that is where we're at now. He refuses to discuss his relationship with Lena with us. He says he is nearly twenty-four and able to make his own decisions," she said.

I realized my words a few minutes before must have uncomfortably echoed his. "I'm sorry. I know that must be a hard situation for both you and Phillip." I felt a twinge of guilt at my reaction to her words earlier.

"Yes. I almost didn't come to New York with Phillip; I was worried about what would happen while we were away. Phillip convinced me that, as Timothy said, he's an adult, and we can only offer him our best advice." She folded up the napkin containing the decimated tea bag. "Trash?"

I nodded toward the bin under the sink. "I think Phillip is right. I'm glad you decided to come."

She came to sit opposite me again and smiled. "I am too." Meredith pointed at my phone, which I had set by my elbow on the table in case Charlie called with news. "I'm ravenous, so if you don't mind—"

"Sure. Mushrooms all right?"

"Yes. And onions too."

I ordered a large pizza to be delivered from Grand Apizza. While I was on the phone, I noticed Bruno nuzzling Meredith cautiously. She reached down and picked him up into her lap.

"Finally. I was waiting for you to decide about me!" She rubbed under his chin, causing him to wiggle in her lap excitedly.

That made me remember I still had to pick up Justin's animals. "The pizza will be here in about thirty minutes. I need to run an errand, but should be back shortly after it comes." I placed some money on the table and told her where I was going. "Please, don't wait for me if you want to dig into the pizza before I get back."

I left Meredith talking to her younger son, Matthew, on WhatsApp and went to Justin's to pick up Jasper and Miss Scarlett. I also packed some T-shirts and pajama bottoms for Justin. I knew as soon as he was able, he would want to get out of the hospital gown he had on now.

Jasper was delighted to see me, and even Miss Scarlett was very cooperative as I loaded her into her carrier.

Jenny was delighted when I dropped off Justin's cat, and I left Miss Scarlett regally surveying her new territory.

When I took him next door to my house, Jasper was thrilled to see Bruno, but I could see Meredith was somewhat taken aback by the two dogs racing around from room to room.

"Will you be all right with me leaving you with these two? They usually calm down after they've gotten their 'zoomies' out."

"No worries. We lost our golden, Holly, two years ago, and I still miss her." She helped herself to a slice of pizza, then said, "Now eat. Then go see your young man."

I wolfed down two slices of pizza, and then I checked in with Charlie. He said that Justin had woken up very briefly but was out again.

"They say that is not unusual, not to worry," he said. "The police showed up, hoping to talk to Justin, see what he remembered, but the doctor told them they would need to come back. He said someone would notify them when he was able to be interviewed." Charlie sounded exhausted.

"Why don't you go home and get some rest. I'll be on my way there soon; I'll stay with him. Is Loretta still there with you?"

"Yeah. She's a trooper. Been getting me coffee and food," he chuckled, "that is, when she's not getting everyone else in the waiting room to tell her their life story. She's made friends with just about all the staff, too." He definitely perked up a little as he talked about her.

"Good. I'll call you with any new developments, okay?"

When I ended my call to Charlie, I noticed I'd missed a text from Sunny

Cody: *Need you to come in tomorrow morning to talk—want to review anything you might have noticed at vet's office. THX*

On the drive to the hospital, I tried to think of everything I saw, any details that might help in the investigation. All I could remember was initially seeing the mess in the exam room when I first walked in. But then my focus had immediately shifted to Justin. Afterward, I noticed that all the drawers had been pulled out, instruments scattered around the room, and the cut strips of adhesive tape on the floor. It looked like whoever broke in wanted to find something to use to restrain Justin. Had they already beaten him and wanted to be sure he wouldn't be a threat if he woke up? The instruments on the floor indicated there had been a struggle. But all this was something I was sure the police had figured out already. I did think of one thing; Lana said whoever broke into their house used zip ties. That means they came prepared to incapacitate anyone they encountered. This time, it looked like they didn't expect to find anyone at the Vet's office.

By the time I reached the hospital, I hadn't remembered anything I thought might be useful to tell Sunny when I spoke to her. I was still going to go into the station tomorrow, though. I wanted to hear what she found out so far. I knew she couldn't divulge certain information, but I was sure she could answer some of the questions I had.

When I reached the Neuro ICU, Charlie had gone home as I suggested. It was later than I planned when I got there, and I knew I wouldn't have much time before visiting hours were over. However, I needed to see Justin at least for a little while again. When I went into his room, a different nurse was at his bedside. She was changing one of his IV bags, and smiled at me as I walked in.

"Hi, you must be Justin's fiancée. His grandfather said you'd be in again this evening."

Charlie said I was Justin's fiancée? I almost laughed. I guess the only one who didn't know that was Justin himself. "Yes. How is he?"

Her name tag read 'Marissa.' "He's stable. He's had brief episodes of alertness so far, which is a good sign."

That was some relief, though I was sorry I wasn't there when he was awake.

I knew that a prolonged coma didn't bode well after a head injury.

"Mr. Duggan said you're a nurse?" Marissa said.

"Yes. I used to work here on a medical-surgical floor, but I work in home healthcare now."

"And you like it? I'm afraid that's not for me. I would never feel comfortable going into the houses of people I didn't know." She smiled again, "No offense."

"None taken." I pulled over the chair to sit next to Justin again, and Marissa left the room.

"Hi. It's me. How do you feel?" I really didn't expect him to answer, but I did notice a slight uptick in his heart rate on the monitor. I was sure he could hear me. I told him about my sister being here now, that I had Jasper at my house, that Miss Scarlett was safe with my neighbors, and that his mother was on her way to see him also. "There is a whole cheering section waiting for you to wake up and get better. So, do your best, okay?"

I could hear the overhead announcement that visiting hours were over. I leaned over to kiss him gently on the forehead, and I saw his eyelids flutter for a few seconds before he was still again.

When I got back home, Jasper and Bruno greeted me at the door, and Meredith was sitting in the living room reading again.

"Just as you said, they did calm down after they got all their energy out," she said. "How did things go at the hospital?"

"Justin is not fully awake yet, but his nurse said he has been conscious for brief periods."

"That's good, isn't it? I know you would know much better than I would."

"Yes. That is good." I didn't add that I really wished I'd seen him awake, however. "Would you like me to fix us a cup of tea?"

"No, thank you." She got up out of her chair and stretched. "It's been a long day. I think I'll head to bed if that's all right."

"You're right, it has been a long day. Let me know if you need anything." I felt guilty, but I was glad she was ready to turn in because I wanted to call Lynn to thank her for helping me out today and get the whole story of what happened when she picked my sister up at the train station. I also wanted to be able to talk about Justin and my worries about him without my sister overhearing.

I was sure Lynn would still be awake. She answered right away.

"How is he? Did the surgery go okay? Did you speak to him?"

"The surgeon said everything went well, and the nurses said he's regained consciousness for a few minutes at a time." I felt my eyes welling up as I continued. "I think he knew I was there, but no, he wasn't really awake."

"He's going to be okay. He's strong, and he has a lot of people pulling for him."

"I know you're right." I took a deep breath. "I want to thank you for picking up my sister on such short notice. She told me that you stayed to get her settled in at my house. That was good of you."

"No problem. She seemed irritated at first that you weren't the one there to pick her up, but she calmed down when I told her what had happened." She laughed. "She did ask how we knew each other, but don't worry, I just said we met through a mutual friend. I'll let you explain who that was."

"Thanks." I chuckled. "To be honest, though, what she thinks of my escapades the past year or so isn't my biggest concern right now."

Chapter Fifteen

The next morning, after breakfast, I fed and walked the dogs, then told Meredith that I needed to run an errand. I promised we would go for lunch at Lenny and Joe's Fish Tale before I went to the hospital to see Justin again.

When I got to the police station, Sunny showed me right into one of the interview rooms.

As soon as we were seated, I told her I hadn't been able to think of anything I noticed or heard that would help in the investigation. "I'm sorry, but I was pretty shaken up."

She sighed. "All right. How is Dr. McKenzie doing? We tried to interview him yesterday, but he was not in any condition to give a statement yet."

"Yes, I heard. I'm going to check on Justin this afternoon." Charlie told me he was getting a ride to the hospital this morning and would update me if there were any changes. "I'm sure the hospital will notify you when he's able to speak to you."

"Yes, that's what they said. Be sure to tell me if he says anything at all while you're with him, though."

"Of course. Was Dr. Reddy able to find out who called the answering service with the emergency?" I wasn't sure she'd tell me, but I knew Dr. Reddy would if she didn't.

Sunny hesitated for a moment. "The operator at the answering service said they got a panicked call from someone who told them they thought their dog was having a seizure, and that they were bringing her right in to the office and to notify the vet on call. They never gave their name."

"What about paperwork? Justin would have filled it out for the receptionist to enter into the computer when she came in."

"There was no paperwork found. Either he never got a chance to fill it out, or as we suspected, he never saw whoever called."

"I don't understand why the operator would notify Justin instead of Dr. Antonio. She said she was covering emergencies."

"The person who took the call was apologetic, but she said she didn't recognize Dr. Antonio's name or know that she was now with the practice. She knew Dr. McKenzie was always willing to cover in a pinch, so she called him."

She was right; if Justin thought there was a true emergency, he wouldn't waste time having the operator call Stella Antonio. He would go himself and find out where the mix-up occurred later. "So, it was pure bad luck that he was the one at the office when it was broken into." As much as I wanted Justin not to have been the one attacked, it would still have been horrible if Stella Antonio had been there. Even if I didn't exactly have any warm feelings toward her.

"Apparently. It still brings up the question of what happened to the dog owner who called."

"Could they have left before the break-in, or maybe the dog seemed better, and they decided it was no longer an emergency?" Justin said that, inconsiderate as it was, it wasn't unheard of for a formerly panicked pet owner to just decide their dog or cat was all right after all, but not notify the vet. "Could you get in touch with whoever called?"

"As I said, the operator at the answering service said she didn't get a name or phone number. I have instructed the staff at the office to notify us if anyone comes in who says they called on Wednesday night, and to find out if they actually showed up or not." Sunny took out her phone as if she had just gotten a text message. "I need to attend to something else right now, but I wanted to tell you that you may have been helpful after all. Your theory about the burglars being interested in stealing valuable animals may not be so crazy. One of the dogs taken from Reddy Vet apparently was a show dog worth quite a bit."

I felt a flash of satisfaction. "What breed were they?"

She looked at her tablet. "One was a champion French Bulldog and the other a young white Labradoodle. The owners are desperate to get them back, and despite the fact we advised them not to, the French Bulldog's owners plan to offer a very sizable reward." She sighed. "I'm afraid of what may happen as we get multiple false tips."

"I have to say, I can't blame them, however." I was certain both Dr. Reddy and Dr. Antonio would also be eager to get both dogs back to their owners.

"I'm sure that wasn't the prime reason for the break-in, but as you pointed out, it's possible that it ties it to the break-in at the Feldmans'." She got up to leave. "Thank you for coming in."

Talking about the missing dogs made me flash back to the day Malcolm had to give Daphne to the Wrights. I thought about the disturbance at the front desk when I was walking in. "Wait. I just remembered something. A few days before the break-in at the vet, there was a client who was very angry about something. I walked in as Justin was trying to calm him down. Their receptionist said he has given them trouble before. Could he have something to do with what happened?"

Sunny made a quick note. "Do you know his name?"

"I don't, but I'm sure the receptionist, Traci, could give it to you."

"We'll look into it, but knowing how people can be, my guess is they may have more than one client who has complaints." She checked her phone again, "I have an urgent message. Let me know if Dr. McKenzie tells you anything."

As I was leaving the station, I got a text from Charlie. *"He's awake! Confused. But knows who I am."*

I was about to text him back when I got a call. "Melanie, it's Meredith." She sounded upset. "The dogs were getting restless, so I was about to take them for a walk again. Jasper saw a squirrel and yanked the leash out of my hand. I don't know where he is."

I was beyond impatient to get to the hospital since Justin was awake, but there was no way I was going to tell him his dog got lost while under my watch. "I'll be home in fifteen minutes or so. Meanwhile, keep calling for

Jasper."

When I got home, Meredith was standing in the front yard with Bruno. He had a guilty look on his face, like he blamed himself for not keeping Jasper under control.

"I'm sorry. There is no sight of him," Meredith said.

"Okay, why don't you stay here in case he comes back, and Bruno and I will drive around and look for him." I took Bruno's leash and settled him in the car. We drove around the neighborhood calling Jasper's name until an elderly woman walking a Border Collie said, "A loose Golden Retriever approached us, but when I tried to grab his leash, he ran that way." She pointed toward Windy Reed Rd.

Bruno and I found him in a standoff with a snapping turtle in the marsh grass on Windy Reed. "Jasper! Leave it." At the sight of me, he came loping over, tail wagging and tongue hanging out of his mouth. His legs and his leash were covered in black mud, and I had to grab a towel from the back of my Subaru to wipe him off. "That's going to have to do for now. I need to get to the hospital to see your daddy—he's awake!"

Jasper began to leap in circles as if he knew what I was saying.

When we got home, I could see the relief on Meredith's face, followed by her look of disapproval at Jasper's not-quite-clean legs. "Someone's been enjoying a bit of mischief, I see."

"Yes, I don't think he's sorry at all about the worry he's caused, either," I said. I smiled as I told her that Justin was awake now. "I hate to ask, but would you mind watching the dogs for a little while longer. I need to get to the hospital to see him." Suddenly, I remembered. "Oh. Lunch. I forgot we were going to go out." I gave her a pleading look.

"Well, of course, you must go. I'll find something here to eat. But this evening, I insist we get dinner out. You're going to need some time to relax, and I did come all this way to spend time with you."

She was right, even though it couldn't be helped under the circumstances. I had been neglecting my sister. "That sounds like a good plan." I looked at the dogs, who were now sleeping under the kitchen table. "I'll be back in a few hours, but if they need to go out before then, you can take them into the back yard. It's fenced in."

Meredith gave me a stern look. "Don't worry, I won't repeat this morning's mistake."

"I only meant…never mind." I realized my words might have sounded as if I was criticizing her, and that we both were still unsure of how to reconnect with each other.

When I got to the ICU and pressed the intercom to ask to be admitted, the receptionist said, "I'm sorry, Miss Bass, but Dr. McKenzie already has a visitor with him. You can wait in the waiting room if you like."

I assumed the visitor was Charlie, but I didn't see Loretta in the waiting room when I got there. After about ten minutes, a very bedraggled-looking Rita McKenzie, Justin's mother, came into the room.

She rushed over to embrace me. "I'm so glad you're here! He seems to go in and out, but he asked for you."

My heart leapt at her words. "When did you get home? Are you all right?"

We took a seat away from the other visitors. "I came straight here from the airport. I was worried sick the whole way. I called my father when I was waiting for my connecting flight from Seattle, and he said the surgery went well and Justin was stable. However, I kept thinking maybe things could still go wrong."

I took her hands. "It's very good that he has regained consciousness. The doctors and nurses will keep a close eye on him and make sure he's improving." I didn't tell her that I wouldn't stop worrying myself until he was home again.

"I still can't believe this happened. My father gave me what information he had, but do you know if the police have any suspects?"

"Not yet, I'm afraid. Did Justin tell you anything he remembered about the break-in?"

She shook her head. "No. He didn't say much." She wiped a tear from beneath one eye. "He just kept saying 'Mom, you're here,' and then he seemed as if he was looking for someone else and said your name. He is still foggy about what happened, I think."

"It may take a little while for him to remember things." I hoped his memory would come back to him soon, though. "You look drained. I can stay with him for a while if you want to go home and unpack and get some rest."

Her shoulders slumped. "Yes, I would love to rest for a while. I feel better now that I've seen him."

I walked her to the elevators and then went in to see Justin. His color had improved slightly. When I walked into the room, he opened his eyes a crack and said, "Hi. What happened?"

I rushed over to kiss him on the cheek and then sat holding his hand. "Some creeps attacked you. Do you remember anything about it?"

He shook his head slightly. "Not really. I know I was at the practice; there was a noise from the back entrance. Some men, two or three. They were dressed in dark clothes." He suddenly gave me a panicked look. "Was anyone else hurt? Were you there? Are you all right?"

I sighed and kissed his knuckles. "No. No one else was there. I'm fine. Do you remember anything else? Did you see what they looked like?"

He seemed to be thinking it over. "Not much. One had a hat, one of those knit ones. He was shorter than me. As soon as he saw me, he pulled the hat down to cover his face. I didn't get a good look. The others had their faces covered. They had on…those stocking caps that cover your face…I can't remember the word." He shut his eyes. "The short man said a word. He said it a couple of times. I don't remember what it was. Somebody grabbed me and shoved me down. I tried to fight, but the others were really big. One of them hit me—a couple of times." He slowly reached up toward his head. "That's all I remember."

He looked exhausted. "That's okay. Why don't you rest now? Maybe in a little while you'll remember more," I said. "When you feel up to it, Detective Cody said she wants to talk to you."

"All right." He squeezed my hand.

He listened as I told him again that I'd picked up Jasper and Miss Scarlett, and that they were being taken care of. He laughed when I told him about Jasper's escapade this morning, then winced and placed a hand over his broken ribs. "How is your sister? Any problems?"

"No. We're getting along just as I expected."

"Hmmm. That isn't too reassuring."

I could see his eyelids drifting closed. "You can take a nap if you'd like. I'll just sit here with you for a while."

He mumbled, "Okay."

His rest was short-lived, as only a few minutes after he drifted off, Dr. Lewis, his neurosurgeon, along with two of his interns, walked in.

"I hear our patient is awake now. Great news!" He gently shook Justin's foot, causing him to pop open his eyes. "Here he is!"

Justin looked confused, "Who...?"

"I'm Dr. Lewis. I was the one who did your surgery." He held out his hand, and Justin slowly raised his right hand to shake it.

"Not bad. Squeeze my hand as hard as you can now." He took Justin's left hand also and asked him to squeeze again. I could see that it took more effort on Justin's part and that his grip appeared weaker. "Okay. No problem, we will work on that. Now raise your right leg for me, then the left."

Again, I could see he was having difficulty raising his left leg off the bed. I felt my breath catch at the look of distress on Justin's face.

"That's a good effort." Dr. Lewis turned to one of his interns. "Send a consult to PT."

I was glad to see that he seemed satisfied with the rest of Justin's neurological examination. "Good. Good progress. I'm going to get physical therapy working with you on strengthening that left side. Keep up the good work!" He and his minions breezed out of the room.

After the doctor left, I could see Justin flexing and unflexing both hands, a worried look plain on his face. "I need to get back the strength in my hand. What if the damage is permanent?"

I wanted to tell him for sure it wouldn't be, but I knew he would know I wasn't being truthful. "It's too early to tell. You said you always tell your clients that often full function may return even if their pet is gravely injured." I said a silent prayer, however.

He gave me a weak smile. "You're right." He grabbed my hand with his right hand.

After an hour or so, his nurse, Maria, bustled into the room with a big smile on her face. "Guess what? Dr. Lewis says you're ready to move out to a regular patient floor!"

Within a few minutes, the nursing team had him packed up and moved to a less intensive step-down neurological unit. I stayed with him, helping him into the pajamas I'd brought, and getting settled in his new room. I stayed until late afternoon when his mother returned to relieve me.

I felt like going home and taking a nap myself, but I had promised Meredith we could go out to dinner.

When I got home, I noticed that Jasper looked much cleaner than he did when I left him. "Thank you for giving Jasper a bath; you didn't have to do that."

Meredith waved away my thanks, though I thought she looked pleased that I had noticed. "It was no bother. I think he and I both felt much better after he had been cleaned up. How did things go at the hospital?"

"Very well! Justin is stable enough now to have been moved out of the ICU." Her comments about Justin ending up with a disability still haunted the back of my mind. I shook off the thought, however. It might take an adjustment, but we would be fine either way.

"That's good to hear. I hope you don't mind, but while you were gone, I took the liberty of rearranging some of your cabinets. I think things are arranged much more conveniently now."

I held my tongue. I would just put things back the way *I* wanted once she left. I noticed a small smudge of soil on the kitchen windowsill where the African Violets Justin gave me last fall used to sit. "Where did you put my plant?" I looked around to see where she had moved it.

"It was dead, so I got rid of it. I thought we could go to a garden center and I'd get you something a bit hardier you could put there."

Admittedly, my African Violet had been going through a tough time lately, but I thought it was starting to look a little better. It certainly wasn't dead! "Justin gave me that plant!" I checked the kitchen garbage can and retrieved the forlorn-looking house plant. I gave my sister a forbidding look. "I'm just going to get some soil to repot this, then I'll get ready for us to go to dinner. Please don't feel the need to fix anything else while I'm gone."

"I think you need to give it a shot with a good fertilizer. Have you fertilized it at all? I'm not too sure the poor thing isn't beyond help, but that could be the problem."

I ignored my sister's unsolicited advice and went outside, fighting not to slam the door behind me. I took the plant to the small shed where I kept my few gardening tools. I couldn't remember when I'd gotten the crumpled bag of potting soil I found, but I peeked into it, and it looked okay to me. It might at least keep the African Violet alive until I could get a new bag.

When I came back in, Meredith said, "I was only—"

"Trying to help. I know." I placed the plant back on the windowsill and went into my bedroom to change.

I was almost ready when I got a call from Lynn.

"Hi. So, how is Justin doing? I called patient relations, but of course, they'll only give you the bare bones of information. They said he's in stable condition."

"He is." I knew one of the reasons Lynn called patient relations before speaking to me was that she wanted to prepare for the eventuality that he had taken a downturn. "As a matter of fact, he was awake, and we were able to talk for a bit." There was a knock on my bedroom door.

My sister's voice came from the other side. "Melanie? Should I take the dogs out before we leave?"

I took the phone from my ear and said, "I'll be right out, Meredith." I had a sudden thought and said to Lynn, "Meredith and I were about to go out for dinner. Would you like to meet us there?" I thought that having Lynn present might prevent further tension from building between my sister and me.

"Yes. I suppose I could. Where?"

I wasn't sure how Meredith would react when I told her I had invited Lynn to crash our "sisters'" night out, but she just pursed her lips and said, "That's fine."

When we got to Chapter One in Guilford, I was able to get us a table near the front window so we could look out at the beautiful town green. I didn't see how Meredith could find fault with our seating, at least.

As we were seated, Meredith looked around. "This is a wonderful view. I just hope those passing by will enjoy their view of us, also!"

I ignored her dig and picked up the menu and studied it. "I'm going to find it hard to choose with so many good choices."

We had just placed our drink orders when Lynn arrived.

Meredith thanked her once again for getting her settled at my house when she arrived, and I finished updating Lynn on Justin's condition. We paused our conversation when the waiter came to take our orders.

"Men in dark masks. It sounds like what Mrs. Feldman described, doesn't it?" Lynn said. "He didn't remember anything about the one whose face he saw?"

"No. Just that he was shorter than him, which puts him at about medium height, I would think," I said. "Not much to go on."

"What do the police think? Have you talked to Detective Cody? Seems like she might agree with your theory now about this being connected to the Feldman break-in."

Meredith suddenly spoke up. "Pardon me, but I think I missed something. Who are the Feldmans? They had a break-in also? Why would that involve you?" She looked at me.

I explained what Lynn and I had witnessed, and that what happened to my neighbor and to Justin had some similarities.

"Here I thought you were living in a safe town, in a safe neighborhood. In any case, I would just concentrate on taking care of your boyfriend and let the police do their work. Much as I hate to bring it up, you said they did find out who murdered your ex."

Lynn got a mischievous look on her face. "I don't know, I think they had a little help in finding Artie's killer."

"You knew Melanie's ex-husband?" Meredith asked.

Just then, our food came, and it gave me a minute or two to compose myself before answering for Lynn. "Yes. It turns out Lynn was Artie's first wife. We met at his funeral."

Lynn and I took turns giving an edited version of how we came to lead the police to finding out who murdered Artie. I was glad to see Lynn was following my cues to leave out the more harrowing details.

Meredith sat listening, the look on her face becoming more incredulous as we spoke. "Good lord! I don't know what to say." She began shoveling her cooling food into her mouth. I couldn't picture my sister ever having eaten so determinedly before in her life.

"As you can see, everything turned out all right. We're fine," I said. I knew now was not the time to fill her in on what else I had been involved in over the past year.

"But you could have told me what happened. You made it sound as if the police handled the whole investigation, "Meredith said.

Lynn said, "I'm sure Melanie didn't want to worry you."

Meredith took a deep breath. "I own a bookshop. I read many, many mysteries. I might have had some insights as to who might be involved."

"But you seem to think that I should have stayed out of it. Let the police handle it," I said. "I thought you'd be upset that I got involved."

Meredith let out a huffing sound. "Well, of course, the correct thing to do would be to let law enforcement handle it. But if you were going to ignore that and go the Holmes and Watson route, I might have also been of help or at least have had a few thoughts on the matter anyway."

Now I realized that even though she would have worried, even more than that, she was hurt that I had excluded her. "I'm sorry."

We were all quiet for a few minutes as we finished eating. Then Meredith said to Lynn, "Were you really married to Arthur before Melanie met him?"

Lynn nodded. "Yes. Melanie tells me you never liked him. You obviously had more sense than we did."

Meredith made a "Hmmm" noise in her throat.

While we waited for our tea (Lynn and me) and coffee (Meredith), I tried to turn the conversation to Lynn's painting. "She had an excellent turnout for a show she had at a local gallery, and she sold a couple of paintings to admiring patrons."

"Congratulations, Lynn. That's wonderful. I'd love to see your work sometime." She smiled and patted Lynn's hand, then turned her attention on me again. "Back to these burglaries. Do you have any idea who may be behind them?" Meredith looked from me to Lynn.

I thanked the waiter as he set my tea in front of me. "I think there may be a connection related to the animals who went missing." I explained about the dogs taken from Reddy Vet and Mrs. Feldman's cat.

Meredith put three sugars in her coffee as well as a huge dollop of milk. "What do the police think? Have you shared your theory with them? I'm sure they may listen, though I don't suppose they would want you involved in investigating the crime."

Lynn's gaze met mine, and I had to look away quickly. I was tempted to tell her about just how involved I'd been in a few investigations over the past year, and that she was right about how enthused the police were about it. Instead, I said to Lynn, "I spoke to Lana Feldman, and she said she and Ernie had some work done on the house recently. She remembered one of the workers was particularly interested in her cat, Nika. She didn't think much of it at the time because the owner of the company is a friend of her son."

"Has she told the police about this?" Lynn said.

"She said she would. I don't know if they've questioned him yet, though."

Meredith spoke up. "But did this person who did the work for your neighbor also do work on the vet practice where Justin works?"

I was a bit confused. Did my sister want me to stay out of the investigation, or was she eager to get involved herself? Either way, she made a good point. "I don't know. Justin never mentioned them having any work done," I said. "I could ask him, or maybe Traci at the front desk would know."

I could hear a chirp as someone's phone announced a text. I was reaching to check mine when Lynn pulled out hers. She smiled as she read her message, then said, "I'm sorry, but I need to go. I have an appointment." She grabbed her purse and said, "I'll explain later." She winked at me as she left.

As soon as Lynn left, Meredith asked, "Who else might have been involved?" She had taken a pen and a scrap of paper from her purse and was making a list.

I told her about the man I saw berating Traci and Justin. "He was very upset, but I wonder if his complaint bothered him enough that it would justify what happened afterward."

"True."

"Also, in both instances, it was three people who broke in."

She scribbled "three" on her paper.

"I thought you were encouraging me to let the police handle the investigation." I smirked at her.

She put down her pen and folded her hands in front of her. "I always thought you were terrible at hiding what you were up to. Obviously, you've gotten better. I strongly suspect the investigation into Arthur's murder was not the only time you have been involved in a police investigation. Since I'm here, and you don't want to listen to my advice, I might as well jump into the soup with you. Also, we are just collecting information, correct?"

"Of course." That was another thing about my sister that irritated me: she could see right through me. When I was young, she had no trouble squealing to our parents on me.

The waiter passed by our table for the third time in five minutes, and I could see the restaurant was now very busy. "I think they are signaling us that it is time to leave." I grabbed my purse and paid. "We can talk more in the car."

Both of us were silent for several minutes after we got into the car, then Meredith said, "If you're going to Justin's practice tomorrow to find out the name of the man who was arguing with him, I wouldn't mind going with you."

I had just been thinking that I should have time to go to Reddy Vet in the morning before I went to see Justin at the hospital in the afternoon. I would have preferred to speak to Traci at the vet by myself, but I also would feel guilty leaving my sister alone again all day. "All right. I want to find out if they did have any construction recently, even something minor, and if so, the name of the company they used." I knew that if there needed to be anything done around the office, it would have been arranged by someone at the front desk.

I glanced over to see Meredith smiling. "Good."

I had been wrong about my sister's reaction to my involvement with crime-solving. She certainly seemed to be all in now.

Chapter Sixteen

I was up early the next day. Rain was predicted later in the morning, and I wanted to walk the dogs before it started. I tried to be quiet, so as not to disturb Meredith. I smelled coffee brewing as soon as I came out of my room.

"Oh, good, you're up. I hope you don't mind. I've made myself some coffee. I was waiting to put water on for tea until I heard you get up." Meredith was bustling around the kitchen.

"No. Of course not." I saw she had eggs boiling, and I smelled toast. I filled Bruno's and Jasper's water dishes and fed them their breakfast. "Thank you for making breakfast, but I just planned on grabbing a yogurt before I took the dogs for their morning walk."

"It's no bother. It will all be ready in a minute."

As I fixed my tea, I looked out the window at the darkening sky and gauged whether I'd have enough time now for that walk before the storm hit.

She placed an egg in an egg cup and a couple of pieces of toast on the table next to me. "After we eat, I'll go with you to walk the dogs."

I was looking forward to that time to sort out what I knew about the two break-ins, and to go over all the questions I had for Traci. My sister must have seen by the look on my face that I was about to insist she didn't need to come with me.

"I could use a walk to stretch my legs, and it will be much easier to manage two dogs if I came along."

I knew I'd have no trouble walking the dogs myself, but said, "Okay. Thank you."

After the mishap the previous day, I thought it would be better if I let her walk Bruno and I took Jasper's leash myself.

We had just started down my road when Meredith asked, "What time does the veterinary office open? We should get there then to interrogate the staff."

"I wanted to give them an hour or so to settle in," I said. "When we get there, I'll introduce you and explain that you were curious to see the practice where Justin works. Afterwards, I can ask the receptionist, Traci, about the irate patient. I'll ask about any recent construction they've had done also, but I want to do it off-handedly. I don't want to seem as if I'm 'interrogating' her."

"Fine. However, I may think of a question or two myself." By the tone of her voice, I could tell she wasn't thrilled with my plan.

We finished the walk in silence. I was right about the storm moving in quickly, and we had to hurry back to the house as the rain started to fall just as we passed my neighbor's house.

The storm let up just as we got to Reddy Vet. I was surprised to see it was Shauna, one of the vet techs, at the front desk, not Traci. "Hi, Shauna. Is Traci out today?"

"No. I'm just manning the desk while she's in back with the man from Apex Alarms. She's showing him the back door where the alarm failed to go off during the break-in." Shauna smirked and leaned in a little closer to me. "Apparently, Traci started seeing the alarm guy a few weeks ago. She was a little flustered when she introduced him to me. I must admit he's cute and seems nice." I saw her look toward Meredith.

"This is my sister, Meredith." I didn't add any more information.

Shauna smiled and greeted Meredith, then said to me, "I heard Justin is doing better. I thought I would go and see him after work. I still can't believe what happened."

Before I could say anything else, Meredith piped up. "I hear that there has been an incident with an unruly client recently, and that he has also been a problem in the past."

I glared at Meredith.

Shauna looked from me to Meredith. "Yes, Traci told me about it, but I wasn't here when that happened, so I don't know much about it."

Just then, Traci came from the back, her face slightly flushed. Alongside her was a very handsome young man in a shirt with the insignia "Apex Alarm Systems" and the name "Keith" over the pocket. Traci is a couple of inches taller than I am, maybe about five-foot-six, and the young man was only about her height.

"Oh, hi, Melanie. How are you holding up? Dr. Reddy has been keeping us updated on Justin's progress." She went to stand behind the front desk next to Shauna.

The young man nodded to Meredith and me, then said to the other women, "Sorry we couldn't get here sooner. Everything should be working okay now, though." He waved to Traci, "I'll call you later," then left.

I watched him as he went out to his vehicle, a plain white utility van. My antenna immediately went up—he was short, and he knew about alarm systems. I repeated to myself the name on his shirt. Kieth. I was trying to think of a way to ask Traci about him when my thoughts were interrupted by Meredith asking her, "Do you think the mystery client who called the night the practice was broken into could have been the man who was arguing with you and Dr. McKenzie?"

Traci said, "I don't know… I guess it could have been. Maybe as a prank to get back at us or something. That would explain why no one showed up."

That was a logical explanation, though I wasn't ready to dismiss that man's involvement yet. "Traci, this is my sister, Meredith. I know you've spoken to the police already, but we were just trying to come up with a reason someone would have broken in here." I could see Meredith open her mouth to say something again, and rushed to add, "Or who might have information about the setup of the office, where the narcotics were kept, and so forth. Have you had any construction done in the office recently, or consulted someone who came in to do a quote?"

Shauna said, "Not that I'm aware."

Traci shook her head, "No. I know Dr. McKenzie and Dr. Reddy were discussing having the rooms repainted, but I'm pretty sure they haven't contacted anyone yet. They wanted to get Dr. Antonio's input on colors first, I think."

I had been gently suggesting to Justin for two months now that the exam rooms could use some freshening up. I told Justin calming shades of blue and green might be appropriate. I suppose it wasn't unreasonable for them to get the opinion of the third vet, but still.

Just then, a woman entered, leading a huge and reluctant Bernese Mountain Dog on a leash. Traci turned to smile at the woman and said, "Hi, Mrs. Cordon! See if you can get Gus to step on the scale for me, and I'll get you right into one of the exam rooms. Dr. Antonio will be with you in a few minutes."

I heard Dr. Reddy call Shauna from the back, and she said, "You know we'll help in any way we can. If I think of anything, I'll get in touch." She hurried away to see what Dr. Reddy needed.

"I'm sorry we have so many questions, Traci. I'm just trying to find out anything that could help catch whoever was responsible for what happened to Justin," I said.

"I understand. If you can wait here, I'll be right back," Traci said to me as she led the woman and her dog down the hall.

As soon as she returned to the front desk, Meredith said, "I was wondering if you could give us the name of the man who acted in a threatening manner toward you and Justin McKenzie. Do you think he would do more than just prank call the practice? Has he been violent before?"

My sister obviously wasn't going to let me take the lead in questioning, as I'd asked.

Traci hesitated a moment. "I'm not supposed to give you any personal information on a client. But no, Calvin Brazen hasn't ever gotten physical. He's just an impatient, nasty-tempered man. Though, he does love his cat." She had been careful, I thought, to say the man's name slowly.

Another client with their pet in a carrier walked in. "Thank you, Traci," I said, and nudged my sister to let her know it was time to leave.

As we returned to the car, she said, "We got the name of the man, but how do we go about questioning him?"

"We don't. I think I should let my friend Detective Cody know and let her decide what to do." I tried to rein in my irritation at how my sister was trying to take over the investigation.

Meredith looked disappointed. "I suppose you're right. Do you think she'll follow up on it, though?"

"Yes." I smiled at her. "You made a good suggestion when you said he may have been the one to call the office that night and then not show up. Even if it turns out he had nothing to do with the break-in, that would be one mystery solved."

"Thank you. I told you I could be of help if you included me in your inquiries." She sounded very self-satisfied.

I thought we had learned something else interesting from our visit today to Reddy Vet. The alarm company would know the system was on the fritz because they had been notified to come to repair it. Keith was driving a white van. Though, assuming the crimes were connected, I didn't know how that tied in with what happened to the Feldmans. Neither Roger nor Mrs. Feldman mentioned that they had an alarm system. I decided I would make a stop at the Feldmans' this afternoon before I went to the hospital to see Justin.

Meredith interrupted my thoughts. "When will I get a chance to meet your boyfriend? Is that what you call him? I realize he isn't in top form right now, but I'd love a brief visit to start to get to know him."

I knew that Justin was as eager to meet my sister as she was to meet him, but I didn't want to just spring her on him. "I'll talk to Justin today and let him make that decision, if that's all right."

"Fair enough."

When we reached home, and Meredith was getting out of the car, she said, "I know you've told him about me, but I hope you haven't painted me in too poor a light."

"Of course not."

She just made a "Huumpt" noise again as she followed me into the house.

I took the dogs out into the back yard to do their business and run around a little, then I grabbed my purse and said to Meredith, "What are your plans for this afternoon?" I had hoped for a sunny day so she could relax on the back patio while I was gone, but although the rain had stopped, the day remained cloudy and humid.

"Oh, I'll just read my book, and I need to call Phillip and see how he is getting on. I know he has a meeting until two, but I'll try and reach him after that."

"Well, give him my best." I still felt some guilt at leaving her on her own so much, though she didn't seem to mind. At least she hadn't said anything to make me think she did.

I stopped at Lana Feldman's to ask about an alarm system, but there was no answer when I rang the bell. When I got to the police station, Sunny Cody came to speak to me, but she made it clear that she only had a few minutes.

"I'm sorry, but there is something breaking, and I need to get back in touch with another officer. How can I help you?" She motioned me to a chair.

I knew better than to ask her what was going on, since I was sure she wouldn't be able to tell me. I could listen closely, though, for clues as to what it was. "I spoke to Traci Cummings at Reddy Vet, and she said that there is a man who is known for giving all of them a hard time. I witnessed an argument between him and Justin and Traci a few days before the mysterious phone call that got Justin to the clinic on the night of the break-in. His name is Calvin Brazen."

She wrote down the name. "Does Ms. Cummings think he might have been involved?"

"She didn't seem to think he would be violent, but admitted he could have done it as a prank or retribution for his gripes with the practice. I don't know if he could be connected to the actual break-in."

She wrote down something else I couldn't read. "I'll look into it. If it was only a crank call, unless it was connected to the attack on Dr. McKenzie and the break-in itself, it isn't a crime." She hesitated a moment. "It may not matter in any case. As I said, there have been developments which I am not at liberty to share."

I opened my mouth to ask if they were connected to the crimes at the veterinary office and the Feldmans', but Sunny cut me off.

"When I can tell you what's happening, I will." She stood up. "I have to get back to my desk now."

I wished I knew what was going on, but I did feel a bubble of hope building in my chest. Not that finding who was responsible for the crimes would bring Ernie Feldman back, or make up for the injuries Justin suffered, but at least the people responsible would be off the streets.

I thought it would be best to wait until I had more information before I mentioned to Justin that there might be some progress in finding the creeps who attacked him. I was in a good mood when I reached the hospital, but when I entered Justin's room, that mood deflated. One of the nurses was in the room checking Justin's vital signs. She looked concerned, and I could tell right away that Justin didn't feel well.

"Hi. We've met before. I'm Betsy. I'm afraid he's had a difficult morning, not to mention now he's spiked a temp." She patted Justin's arm. "I was just about to give him the antibiotics Dr. Lewis ordered." She connected the bag of fluid containing the meds to his IV. "The doctor will be stopping by later after he finishes with surgery to check on you," she said to Justin. "I'll be back shortly when that's finished infusing. Call me if you need anything in the meantime."

After she left, I pulled the chair up to sit by Justin's bed. "How do you feel? Can I pour you a glass of water or anything?"

He gave me a forlorn look. "They had me up walking before. My leg was like a sack of sand."

I noticed right away his words were slightly slurred. "You mean it was hard to move it? Were you able to put weight on it?"

"Yes, but it felt like I was dragging it." He said "yes" like "yeth," and "id" instead of "it."

I tried not to show how alarmed I was. He could have developed another clot on his brain if a small vessel had ruptured due to the surgery, or maybe it was just because he had a fever that caused his speech to be altered. The leg worried me, too. "What did your physical therapist say? I know it can take a little time to get function back." He knew that, too, but I wanted to console him somehow.

"Said it was okay. Keep trying." He looked angry now. "My words aren't coming out right!"

I took his hand. "Try to relax. The doctor will be here in a little while. Do you want me to get your nurse? I could ask her to call someone to come to see you in the meantime?" Betsy said Dr. Lewis was in surgery, but I knew someone on his team had to be covering his patients.

Justin sighed. "No. I'll wait."

A short time later, Betsy came back into the room. "I spoke to one of the interns on Dr. Lewis's team to let them know what's going on, and they said he wants you to go for an MRI. Transport will be here shortly to take you."

I felt some relief that they were going to look more deeply into the change in Justin's condition.

Justin looked too miserable for me to quiz him about Mr. Brazen and whether he thought he could be involved in the break-in, or about any updates or expansions to the clinic. In any case, as Sunny Cody hinted, I hoped they were close to arresting whoever did this to him.

When the transport person came to take him for the MRI, Justin said, "You don't have to wait. You can leave if you want." His words were clearer now, only a couple slurred.

"No, I can wait. I want to be here when you get back." As I waited, I examined all the floral arrangements in his room and went around reading the cards to see who they were from. I recognized the bouquet I had brought and saw next to it a lovely one from his mother and another from his grandfather. There was, of course, one from the staff at Reddy Vet, but I noticed a bouquet of sunflowers sent by Stella Antonio. The card read "Missing you—at the 'office.'" I should have been pleased at the thoughtful gesture, but was instead annoyed. What did she mean by the way the card was phrased? I kept flashing back to the day Malcolm brought Daphne to the clinic and she seemed more familiar than appropriate with Justin. He had never given me any reason to be jealous, but I still felt insecure about the new partner in the practice. She was beautiful and obviously found Justin attractive.

When Justin got back from his MRI, he looked exhausted. I tried to entertain him by telling him about my dinner with Meredith and Lynn and how gobsmacked my sister was to learn Lynn had also been married to Artie. However, in spite of his attempt to listen and an occasional smile, I could see he was ready to fall asleep. I sat quietly then and waited for Dr. Lewis to arrive.

Justin woke up just before Dr. Lewis came in. The doctor was still in his scrubs and surgical cap. "Well, the MRI looks good. I don't see any new bleeding or clots. Sometimes there can be an effect of the initial injury, or due to the surgery, we don't see right away. Let's see what happens with your speech in the next day or two and take it from there. As far as your left leg—just keep at it. I think movement will improve over time." He patted Justin's shoulder and left.

"It's good that there is no new bleeding," I said.

"Yes." He didn't seem convinced.

Just then, his mother and grandfather came into the room. I had called Charlie and Rita while Justin was out of the room for his MRI to let them know what was going on.

After I greeted them, I said, "I'll leave you two to visit. I better get home and keep my sister company before she thinks I've totally abandoned her." I decided to wait to bring up the subject of Justin meeting Meredith for the time being.

On the way home, I stopped at Mrs. Feldman's again. She confirmed that, no, they didn't have an alarm system before the break-in. "But Roger has called someone to install one now. They're coming tomorrow."

No matter what was happening with the official investigation, I didn't think it would hurt to speak to whoever showed up to install the system.

Chapter Seventeen

eredith was waiting in the kitchen for me when I got home. "I spoke to Phillip. He said things are going well with the project, but he needs to attend some kind of banquet tomorrow night, and he wants me to go with him. Apparently, all the other spouses will be attending."

"You don't sound happy about the prospect," I said.

She sighed. "I hoped we could have a longer visit, and I never did get a chance to meet your Justin."

I was about to point out that New York was only a couple of hours away when she said, "I do miss Phillip, but after a day or two, I'm sure I could come back here to stay longer. We just got a couple of good leads on who might have been responsible for the crimes, and I would love to continue to help you."

She had come up with some good insights, but I really wanted to follow up on the information we had myself. While her questioning technique had a bit more grace than a bull in a china shop, I could see her direct manner set people on edge. On the other hand, it had been a long time since we'd been able to spend time together, and I could try to tactfully set boundaries on how involved she could be. I was supposed to be leaving the investigation to the police anyway. "Yes, I would love it if you could come back and stay a little longer."

"I plan to catch the 10:30 train to New York tomorrow, so I'll need you to be ready to leave here at 9:30. I don't like to cut things too close," she said.

"All right." I wanted to be sure to be home when the alarm company came to install the system at Lana Feldman's. With any luck, Traci's new boyfriend, Keith, would be one of the technicians. If not, I still might be able to find out if his coworkers knew anything about him. However, there was no way I could refuse to drive Meredith to catch her train. I only hoped that the alarm company would still be at the Feldmans' when I returned.

"I'll let Phillip know to expect me by early afternoon." Meredith paused with her phone in her hand. "You will call me if you find out anything interesting before I come back?"

"Yes, of course."

Meredith nodded, as if satisfied with my answer. "How is Justin, anyway?"

I felt reluctant to discuss today's setback. "He's coming along."

"Good." She went into her bedroom to pack and make her phone call.

* * *

I was in the car returning from the train station the next day when I got a call from Sunny Cody.

"I wanted to let you know before you heard it on the local news. There's been an arrest in the rash of break-ins in the surrounding towns."

My heart rate sped up. "That's fantastic! Did they get all three of the men involved?"

"Branford police made the arrest. They said it was two brothers who have a long record, including two for B and E. They arrested them when they tried to sell the painting stolen in Branford to an undercover officer."

That must be the painting stolen from Mrs. Paine's friend. "But Justin said there were three people. So did Mrs. Feldman."

"I know. It's possible there was a third person working with them, but if so, they aren't admitting to it."

"What about the dogs stolen from Reddy Vet, or the items they took from the Feldmans'? Was there anything found to link them to those crimes?" My initial excitement fizzled away.

"No. Personally, I'm not sure these are the guys who were involved in those crimes. But our departments are continuing to work together to determine if they could be connected. I'm sorry, I wish I could say with certainty that we caught the people involved with the break-in at the vet and your neighbor's. As I mentioned, the arrest will be on the news, so I wanted you to hear it from me."

"Thank you." Sunny and I met when she investigated my ex-husband's murder, and since then, through my involvement in a few other investigations. When I took care of her after a work-related injury, we had also developed a friendship of sorts. I knew she skated a thin line between what information she could share and what she could not. "Did you get a chance to speak to Mr. Brazen to find out if he was the one to call the practice the night it was broken into?"

"Yes. He denied calling and was quite offended that anyone could think that he would do such a thing. Despite his prickly temperament, his response seemed genuine."

I had hoped we had at least solved one mystery surrounding the break-in. "All right. Thank you for the update." I was sure she could hear the disappointment in my voice.

As I approached my house, I could see a white van in the Feldmans' driveway, and my hopes rose again. Then I saw the logo on the side: "SUPRA ALARMS." It was not the same company Reddy Vet used.

I saw Roger Feldman standing by the van, talking to a man in a khaki shirt. I pulled over and got out of the car. As I approached the two, the man from the alarm company turned and went toward the house. "Hi, Roger. Your mother mentioned to me that she was having an alarm system installed."

"Yes, shutting the barn door after the horse is out, as they say. But I'll feel better knowing she has one now at least."

I tried to think of a way to bring up the subject of his friend's company, the one that installed her new windows. "I was thinking about how, of all the houses on the road, your parents' house was chosen to rob. It's as if whoever broke in knew what they wanted to steal, and who lived here." I realized after I said it that my attempt at subtlety failed miserably.

Roger gave me a sharp look. "My mother told me that you questioned whether someone from Frank's company was involved. No way. I've known

Frank for years, and he's particular about who he hires."

It was obvious he was irritated that I would even suggest such a thing. "Okay. I just was trying to think of people who would have had access to your parents' house."

He didn't respond to that, but said, "Thanks for checking in on my mother. She really appreciates it, and so do I." He nodded toward the house. "I better go in and check on how things are going in there." He gave me a stern look again. "Don't worry, I plan on staying until they're finished with the job and will keep an eye out for any suspicious behavior." He marched toward the house.

Despite Roger's reassurance, I thought it might still be worth a visit to Rockwell Construction at some point to talk to his friend Frank.

* * *

When I got to the hospital that afternoon, Justin looked flushed and was slightly out of breath. "You just missed my physical therapy session."

"Oh, sorry, how did it go?" I was glad to hear his speech seemed more natural, a little slower, but no slurring. The antibiotics must have helped because he was much better than the previous day.

"Carly said I'm doing better. I was able to move my left leg a bit easier, but it still lags way behind my right." He looked disappointed.

"But that's great! You know it's going to take time to get back to the way you were."

"I know. But I need to get back to work. They're getting swamped with me out of service. Stella said Martin has been able to get extra coverage from Bill Hobbs in Branford and Ken Seymour in Durham so far, but they have their own practices to keep up also."

My ears perked up at one thing he'd said. "Stella Antonio was here?" I looked around as if to see evidence of her presence.

"Yes, she stopped in to see how I was doing. She and Martin Reddy both. Well, not together. Someone had to be seeing patients." He must have seen the look on my face. "What's wrong?"

"Nothing. I hadn't realized you two had become friends, is all." I tried to keep my tone off-hand.

"Not so much friends, but we *are* colleagues." He gave me an amused look. "Does her having come to see me bother you?"

"No. Of course not. I'm glad she did." I quickly looked away from him so he wouldn't see the truth.

"Anyway, she had some good news to share. The owners of the French Bulldog, the Dolans, got their dog back."

"That's wonderful! How? Have they notified the police?" I would have thought Sunny would have shared this news with me.

"Stella said the Dolans told Dr. Reddy that the offer of a reward did the trick. They said a man brought the dog to them after seeing it wandering around his neighborhood. Mr. Dolan said the man told him he immediately recognized the dog's picture from social media and so contacted them."

"Did the Dolans give a description to the police of the man who returned the dog? The story he gave them sounds a little fishy, doesn't it?"

"Stella didn't say if they notified the police. She did say that Martin was visibly relieved. He offered the Dolans free vet care for the rest of the dog's life as compensation for him having been taken while in our care.".

"Wow! That's certainly generous, but it wasn't the practice's fault or yours either!"

"I know. They refused his offer anyway. They've been clients of Reddy Vet for years with all their dogs, and they assured him they didn't blame us for what happened."

I planned to check with Sunny Cody myself to see if they were notified of the dog's recovery, and if they had questioned the Dolans about the man who "found" the dog.

"How are things going with your sister? Is she okay with you spending time fussing over me?" I could see a twinkle in his eye as he asked.

"She has been very good about that, in fact. She's had to return to New York to help out her husband for a few days, but she's planning to return and is desperate to meet you." This time, I gave him a mischievous look.

"Be sure to warn me when you plan to bring her so I can be on my toes. I want to be ready to field any zingers she may throw my way." He laughed. "Anyway, I think they're getting ready to send me to a rehab facility for a while to work on my walking." He flexed his left hand. "At least this hand is almost back to full function, and I'm finding my words better." He looked at me for confirmation.

"Yes, definitely." I beamed. He really was making wonderful progress. I planned on warning Meredith not to make any comments to upset him.

Charlie, Loretta, and Justin's mother, Rita, came to visit Justin in the late afternoon. I could see that Loretta was becoming even more of a fixture at Charlie's side, and that made me happy.

"I need to get home and take care of the animals now, but I'll call later." I bent to give Justin a quick kiss. "Jasper misses you. You need to hurry and get better."

* * *

After I fed and walked the dogs, I called the police station to find out if Sunny had gotten a description of the man who returned the Dolans' dog and claimed the reward.

"You caught me just as I was leaving," she said.

I asked about the so-called "Good Samaritan" who returned the dog.

"It does sound suspicious, but unfortunately, the description they gave of the guy was not very helpful: on the short side, but not too short, dark, or sandy brown hair, sunglasses, or maybe they were regular prescription glasses. He was wearing either a green or brown T-shirt. The husband and wife each gave different descriptions. They both admitted that they were more focused on the dog. They apologized for being so poor at describing him, but they also pointed out the reward promised cash and no questions asked if the dog was returned. So, they were careful not to act too inquisitive."

I sighed. "That's too bad. You're continuing to investigate this as a separate crime from the one in Branford, aren't you?"

"Yes. Unless we can find something to link them."

"Anything else you can share about what is going on with the investigation?"

She was silent for a beat or two. "Katie says hi, and my dad wants to know when you are coming back to work. According to him, he didn't get on very well with the nurse who was covering for you this week."

Obviously, I wasn't getting anything else out of her. "Tell your dad I'll be back before his next scheduled visit."

I was planning to turn in for the night when I got a text from Meredith: *Dinner elegant but boring. Any new developments? Justin okay?"*

I texted her back the news that one dog had been recovered, but no clues as to who took him; and Justin was ready to meet her when she returned.

She texted me right back: *Be back in three days. Promised P. I would go to another function with him—fundraising so necessary. Forming plans how can interrogate our suspects.*

I still couldn't get over my sister's apparent interest in sleuthing after how worried I'd been that she would disapprove of my own involvement. I did think she was going to have to work on her techniques, however.

* * *

Justin's mother picked up Miss Scarlett from my neighbor's the day after her return home from her shortened cruise, but we both agreed that it would be better if I kept Jasper until Justin got home from the hospital. Rita's cat, Grumpus, did not tolerate dogs in any way, shape, or form.

I had just gotten home after walking the dogs at Hammonasset Beach State Park when Charlie called me. "I was hopin' you could drive Rex and me to the dog groomer. Rex is looking pretty raggedy these days. Needs his nails cut, too. Loretta is going out of town to visit her daughter, and Rita has an appointment to get her own hair gussied up."

I checked the time. I had planned on trying to talk to Frank Eastman, Roger's friend, this morning. However, if we weren't too long at the groomer's, I could still squeak in a trip to the construction company before I went to see Justin at the hospital. "Sure. I'll be there in twenty minutes."

When we got to Sleek Pet, Rex became visibly excited, yipping and walking faster than I had ever seen him move. Charlie chuckled. "Poor old guy, he loves the way the girls fuss over him here."

Charlie and I had permission to stay with Rex for his appointment. We spent the time chatting with Kim, the groomer, as she washed, blew-dry, and brushed Rex. I swear the little Pomeranian smiled throughout the whole process.

"There." Kim handed Rex back to Charlie. "Always a pleasure working with this little guy. Not like some of our customers."

I thought about the dog who was still missing and wondered if Kim had heard something. "The dogs themselves, or their owners?"

She laughed, "Sometimes both."

"This may sound odd, but have you had any clients lately where the dog didn't seem comfortable with the owner? Or the owner seemed to be not very engaged with their dog?"

Rex had started to squirm a little in Charlie's arms. "I'm gonna take this guy outside. His bladder isn't what it used to be." Charlie gave me a look that told me he had picked up on where I was going with my questions. "I'll meet you outside."

Kim gave Rex a final kiss on the head. "Yes, to what you were asking. It's more that some of the clients just don't seem to be as close to their dog as I would expect. Though, sometimes it's that they are bringing the dog in as a favor for someone else, and it's not their dog." She shook her head. "I've seen some crazy things, too. I had a funny incident yesterday. A lady brought in a young Black Labradoodle, and as I'm bathing him, I can clearly see white roots peeking out from the dog's fur. The dog had obviously been dyed black."

"What did she say when you asked her about it?"

"Well, she acted shocked at first, then angry. She said she had been very clear to the breeders she contacted that she was looking for a black Labradoodle and would pay extra for one."

"Did she mention how long she has had the dog?" I tried to hide my mounting excitement.

"No. I got the impression she had just gotten him, though. Why?"

I told Kim about what happened at Reddy Vet and the rash of other dog disappearances.

"That's horrible! I did hear about what happened at the vet, and I was shocked." Kim looked upset.

"Did the woman tell you where she got the dog?"

"No, but wherever it was, she seemed upset with them."

"Would you be able to give me the woman's name and phone number? Maybe I could find out where she bought the dog."

I could see Kim was wavering about whether she should do that. "I don't know. I'm not sure if the woman would be angry if she found out I gave you her information."

"But if she's unhappy with the breeder or whoever sold her the dog, she may be glad to have them exposed as dishonest."

"I guess you're right. I would hate to have someone else the victim of an unscrupulous breeder," Kim said. The look on her face told me she had made her decision.

A woman leading a Skye Terrier came into the shop just then. Kim said, "Hi Mrs. Duffy. I'll be right with you." Then she said to me, "I'll get you that name. I just hope it helps."

When we got back in the car, Rex immediately curled up on the back seat and fell asleep. Charlie said, "Well? You find out anything?"

I told him about the dyed dog, the same breed as one of the ones stolen from the vet's office, and that I had been able to get the name of the woman who brought him in.

"You going to question her by yourself? What if she's involved in this whole setup? I can go with—"

"No. Thanks, but I have a better idea. I want to go see this woman as soon as possible, but I also told Justin I would be there at two p.m. for his physical therapy session. If I can get the name of the breeder or whoever sold the woman the dog, do you think you could do an internet search for him and see what information is available?"

Charlie gave me a disgusted look. "Just because I'm old don't mean I live in the dark ages. I'll Google the place, and I also might have a contact or two with some information."

"Good. Thanks."

As I dropped Charlie off at his house, he said, "Get me the name of the guy who sold her the dog, and I'll get back to you as soon as I have anything."

My visit to Frank Eastman would have to wait. Charlie's point about it not being safe to go alone was well taken, though. I had learned the hard way that bringing backup was always a good idea. I called Lynn.

"You're lucky, I just got cleaned up after a particularly productive morning painting. I'd love to go with you. What's our cover story?" Lynn sounded excited.

After I spoke to Lynn, I realized it might be a good idea to call and make sure the woman was at home before I just showed up at her door. She was wary at first, but when I made up a story about how a breeder had scammed me when I got my dog, she agreed to let me come and speak to her.

Once Lynn was settled in the car, she said, "So...I was dying to tell you something the other night. I've been seeing the nice-looking guy who bought my painting that night at the Branford Arts and Cultural Alliance. His name is Brian Johnson."

I gave her a startled look. "What! That's great, but do you think—"

"I know what you're going to say, I'm taking things slow this time. It's strictly casual at this point."

"Uh huh." I glanced over at her.

"I swear!" She cleared her throat. "So, you said when we speak to this woman, our story is that we've been scammed by a dishonest breeder, also? What's her name?"

"Heidi Grange. I told her I had gotten a dog that wasn't what I'd been promised. I didn't mention the theft of the dogs from Reddy Vet, and that there's a possibility her dog could be one of them."

"And what if we find out it is?" Lynn asked.

"I want to get the dog back to its rightful owner, but more importantly, I want to find out who sold it to her and how they're connected to what happened at Reddy Vet. I told Charlie I would call him with the name of the kennel or person who sold her the dog, and he is going to do some digging to see what he can find out about them."

As we pulled into the driveway at the address Ms. Grange gave me, the hopeful feeling I'd felt earlier was dampened. I thought about Malcolm and Daphne, and I realized I might just have to tell another person their dog did not actually belong to them.

I could hear barking in the background when Heidi Grange opened the door. She called over her shoulder, "Walter! Quiet!" She eyed Lynn and me silently for a moment, then said, "Are you the woman I spoke to on the phone about the dog? Come in."

I introduced myself and Lynn, then said, "I'm sorry to bother you, but when I heard your story from Kim at Sleek Pet, the anger I felt at what happened to me flared up again. I heard you were duped by the breeder you bought your dog from." I did feel a bit guilty about misrepresenting myself to the woman, but if it helped track down who plundered Reddy Vet and sent Justin to the hospital, it was certainly worth it.

Lynn piped in, "It happened to me, too." She quickly glanced at me, then said, "We wondered if it was the same person who sold all of us our dogs under false pretenses."

I nodded approval to Lynn.

Heidi motioned us to follow her into the kitchen, where a black puppy was restrained behind a doggie gate. "Coffee? Tea?" After she took down the gate and entered the kitchen, the puppy jumped up to put his paws on her thighs. She looked annoyed and pushed him down, brushing off her slacks. "Stop it! Go lie down. Here's your toy." She threw a squeaky toy into another room.

Lynn and I looked at each other. Maybe it wouldn't be so hard to separate Ms. Grange and the dog if my suspicions were correct.

As she put the water on to boil, she said, "I was hesitant to even get a dog, but my husband had been pleading with me for some time. We've had some…difficulties…recently, and I hoped to cheer him up by surprising him with the dog when he got back from his business trip." She took down three mugs and filled hers with coffee and ours with tea bags. "He had a black poodle when he was a boy. That's how I ended up with Walter." She flipped her hand at the dog, happily chewing on his toy in the next room. "Now I find out he's neither a pure-bred poodle as I was told, or even black!" She shook her head. "He wasn't cheap, either."

My sympathy for her was fading by the moment. "Same here. My dog turned out to not be the breed I was assured she was, either." I changed the dog's sex because it seemed too disloyal to Bruno to even pretend he was not the dog I wanted. I had no more story prepared about my fake dog, and luckily, Heidi did not seem too interested in my experience anyway.

"I tried calling the breeder when I found out he had sold me a dog under false pretenses, but I was only able to leave a voicemail. So far, no callback."

I took out my phone. "What was the name of the place where you got Walter? I wonder if it was the same place where I got my dog."

She took out her own phone and scrolled through it. "Dandyboy Farm." She looked up at me. "You?"

I tried to look disappointed. "No. That doesn't sound right, but maybe I'm not remembering the place correctly." I typed the name of the kennel into my notes. "Where was this kennel? Maybe if you describe it, something will ring a bell."

She snorted. "Woodstock. Way in the back of beyond, up in the northeast corner of the state. That's one of the things that, when I think back on now, makes me feel more the fool. I didn't see any other dogs while I was there, though I did hear another one barking. The guy I bought the dog from said he was in the process of moving his business, and most of his dogs were at his new facility. I didn't question him; all I focused on was getting the dog I wanted. Like I said, I planned to surprise my husband. He'll be surprised, all right. By how stupid I was."

I did feel a little sorry for her now. "When did you get Walter?" I held my breath as I waited for her answer.

"Three days ago." She looked from me to Lynn. "So what do you think I should do? What did you both do?"

"I think you should call the police and report the man who sold you the dog." I looked over at Lynn. "That's what we did."

"The police said they would look into it, but then we never heard back."

Lynn shrugged. "However, we decided to keep our dogs after all."

I shot Lynn an amused look. I should have known there was no way she would let us give up our imagined dogs.

"I'll call, but I think this whole thing was a big mistake anyway. You can probably tell, but I'm not really a dog person."

We got up to leave. "I'm sorry this happened to you. Thank you for talking to us. I'm not sure we were duped by the same person, but sometimes it helps to find out you weren't the only one that happened to. I would call the police, though, and tell them what happened."

As she walked us to the door, Heidi gave Walter a disgusted look. "I suppose I need to take you out now to do your business. Yeesh!"

"Poor Walter!" Lynn said when we got back into the car.

"Maybe not. I'm all but certain he's the dog taken from Reddy Vet, and I'm going to call Sunny Cody and let her know what Heidi Grange told us. If we're right, at least he'll be reunited with his rightful owners."

As I drove Lynn home, I asked, "So tell me about this Brian you've been seeing? What does he do? Have you been out with him a lot since you met him at your art show?"

She laughed. "So many questions! As I said, it's nothing serious, we've just gone out a few times. As to what he does, he said it's something in finance, I'm not sure what. He said it was boring and he'd much rather talk about what I do. He said he just recently became interested in art. He asks me a lot of questions about it. He really listens and seems interested, too. As to having been married, he said he's been divorced for three years, no children with his ex. He's just…nice."

I recognized the glow in her cheeks. "Good. Just be careful."

"Yes, Mom."

Her comment, though meant jokingly, stung a little. Lynn was several years older than me, and I really wasn't trying to mother her, just look out for her welfare. She had been hurt several times before. Also, I heard echoes of my sister's advice to me.

"Speaking of love interests, how is Justin doing? I mean, really." Her voice was concerned. "I thought I might go see him tomorrow morning before a class I'm doing in New Haven."

I took a deep breath. "He's doing much better, but I am worried that he might have some residual effects from what happened to him. He doesn't have full function in his left leg, and though his motor control in his left hand is getting better, I worry if he'll get it all the way back. It would kill him if he couldn't do surgery any longer." I looked over at her. "When you go to see him, don't let on that I'm worried, though."

"I promise, I won't." As she got out of the car, she smiled. "Call me anytime you want back up."

I called Charlie as soon as I got home and gave him the name "Dandyboy Farm" to check out. I repeated the story Mrs. Grange gave me about the place and the guy who sold her Walter.

"Sounds pretty suspicious to me," Charlie said. "Wanna bet there is no such place listed when I go online to check it out?"

"That's what I'm afraid of, too. She didn't get the name of the supposed breeder, either."

Charlie was quiet for a few minutes, like he was thinking. "She said the place is in Woodstock? I'm trying to think of the guy I used to know who investigated animal complaints for the state in that area. Maybe he knows something about this kennel. I'll check into it."

I got to the hospital just before two p.m., and had just begun telling Justin about my experience with Mrs. Grange when Carly, the physical therapist working with him, came in.

"I'll tell you the rest later," I said to Justin, then introduced myself to Carly.

"Great! I'm glad you could make it," she said. "I hear you're a nurse, so you'll be familiar with a lot of what we're trying to do here. Today we're going to focus on getting the dexterity and strength back in that hand."

She had Justin squeeze a stress ball and practice picking up a pen. "Now for some fun!" She took out a bag of modeling clay and had him roll it into balls and snakes. I could see small beads of sweat forming on his forehead as he concentrated.

At the end of the session, she said, "Good work! You are definitely improving. I'll leave the ball and clay; keep practicing with them. We'll work on moving your left leg tomorrow."

After Carly left the room, Justin said, "So you think the dog she bought from this supposed breeder is the one taken from our practice? Did you notify the police yet?"

"Not yet."

"What did the dog look like? I know you said he was black now, but other than that."

"Mostly, I noticed how friendly he seemed, and that he wanted to be loved. He looked to be about nine or ten months old, and he definitely looked like a labradoodle versus a full-bred poodle. Mrs. Grange admitted to not being a dog person, so I could understand her being fooled. I wish I could think of something more specific."

Justin took my hand. "No. What you described makes me think you are right, and this is the dog that was stolen."

"She said she would call the police herself, but maybe I'll call Sunny Cody and check to be sure."

Charlie called me back as soon as I got home. "Big surprise, but I did find an address online for Dandyboy Farm."

"Great! Let me get a pen so I can write it down."

"I'll give it to you, but I wouldn't get my hopes up. I remembered the name of the guy I know from up there who was in Animal Control. He said the place was owned by a guy named Andy Phelps, a reputable breeder of Scottish Terriers. The problem is, Phelps died about seven or eight months ago, and the place is empty now. Or is supposed to be."

Chapter Eighteen

I called Sunny Cody the following morning to tell her about what I found out at Heidi Grange's. She confirmed that Mrs. Grange had already called about Walter.

"Did Mrs. Grange give you a description of the man she bought the dog from?" I asked.

"Yes. Medium height, medium build. It looked like dark hair, but he was wearing a baseball cap, and he had on sunglasses, so no idea about eye color."

"So, nothing specific." I couldn't hide the disappointment in my voice.

"When I told her that we suspect that her dog was stolen, she didn't seem too surprised, or too upset at the prospect of having to give him up. She agreed to bring the dog here, and we have notified the Clarks, the family whose Labradoodle was taken. They're meeting her later this morning to confirm he is their dog," Sunny said.

"I'm glad. When I told Justin about him, he said the dog sounded like he was about the same age as the one taken from their clinic, and even though his appearance has been altered, he's sure it is the Clark's dog. Did Mrs. Grange tell you where she purchased him, because I have—"

"She gave me the name Dandyboy Farm and an address. Woodstock is covered by the State Police. I've notified them that we suspect someone is selling stolen animals out of the former kennel, and that whoever it is may be wanted in connection to crimes here."

I felt a sense of relief. This could bring us one step closer to finding the criminals who broke into Reddy Vet. "Good, will you let me know if they find the guy who is running that operation?" I knew I was pushing my luck by asking her to give me information that shouldn't be public yet. I hoped she would forgive me for playing my sympathy card. "Justin could have been killed. I'll feel better once I know the people or persons responsible have been arrested."

"When I spoke to Trooper Goodman at Troop D, he said someone would take a ride by when they have a chance and check the place out. However, he said right now they were pretty backed up with a major incident in Putnum. As soon as I hear anything, I'll let you know."

I wished I knew just how long it was going to be before the state police would be able to get to Dandyboy Farm. I still wanted to talk to Frank Eastman at Rockwell Construction and find out more about the men who did the work on the Feldmans' house, but I felt like Dandyboy was the most concrete connection to the break-in at Reddy Vet yet. I looked at Bruno, who was watching me as I paced the floor, trying to decide what I should do. "You know I want to take a ride to that place and check it out myself. It's possible that whoever sold Walter to Heidi Grange is still using it."

Bruno sat patiently as I voiced my obviously dangerous plan. "I know. But I won't go alone, and I promise not to confront anyone if they're still there." He came over and licked my hand, a gesture I chose to interpret as permission.

I put a call in to Lynn again. "Want to take a ride to check out Dandyboy Farm with me?"

"I'd love to, but this morning is the class I teach at the senior center."

I needed to go back to work soon, and Meredith was due back the next day. While I knew she would be eager to help me check out the other leads I had, I didn't quite trust how Meredith would handle this situation. "That's okay, I'll take Bruno with me, and we'll take a quick ride by, just to see if there are any cars there." Bruno got excited at the mention of his name.

"Whoa. Whoa. I can reschedule my class. There aren't exactly any Rembrandts in attendance, and they will be just as happy if the director, Jane, lets them smear paint on a few canvases, whether I'm there or not. I know you, and if you do find someone there, the temptation to talk to them will be too great to resist. Bruno is an excellent bodyguard, but I am not letting you go to some secluded place without someone who can use a cell phone to call for help. Especially if there is any chance the guys involved in the two break-ins may be there."

I felt immediate relief. I knew she was right, and that planning to go alone was beyond foolish. "Okay, Thanks. I was going to leave soon. Can we pick you up on the way? We can use the cover story of you wanting to buy a dog if we find anyone there. We can say we heard about them through a friend."

"I thought we were going to just take a ride by?"

I didn't answer. I flashed on how Justin looked when the paramedics were rushing him to the ambulance.

"If we do find anyone there, we call the police right away," Lynn said.

"Agreed."

It took close to an hour to get to Dandyboy Farm. Mrs. Grange wasn't kidding when she said it was in the middle of nowhere. We passed several fields where cows and horses were grazing, and I made a mental note to stop at one of the many farm stands along the roadside on our way home. We passed multiple places selling lettuce, peas, and early beans. Most tempting of all, though, were the strawberries, which were in peak season.

"There it is!" Lynn said as we drew up to a long driveway with a sign for "Dandyboy Farm—Breeder of Champions" swinging from a post at the entrance.

The sign was faded and peeling, and there were no buildings visible from the road. A rusty chain hung from another post on the other side of the dirt and gravel driveway, but it was no longer blocking the entrance.

I looked around as we slowly drove up the potholed driveway. "It looks like this might have also once been an actual farm as well as a breeding kennel," I said.

"I bet you're right. It's a beautiful place. I wonder when they decided to start breeding dogs."

As we approached, we passed a barn that looked like it had been converted into a kennel. There were outside runs jutting from the side. A newer-looking kennel building sat a short distance from the barn. We continued toward what was a lovely, though well-worn farmhouse with a porch overlooking the surrounding fields. One of the fields had been fenced in, I assumed to allow the dogs to run and get exercise. It was now covered in knee-high grass and weeds. There was a rusty-looking tractor sitting in another field, but I didn't see any other vehicles. Bruno had started to get excited, letting out small yips as soon as we drove past the barn/kennel.

I stopped the car. "It doesn't look like there is anyone here right now, but let's be sure."

I put Bruno on his leash, and Lynn and I both crept up the stairs to the front porch of the house. I called out, "Hello! Anyone home?" There was no answer, so Lynn and I each peeked in a window, while Bruno sniffed the porch intensely.

"Looks empty. I can't tell if it has been used recently or not," I said. I gingerly tried the door to see if it was locked. It was.

Lynn turned to me. "I'm getting a creepy feeling. I know you wanted to get a look at whoever sold Walter to Mrs. Grange, but if someone is still using this place, I don't want to get caught sneaking around when they come back."

I knew Lynn was right. My idea of using a fake story to explain our presence seemed silly now. "Okay, but let's see if we can check out the rest of the place before we leave."

We went to the barn next. It had indeed been converted to house the dogs Mr. Phelps bred. There were six kennels, a grooming station, and what looked like a puppy play area. The kennels were outfitted with plush doggie beds and had wooden half gates, which could be closed to contain the dogs. Three of the six kennels looked like they hadn't been used in a while, the beds dirty and two with the stuffing hanging out, but three on the right side of the building had water and food dishes and looked like they had been cleaned out recently. I checked to be sure the door was closed behind us and let Bruno off-leash to check out the place as we continued to sniff around ourselves.

"Someone definitely has been keeping dogs here recently," I said. I walked over to the grooming area and found a mix of various colors and textures of dog hair swept into the corner. "Charlie said Mr. Phelps bred Scottish

Terriers, but whoever was using this place was using it to keep more than one kind of dog." I peered into the trash bin under the grooming table. "I think this confirms that this is where Walter became a brunette." I held up a plastic bottle of black hair dye. Bruno ran over to where I was standing and began to scratch at something on the floor. I told Bruno to leave it and bent to pick it up. It looked like the remnants of an old chew toy, but next to it was a scrap of metal. It looked like it could be a dog tag, but it was crusted with dirt and scratched, so it was difficult to read what it said. I was able to make out that it was a rabies vaccine tag and could read some of the numbers, but the name of the vet was unreadable.

Just then, there was the sound of a car approaching up the long driveway. Lynn and I looked at each other. I shoved the rabies tag in my pocket and put Bruno back on leash. I took a deep breath as Lynn and I stepped out of the barn, ready to go to Plan B and give our story about wanting to buy another dog. We were greeted by a cloud of dust as whoever it was raced back down the dirt-and-gravel driveway.

"Did you see what the car looked like?" Lynn asked.

"Not really, from the back I would say it was an SUV, though."

"Could it have been the State Police checking the property?"

"No," I said. "If it was the police, we'd be answering some pretty direct questions by now. Whoever it was didn't want us to see them." I thought for a minute. "It could have been the criminals bringing more dogs, or maybe they found out the police were notified about this place and are trying to clear out anything that would connect it to them." This last thought made me anxious. If the state police didn't get here soon, any evidence to connect them to the crimes at the Feldmans' and Reddy Vet could be gone.

"You're not thinking of waiting to see if they come back, are you?" Lynn sounded incredulous.

I let out a frustrated sigh. "No. If we're right, they're probably watching from somewhere to make sure we leave before they return." I debated calling Troop D to report the car we saw, but I had exactly zero information about it, not to mention having to explain what we were doing there to begin with.

I told Lynn to watch for any cars that could have been the one at the farm as we drove down the narrow road leading from Dandyboy Farm. However, we didn't pass anyone for a mile or more. Suddenly, a dark blue SUV came barreling around a curve up ahead and had to swerve to miss us. I pulled the steering wheel hard to the right and brought my car to an abrupt stop at the side of the road, inches from a ditch running alongside it. I looked in the rearview mirror to see that the SUV had also stopped briefly but then roared off again.

I looked over to see Lynn with a hand on her chest. "That was close!" She glanced out her passenger side window to the ditch, which was merely inches from our tires. "Good driving!"

Bruno let out a couple of barks from the rear seat where, luckily, he was in his restraint. I took two deep breaths to calm myself and made sure there were no more cars coming out of nowhere before I carefully pulled back onto the road. "Maybe I'm just being paranoid, but did that car look like the one we saw at Dandyboy Farm?"

"I didn't get enough of a good look at the one we saw earlier to say." Lynn was quiet for a moment. "Besides, we are quite a way away from Dandyboy; it could be that the car that nearly hit us was just some kids who are used to driving way too fast on nearly deserted roads."

"Maybe." I tried to shake the disappointment I felt at not finding anything useful at Dandyboy Farm. We stopped at one of the farm stands we had passed earlier, and I bought lettuce, peas, and some delicious looking strawberries. It would be nice to have some locally grown produce to serve Meredith when she came back, and the thought of strawberry shortcake almost made me feel more optimistic.

Chapter Nineteen

When I picked up Meredith at the train station the following day, I could tell right away by the tight set of her mouth that she was annoyed by something. I wasn't late, so I didn't think she was upset with me. "Hi. How was the ride?"

"Terrible! The train was stuffy and crowded. A young man got on at the stop right after Grand Central and chose the seat next to me. He had a bag that was obviously oversized and insisted on trying to shove it into the overhead. This took several minutes with him mumbling obscenities the entire time. When he finally sat down, he jiggled his leg in time to the music he was playing on his phone, and in spite of the fact he was using headphones, the music was turned up so loud I'm certain everyone in the train car could hear it. I asked him politely to turn down the volume, but he called me—I won't even tell you what he called me." She shrugged as if to loosen her shoulders. "I need a glass of wine, or at the very least a cup of tea."

Unfortunately, her bad mood put a crimp in my plans for the morning.

Meredith looked over at me, and my disappointment must have shown on my face. "What's happened?"

"It's nothing. Just that the hospital is only a few blocks from here, and I thought we could stop by on the way home so you could finally meet Justin. But why don't we go home instead, so you can have some tea and relax for a bit? We can visit him later." I had warned Justin of my plan, and he was eager for the big meeting, but I thought it might be better to call him and let him know we wouldn't come until later. After listening to her rant, I wanted Meredith in a more affable mood before they met.

"No. Let's go now. I assume there is some sort of cafeteria or coffee shop at the hospital. We can get a cup of tea there."

I hesitated before answering. "All right." I told myself once again it didn't matter if she hit it off with Justin or not; it wouldn't change things. Besides, I was used to handling her disapproval.

As soon as we sat down in the hospital atrium with our tea and scones, Meredith asked about what was going on with the investigation. I told her about the two dogs that were recovered from the break-in at Reddy Vet.

"That's wonderful! I wish I'd been here to go with you to visit the Grange woman, though. Did she give a description of the man who sold her the dog? How about the people whose dog was returned by the good Samaritan?"

"No. Both gave descriptions so vague or contradictory that they're of little use," I said.

"I've read about how unreliable witness descriptions can be. But if I'd been—"

My phone began to vibrate on the table, and I checked the screen. "I need to get this. It's Detective Cody."

Sunny got right to the reason for her call. "I wanted to let you know that Trooper Goodman got back to me. He said one of his officers took a ride out to Dandyboy Farm, but it was deserted, just as expected. He said there was some evidence that someone had been there recently, but it looked like whoever it was had moved on. I know that's not the news you hoped for, but they did follow up on the lead you gave us."

I didn't tell her that I had already checked out the place myself and had come to the same conclusion. "All right. Thank you for getting back to me."

Meredith gave me a questioning look. "What was that about?"

I told her about Lynn's and my trip out to Dandyboy Farm. "I'm sorry, I couldn't wait for you to get back. I didn't even want to wait for the police to get around to checking it out. It looks like whoever was using the place left and got rid of anything that could connect them to the crimes." The dog hair and dye we had found only confirmed that whoever was there had used it as a base to sell dogs illegally. I had hoped the police would find something more.

Meredith interrupted my thoughts. "How did whoever was operating out of the kennel know it was vacant? You said the owner has died, but did he have people who may have worked for him or with him?"

"I suppose neighbors would know Mr. Phelps had passed, or if he had an obituary in the local paper, it could have tipped someone off."

"I guess that's true."

"As far as someone working with him, I had assumed he operated the kennel alone, but if he had a number of dogs, you could be right; he must have had some kind of help. Also, there were customers and any other services he used to help run his business who would know about Dandyboy Farm being empty now, so following that line of investigation might not help us at all." I was interrupted by my phone dinging with a text. "That's Justin. He wants to know if we are on our way. We should go up to see him now."

We found Justin up in a chair by his bed, and he greeted us both with a smile that could melt any heart. After giving me a kiss, he extended his hand to Meredith. "I'm so glad to finally meet you. Melanie has been so happy that you're here and has been telling me all about you."

I could tell by the look on Meredith's face that Justin's charm was getting to her. "I'm glad to finally meet you, also. Melanie has been keeping such a close guard on you, I was beginning to worry what I would find when we did meet."

Justin chuckled. "I hope I'm not as bad as you feared."

I pulled over the other chair in the room so Meredith could sit. "I only wanted to be sure Justin was up to visitors. That's why I held off introducing you." I tried to keep the irritation out of my voice. "I'm going to see if someone can bring us another chair. I'll be right back."

The floor was very busy, and it took several minutes to find someone who could help me. When an aide and I returned to Justin's room with a third chair, I could see he was upset about something.

Meredith was talking. "...so she said they didn't find anything. I plan to help with any further investigation..." She looked up as I came back into the room. "Oh, you're back!"

"What's this about Lynn and you going by yourselves to the kennel where one of the stolen dogs was sold?" Justin asked. "That could have been dangerous if those guys were still there." He took a deep breath and glanced from me to Meredith. "I know you're determined to find out who is responsible for this," he motioned to his head and leg, "but please, this time, let the police take the lead."

I didn't want to upset him anymore, or to discuss this in front of Meredith, so I kissed him on the brow. "I understand." The look he gave me told me we would talk about the issue later.

I tried to redirect the conversation. "So, have they told you when you'll be transferred to the rehab facility?"

"They said tomorrow or the next day. I don't plan on being there long, though. I want to get back home."

Meredith butted in with, "You really must follow the regime they set up to the letter, and you can't push yourself too fast either. I have an elderly friend who had a stroke, and she was determined to walk without the walking frame she was supposed to use. She fell and broke her hip, and after surgery, ended up back in rehab for two months."

I scowled at her. "Justin is not elderly, and I'm sure he isn't in danger of breaking a hip."

"Thank you, I promise to do as I'm told." Justin took my hand and gave it a gentle squeeze.

"After you get home, I'll see about taking some more time off," I said.

He smiled. "Thank you, but my mother has volunteered to come to stay with me until I can get around better on my own."

"All right. I'll still need to make frequent visits to check on you, though."

"Of course." He leaned toward me to give me a kiss.

Meredith coughed softly. "I need water. I think I saw a drinking fountain in the hallway." She smiled at us, then left the room.

As soon as she left, Justin said, "She's not so bad. I like her."

"I'm glad. You looked a little ruffled when I got back from getting the chair, though. Did she say something to upset you?"

"Just that she was telling me all about how you've been investigating some of the leads you've found concerning the break-ins. She seemed very excited to help you." He paused to take a deep breath, "Talking to your neighbor's son, even going to see the woman who bought the stolen labradoodle, and then giving the police the information, was all right. But you and Lynn going to Dandyboy Farm by yourselves has me really worried."

"I know, but as it turned out…" There was some throat clearing outside the doorway, and Meredith walked in again. "One of the nurses got me a cup of water from their break room. To be honest, I don't love drinking from a public drinking fountain." She shuddered. "Did I miss anything I should know about?"

Both Justin and I said, "No."

Justin asked Meredith about her bookshop in Bloomsbury, her boys, and how it felt to be back in the States for a while. Before I realized it, we had been chatting for over an hour, and Justin and Meredith seemed to be getting along just fine. I felt silly for worrying.

There was a quick rap on the door, and Carly, Justin's physical therapist, entered. "Hi! Time to get up and do some walking!" She looked at Meredith and me and said, "You can stay, if Justin doesn't mind."

I realized Meredith hadn't had a chance to get to my house to unpack, and we hadn't had anything to eat for lunch except tea and scones. Also, I was hesitant for her to watch Justin as he did his physical therapy. He was using his left leg much better but still needed a walker. I didn't want to listen to her prognosis for his recovery. "No, that's all right. We were about to leave anyway."

On the way back to the car, Meredith said, "Justin seems delightful. He obviously cares very much about you."

I smiled at her. "He likes you, too. I was glad to see you both get along so well."

She paused before she opened the car door to get in. "I worry that he might be a bit controlling, though."

I was speechless for a few seconds. I could certainly remind her that the same term could easily be applied to her. Instead, after I got behind the wheel, I said, "What do you mean?"

She shrugged. "I picked up on his displeasure with you doing any investigating of the break-in at his clinic. He all but told you to stop."

"He's just worried. We've discussed this before, and he understands my need to get involved. He was just reminding me to be careful." I was hurt that she had any criticism of Justin, even though in the past I had accused him of the same thing.

"We still are going to continue to look into who was involved, aren't we?"

It was hard to determine if she was asking me or telling me. "Yes, but—"

"I know, we will be cautious."

I had planned to say that she had to follow my lead, but instead just said, "That's right."

When we got back to my house, I could see that Meredith was thrilled that Bruno and Jasper greeted her nearly as enthusiastically as they did me. She put down her bags and squatted down to pet both of them, not seeming to mind at all that Jasper was giving her sloppy kisses. Laughing, she said, "I do miss having a dog. Once we are back home, I have to have a talk with Phillip about getting one again."

Seeing her acting so loving toward the dogs made me reconsider what I was planning to do that afternoon. I remembered Malcolm saying he met the man selling Daphne somewhere, and I strongly suspected it could be the same man who sold Walter to Heidi Grange. I thought he said he met the guy who sold him his dog someplace several towns away. He would no doubt be able to give a description of the man he met. But I wanted to speak to him alone. I knew he was still sensitive about losing Daphne, and even though she had suffered the loss of her own dog, I didn't want to chance Meredith saying something to upset him.

After Meredith got settled in again, and we had lunch, I said, "Why don't you relax for a while. I need to pick up some dog food, and I promised to stop by and speak to a friend. We can discuss who we think might be worth speaking to about the break-ins when I get back."

"That sounds like a good plan. I am tired. Maybe I'll sit outside on your patio for a while. I brought along a new mystery I've been dying to start reading." She stretched and yawned. "Or maybe I'll take a quick nap."

* * *

I knew Malcolm would be working, but I was sure he would spare me a few minutes if I asked to speak to him. When I approached the front desk at Highlife Dermatology, Bethany smiled at me. "Hi, Melanie! I didn't realize you had an appointment today." She started tapping my name into her computer.

"Actually, I don't. I was wondering if I could speak to Malcolm Devlin if he has a few minutes between patients."

She checked his schedule. "He should have time to speak to you after he's through with the patient he's with now." Her face clouded over. "I heard about what happened to your...Dr. McKenzie. I'm so sorry. How is he?"

"Thanks. He's healing and may be ready for discharge soon." Another patient walked in then, so I took a seat. After she finished checking the patient in, she called Malcolm and then told me I could meet him in his office.

"I didn't expect to see you today." Malcolm gave me a quick hug. "What's up? How is Justin?"

"He's much better."

"Good. No progress in finding who broke into the practice, though?"

"No. That's kind of why I'm here. I wanted to ask you some questions about the guy who sold you Daphne, if you don't mind."

He winced when I mentioned Daphne. "Sure. Go ahead."

I told him that they had recovered both dogs stolen from Reddy Vet, and how Heidi Grange bought Walter from someone who said they were moving their business, so he was the only dog on the premises at that time." Malcolm shook his head and snorted. I continued, "She said she went to a place called Dandyboy Farm in Woodstock. The owner of the place once bred Scottish Terriers, but has since passed away, and it should be deserted. I never asked, exactly where did you meet the guy who sold you Daphne?"

"It wasn't at a farm, but it was in Putnam, which is right near Woodstock. He had me meet him at a parking lot in a strip mall where half the stores were abandoned. I thought it was weird, but he said his place was a mess as he and his wife were packing to move, plus he said he needed to get something at the hardware store anyway. I noticed there was a hardware store there that looked like it was still in business." He shook his head. "I can't believe I was so stupid. There were so many clues he wasn't on the up and up. He wanted cash and seemed very eager to close the deal. I attributed it to him being a lousy dog owner because he didn't even pat her or say goodbye, good luck, or anything before he handed her over. Mostly, I remember looking at her and knowing there was no way I could walk away without taking her."

"What did this man look like? Mrs. Grange gave a description of the man who sold her the Labradoodle, but she said she didn't notice anything specific."

Malcolm thought for a moment. "I might recognize him if I saw him again, but maybe not. He was on the short side of medium height, had on a Red Sox cap. I would say his hair was dark, and he was thin, but didn't have a wiry build. He was wearing sunglasses, so I didn't get a look at his eyes."

Everything Malcolm described fit with what we had so far, but there was nothing distinctive to help identify him.

"Wait. I remember he had a scar on his left wrist. He must have seen me looking at it, because he said not to worry, it wasn't from Daphne. He laughed and said he hurt his arm at work. It sure looked like a healing dog bite to me, though."

Malcolm's phone rang and after he answered it he said, "I'm sorry, but my next patient is waiting. I'll call Detective Cody if I think of anything else that might help catch whoever is behind this whole thing." He grinned, "And of course I'll let you know, also. Give Justin my best."

A dog bite scar was at least something to go on, and Mrs. Feldman said Nika put up a fight when the burglars grabbed her. Cat bites were notorious for becoming infected. One thing was for sure: whoever these people were, it didn't sound as if animals liked them very much.

On the way home, I stopped at the store to get the makings of a salad for our dinner as well as the dog food I needed. The day had heated up quite a bit, and I found the thought of chicken on the grill to go with the salad a good choice for dinner. Meredith was just waking up from a nap when I got home.

"I tried sitting out on the patio, but got too warm. That quick nap did make me feel better, thank you for suggesting it." She looked at me levelly. "I assume the friend you went to see had something to do with getting information that can help with our investigation. What did you find out?"

I knew I might as well accept the fact Meredith was going to be in this with me. I told her what Malcolm said about the man who sold him Daphne having a healing dog bite.

"Good! Whether they are connected to the break-ins or not, someone who would steal a dog deserves it. Do we have time to go and speak to someone else today?"

"I think we'd better wait until tomorrow." I thought we could find out from the man who owns Rockwell Construction, Frank Eastman, who it was that worked on the Feldmans' house." I cleared my throat. "It might be best if you let me take the lead when we question him. You could write down the names he gives us." This wasn't the first time I'd asked her to let me be in charge of what we asked. I really hoped she'd listen this time.

Just as Meredith and I were making our dinner, I got a text from Justin. *Will be transferred to rehab facility tomorrow AM (so they say anyway!) will call when I'm settled in. stay safe please. XX"*

I texted back *okay will wait for your call before coming to visit. Will be careful— meredith on the case with me! XX*

Chapter Twenty

On the way to Rockwell construction the next day, I tried to think of a subtle way to ask Frank Eastman about the crew who installed the window for the Feldmans. When we reached the office, I asked to speak to Mr. Eastman, and his office manager said she would get him for us.

Frank Eastman was tall and thin. He looked to be in his fifties, and from his clothes and work boots, it looked like he was used to helping his men with jobs, not just supervising.

After we introduced ourselves, and before I could say anything else, Meredith said, "My sister is considering some work on her house, and we hear your company did such a good—"

Frank held up his hand. "No need for ploys to get information. Roger Feldman called me and told me he thought you might come here asking me questions." He looked at me, "I feel sick about what happened to Mr. and Mrs. Feldman. I've known them for years. I can understand you wanting to find out who was responsible, but two of my long-time employees, good guys, did the job. They were as upset to hear about what happened as I was. They had nothing to do with it."

"I believe you, but you wouldn't be able to give us their names, would you? I'd like to ask them a couple of questions myself," I said.

He looked annoyed, but said, "Fine, but I'm telling you they had nothing to do with it." He turned to his office manager and said, "Is Hal still here? Call him and tell him someone needs to speak to him." He said to me, "Hal Foster is one of the guys who worked on the job; Manuel Rojas is the other.

Manuel is out on a job now, but he was away on vacation at the time of the Feldman break-in."

A short, sturdy-looking young man came into the office. "Someone wanted to see me?"

I immediately looked him over for a bandage or obvious wounds. I noticed he had a nasty-looking scratch on his right forearm, though it looked fresh. "Hi, I'm Melanie Bass, and this is my sister Meredith. I'm a neighbor of the Feldmans. I understand you did some work on their house a few weeks ago?"

"Yep. Lovely old couple. It was horrible what happened to them." He shifted his weight from one leg to the other. "What can I do for you?"

Meredith started to open her mouth, but I held up my hand to her and said, "Mrs. Feldman said one of the workers really admired her cat, Nika."

He chuckled and said, "Yeah, that was me. I wanted to get a kitten for my girlfriend, so I asked about their cat. It's beautiful, I knew my girlfriend would love one like it. I asked Mrs. F where her husband got it. When I found out what he paid, though…whew! Too rich for my blood. I decided to go to the animal shelter instead."

I motioned to the scratch on his arm. "How did that happen?"

"Our new kitten. She's a little hellion, but Cindy loves her. She looks a lot like the Feldmans' cat, but she's not a real fancy purebred. I told this guy I got acquainted with at the animal shelter what I wanted, and a few days later, he contacted me and said I should come down and look at one that just came in." He paused for a minute. "It cost me a bit more than I thought most rescues charge, but I was happy to pay. He said it was because she was such a special kitten, and I better grab her before someone else did."

My ears perked up. "Do you remember this guy's name?"

"I think it was Luc; I don't know his last name."

Meredith had her pen and pad out and was jotting this down. "What's the name of the shelter?"

He smiled at her. "You looking for a cat, too?"

"Yes, something like that." She wrote down the name and directions he gave us.

Hal shifted on his feet once more, then said, "I have to go; my partner is waiting in the truck. Tell Luc I gave you his name. He'll help you find what you're looking for."

When we got back into the car, I punched the address Hal had given us into my GPS. It looked like the place we were looking for was seven miles north of us. He said it was called Rhonda's Rescues. When we came to our destination, it turned out to be a small but very well-kept property. There was a fenced-in yard in which three healthy-looking dogs were playing. I noticed two small buildings, one marked "Pretty Kitties" and another "Handsome Hounds."

We followed a sign that pointed to the office and approached the front counter. "Hi, is Rhonda around?" I asked.

The teen behind the counter said, "Yeah, I'll get her," then yelled, "Mom!" toward the back of the building.

An attractive blonde-haired woman in her late forties came out to talk to us. I gave her our names and said, "We understand a man named Luc works here."

Meredith interrupted and said, "We were hoping to speak to him. Is he here now?"

Rhonda shook her head, "No. He doesn't work here; he volunteers, and he pretty much comes whenever he wants."

"Do you know how I could reach him?" I asked.

She gave me an assessing look. "He didn't offer much information when he started volunteering here. As you can see, I run a small operation—I'm licensed and all to take in dogs and cats—but I rely on animal lovers and my own family to help out. I don't press my volunteers for information." She seemed a bit defensive now. "I have two volunteers helping me out today; maybe they can help you."

Meredith answered for me, "Yes, that may be useful."

Rhonda led us to the "Pretty Kitties" building, where two young women were working. One was cleaning out litter boxes, the other holding and petting a bright-eyed tiger cat. As we walked in, I heard the one cleaning the litter say, "After this one, we switch, okay?"

Rhonda introduced us, then said, "I need to get back to the office. Let me know if I can help you with anything else."

"I have one more question. I understand your adoption fee is a bit more than most shelters charge. I was wondering—"

She straightened up, obviously very offended. "We provide excellent care! I don't think you can put a value on a companion you will have for a lifetime!" She huffed and said to the girls, "I'll be in the office if you need me." She looked Meredith and me over one more time before she left.

When I asked the girls if they knew Luc, they looked at each other. The tall red-headed one said, "We don't know him, but we know who he is." Her friend added, "Yeah, we try not to have anything to do with him. Like, if he's here, Bridget and I find a reason to leave whatever building he's in and work together in the other one."

Meredith asked, "Why is that?"

Bridget looked at her friend and shrugged, "I don't know. I just get a bad vibe."

"Do you know when he'll be here again?" I asked.

Both girls shrugged. "Like we said, we don't really talk to him."

"What does he look like?" Meredith asked. I had to admit, we were working well together now.

"I don't know. Just like a guy. Maybe thirties or forties, brownish hair. He's kinda short." Most guys would look short to Bridget, though; she looked like she played basketball.

I thought of something else. "Does he have any bites or scratches on his arms?"

Both girls held out their arms, "We all have scratches. These poor things can't help it; they weren't always treated well before they ended up here."

I thought of one more thing to ask. "Did this Luc ever show up with a dog or cat that he said he found or that someone gave him to bring here?"

Bridget's friend answered this time. "Like we told you, we try to keep away from the guy. Most of the animals we get are because people know Rhonda takes in unwanted animals, and they call her to check if they can bring them here. I do remember a couple of times we'd show up to volunteer and there was a new cat or dog we never saw before. Luc might have been here some of those times."

Bridget added, "But they could have been drop-offs, too." She headed toward the next cage where an orange tabby was meowing plaintively.

I signaled to Meredith it was time to leave. "Well, thank you for your help. Do you think you could call me if Luc comes in to volunteer while you're here?" Meredith handed me a slip of paper with both our phone numbers on it. I held it out to Bridget. I could see she was hesitant to take it. "I want to talk to him about a cat," I added.

She took the paper and put it in her pocket. "Okay, but Rhonda would be a better person to help you with that."

On the way to the car, Meredith said, "That was helpful, wouldn't you say?" She seemed almost giddy.

I tried to tamp down my own excitement. I told myself we only had a first name, and the description the girls gave of this Luc made him sound average-looking. However, that fit with the description Malcolm gave, as well as what the owners of the stolen dogs said. "I just wish we had more information on this Luc, so we could speak to him."

"Do you think those girls will call when he comes in next?"

"I don't know. I hope so," I said.

Meredith turned to look at me as we drove away from Rhonda's Rescue, "Where next? Do you think we should follow up on the man your detective said denies making the late-night call to Justin's practice?"

"I'm not sure that wouldn't cause more problems. Detective Cody said they interviewed him already, and she seemed convinced he wasn't involved. I've seen him when he was angry, and I wouldn't be surprised if he complained about us to the police. As it is, I'm treading on thin ice—and taking you with me. Our best bet is to try to stay under the radar until we have something concrete to report to the police."

Meredith looked disappointed. "All right. If you say so." She mumbled something under her breath.

"Besides, if he did make that call, it was likely as a crank call, and it doesn't help us find who really is involved." We were quiet the rest of the way home. I was trying to think of a way to track down this Luc we had heard about. "It's a long shot, but one of my friends from Coretrack Homecare volunteers at our local animal shelter. It's possible she's met Luc if he also volunteers there," I said.

"Good idea. But I think you should get in touch with her immediately. We need to get any information about him we can before he goes to Rhonda's again and finds out someone was asking about him."

I gritted my teeth. "Yes. I know. I'll get right on it."

I called my friend Hannah as soon as we got home, but she didn't remember ever meeting anyone named Luc. "I've been there a long time, and we have a regular schedule of when we are to come and how long our shift is. Plus, the director of the shelter vets all new volunteers, and we are required to give contact information. I'll ask, though. If this Luc does volunteer there, I probably can get you a last name and contact information."

"Thank you, Hannah. That's very helpful."

"Any luck?" Meredith asked.

"No, afraid not." I checked my phone for any missed messages or phone calls. "I expected to hear from Justin by now. I wonder how things went with his transfer to the rehab facility." I decided I had better call him.

"Hi. How did it go? Are you settled in?" I asked.

"I was about to call you. Change of plans. The doctor decided to discharge me to home. He's prescribing daily in-home PT and OT for now. It took some time to get all those services in place. We just got here a little while ago."

"So, you're at your house now? That's fantastic!" I could see Meredith giving me an inquiring look.

By the sound of his voice, I could tell how happy he was. "It feels so good to be home, to be able to sleep in my own bed again!" He lowered his voice a little, "Speaking of which, when can you come over? I need my favorite homecare nurse to check on me."

I laughed and said, "I'll be there shortly. Meanwhile, don't give your mother a hard time."

"I wouldn't dare!" I could hear his mother's voice in the background, then he said, "When you come over, why don't you bring Jasper. I miss the big lug. Miss Scarlett seems to prefer my mother to me now. I think it's going to take some time for her to forgive me for being away."

When I ended the call, I told Meredith what Justin had said and that I was going to check on him and bring Jasper back home.

Meredith helped me gather Jasper's food and water dishes, then bent to pet him and scratch his ears. "You're a love, aren't you, a real silly boy." She smiled at me and said, "I'm going to miss him. Is Justin sure he can handle him while he recovers?"

"I'm sure he'll manage. Plus, I'll take Bruno with me, and I can walk Jasper for him over the next few days. Better still, you could come to help if you want to."

"I'd like that."

No matter how he felt about it, I knew Phillip didn't stand a chance against my sister – I was certain they would be getting a new dog once they returned home.

Bruno eagerly followed Jasper and me to the door. "Okay, I know you missed your buddy Justin, too," I said, and clipped on his leash. I turned to Meredith. "We'll be back by dinnertime."

Chapter Twenty-One

When I got to Justin's, Bruno rushed to lick his hands and put his paws on Justin's knees. However, Jasper was so excited to see Justin and to be home, it took both Justin's mother and me to calm him so he wouldn't hurt our patient.

After Jasper gave him many kisses and fetched every toy he owned for Justin to toss for him, Justin's Mom, Rita, said, "I'll take both of these guys outside for a few minutes. I'm sure you two want to talk."

I sat on the arm of Justin's chair and gave him my own enthusiastic welcome home. Afterward, I said, "I was so frightened when I saw what happened to you that day." I could feel myself choking up a bit.

He kissed me again. "I'm sorry you had to see me that way. I'm just thankful to even be here today. I only wish I had a sharper memory of exactly what happened."

I was about to tell him about what I suspected about Luc, when there was a loud scratching at the kitchen door, and I could hear Rita saying, "All right! You can go in and see your daddy again." Jasper burst into the room and ran in excited circles. Rita and Bruno followed closely behind.

Justin called Jasper over to give him a belly rub, and that helped to quiet him down. Bruno came to sit by my feet, but I noticed him watching Justin closely.

After calming Jasper, Justin straightened up and said, "Let me show you what I can do now." He picked up a pencil and piece of paper from the side table near him with his left hand and wrote a few wobbly words. "Not bad, right? Especially since I'm right-handed." He beamed like a kindergartner who had just learned the alphabet.

"I'm impressed," I said.

"That's wonderful!" His mother came to give him a hug.

"Wait! Watch this!" He stood up shakily but then used his walker to cross from his chair to the sofa. It looked like he still had to use a lot of effort to move his left leg.

He was a bit out of breath after he fell back onto the sofa. "Walking still needs work. My physical therapist is coming tomorrow, and I hope he is as good as the one I had in the hospital."

"If it's Tyler Ward, I can vouch for how good he is. He seems to always get the best effort out of his patients."

That seemed to reassure both Justin and Rita.

Talking about his therapist coming to the house reminded me that I needed to call my manager, Judy. When Justin was injured, I called her and asked for an extension on my time off, and she readily agreed. But I knew the time had come for me to go back to seeing patients.

Rita made us tea and coffee, and we sat and listened as she told us about her Alaskan trip—what she had of it anyway, before it was cut short. When she had finished showing us the photos she took, I finally mentioned the trip Meredith and I took to Rhonda's Rescues, and that I was suspicious of one of the men who volunteers there. "He doesn't come regularly, and two of the young women said they find something dodgy about him. When I asked Rhonda, she didn't have any information on him."

"This trip was just to ask questions, right? I don't want you to confront the guy, especially if someone has gotten a bad feeling about him."

"No, I haven't had any contact with him. As I said, he wasn't there, and there was no information about how to find him either."

"But if we do find out any information on him, it would be something I think we better let the police look into." Justin looked as if he was thinking for a minute. "I'm pretty sure I had a client once who said she got her dog from Rhonda's Rescue. The dog was in good shape, but I'd never heard of that place before. I guess I could ask around at some of the other practices in the area and see if they have any info on it."

"Okay. Great." I was pleased that "we" were going to investigate it further. I looked at the time and said, "I promised Meredith I'd be home by dinner. I'll be back tomorrow. Meanwhile, is there anything you need me to do or get for you?"

Justin reached down to pet Jasper again, "Actually, there is. Jasper is due for his monthly flea and tick med, and I'm all out. Would you mind stopping by the practice and picking more up for me?"

"I'll be glad to," I said, "I need to get Bruno his med, too. I'll pick up their meds tomorrow."

* * *

I found Lynn and Meredith out on my patio sipping ice-cold glasses of lemonade when Bruno and I returned home.

"Hi! I just thought I'd check in and see what you two were up to this evening," Lynn said. "Meredith was just telling me about the tip you got that led you to that animal rescue place. Good work."

I let Bruno off-leash to run around the back yard, then poured myself a glass of lemonade. "Thanks. I'm not sure if this Luc is connected to the break-ins, but I wouldn't be surprised to find out he's responsible for the 'rescue' of somebody's unguarded pet."

"So, what now?" Lynn asked. "Is there any way to find out more about this guy? If he is responsible for 'finding' animals and rehoming them for a significant fee, do you think the woman who runs the rescue knows about it?"

"She did seem to tense up when we mentioned Luc's name," Meredith said.

"I agree. I don't think she liked us coming there and asking a lot of questions. Justin said he would call a few of his colleagues in the area and see if they have had dealings with her. All the animals in her care looked to be in good health, so she must be getting them veterinary care."

Bruno ran up to me then and sat in front of me, then reached out to tap my knee with a paw. I laughed, "He's letting me know it's dinner time. After I feed him, I thought we could throw something on the grill. Do you want to stay for dinner?" I asked Lynn. "Unless you have plans with Brian?"

Meredith said, "Who is Brian? I haven't heard about him. Is he your boyfriend?"

Lynn said, "Well, not exactly my boyfriend, though we have been seeing each other. But no, I don't have plans. Brian said he needed to be away for a week or so. Some business deal he's working on. So, I'd love to stay."

"Hmmm. You don't think that Brian has another family he's hiding from you or anything, do you?" I was only half kidding. Both Lynn and I had been deceived by Artie Krapaneck, who had dated me while still married to Lynn.

Lynn laughed, but then looked uncertain for a moment. "No, of course not. I don't think he's hiding anything from me. Anyway, it's nothing serious for now." I could see I'd planted a seed of doubt in her mind, though.

Meredith and I glanced quickly at each other. "I'll go take care of Bruno, then I'll bring out the burgers and corn." I felt sorry for worrying Lynn, but I didn't want her caught up in another disastrous relationship.

When I came back out with the food, I said, "I'm sorry if I upset you, Lynn. I just—"

She smiled and held up her hand to stop me. "I know in the past I haven't had the best judgment concerning men. I appreciate you looking out for me."

I heard Meredith clear her throat, but ignored it.

We spent the rest of the evening pleasantly, sitting outside talking until it got dark and then watching Bruno chase fireflies. I was glad to see that Meredith and Lynn were becoming friends and felt comforted by the fact that Justin was out of the hospital and recovering.

Chapter Twenty-Two

The next morning, before I went to Reddy Vet, I called Judy at Coretrack Homecare to speak to her about coming back to work. She listened as I told her Justin was doing better and that while my sister was still visiting, she had settled in and would do fine on her own while I was at work. "I really appreciate you giving me extra time off, but I think I'm ready to come back to work now."

"I'm so glad to hear that your…Justin…is doing better. That whole experience must have been a nightmare for you. We'll be glad to have you back, though. I might be able to give you a lighter schedule for a couple of days. Things have settled down here for at least a little while."

"Thank you. That'll be great." While I was eager to get back to work, I would be happy to have more time to spend looking after Justin and with my sister. Not to mention, time to follow up on any information Justin got on Rhonda's Rescue, or the mysterious Luc.

As we were eating our breakfast, I let Meredith know my plans for the morning. I assured her I was only going to pick up medications at Reddy Vet and had no plans to snoop around anywhere else.

"Good. I think this whole investigating business has helped forge new bonds between us, wouldn't you agree?" She smiled at me. "Sister sleuths!"

I laughed. "I'm not sure I'm ready to hang out our shingle, but you have a point about new bonds forming."

Meredith took a last sip of her breakfast tea. "It was difficult, I think, when we were younger, with the age difference between us. It was a shock when Mother told me I was going to have a little brother or sister."

I realized that must have been difficult; she had been used to being an only child until I showed up.

Meredith got up to put her cup in the sink. "Then of course, Mother and Father babied you so much it was hard to tolerate."

"What! They never babied me! And I had to put up with them constantly holding you up to me as a good example! All my life, I felt like I had to measure up to you." I started to breathe rapidly. "It took me a long time to accept that I was my own person and could live my life my own way."

"Funny. I don't remember things that way." She gave me a tight smile. "But let's not argue now, all that is in the past anyway."

I wanted to snap back, "No! You're still telling me what to do and trying to take over my life today!" but I held my tongue. I didn't think she would acknowledge that anyway, and I was trying to keep things pleasant while she was here.

"Right. Well, I need to get to Reddy Vet. I'll be back after I drop off Jasper's meds." Sensing my anger, Bruno had come to sit by my leg. I pet him to reassure him I was all right, then left, closing the door firmly behind me.

When I got to Reddy Vet, the waiting room was empty, and I could see Traci and Shauna whispering at the front desk. I walked over to where they were standing and murmured, "What's going on?"

"Stella is in one of the exam rooms with a guy. We're pretty sure it's her boyfriend," Traci said.

"Oh, I didn't realize Stella was seeing someone." I tried not to let on how pleased I was to hear that.

Traci nodded, "He's been in a couple of times asking to speak to her. When he leaves, she always looks a little flustered."

Shauna said, "I asked her about him the other day, and she started to blush a little and said, 'Oh, he's just an old friend,' but I could see there's something more there."

"I say good for her!" Traci said.

Yes, good for her. I felt a little silly now for thinking she had designs on Justin. "Did Justin call and let you know I'd be picking up Jasper's medication as well as Bruno's?"

"Yes. I'll get them for you," Traci said.

The front door opened, and one of my former patients walked in, a cat carrier clutched in her hand. "Melanie? Hi. Brenda Loomis. Remember me?"

"Of course." I was talking with Mrs. Loomis when I saw a man come out of the back, where the exam rooms are, and walk by us. He waved quickly to Traci as he left. He looked a little familiar, and I realized I'd seen him here before, patiently waiting to see Stella. I'd have to ask Justin what he knew about him, and if Stella had been in a serious relationship all along.

Just then, Stella came out to the front desk. "Hi Melanie. I hear Justin is home now. We can't wait until he is well enough to come back." I noticed her color did look a little higher than usual.

"He's eager to get back to work, too, but he's still got a way to go before he's ready."

"Of course. Well, tell him I said hi." She had Mrs. Loomis follow her back to one of the rooms.

I left feeling more kindly toward Stella Antonio than I had since I'd met her.

Chapter Twenty-Three

When I got back home, I found Meredith working at the counter, cutting up the makings of a chicken salad for our lunch. Neither one of us mentioned our spat earlier.

"How did things go at the vet? Anything interesting going on there?" Meredith asked.

"As a matter of fact, yes. I found out Stella Antonio has a boyfriend." I couldn't keep the satisfaction I felt out of my voice.

"Is she the attractive woman vet I saw when we were there questioning the receptionists? Why is that such good news?" She gave me a piercing look. "You don't think there was anything going on between her and Justin, I hope."

"No, of course not." No way I was going to admit to her I'd been suspicious of Stella's intentions toward Justin. "I completely trust Justin. I'm just happy for Stella."

"Well, good. I know I would hate to have to worry about any female co-worker of Phillip's having designs on him." She put the chicken salad in the refrigerator, then turned and said, "I've been thinking. Since you're going back to work, I thought I might rent a car for a few days. That way, I have some way of getting around while you aren't home. I could also help by doing the shopping or running other errands for you if you like."

"That's very nice of you, and I don't blame you for wanting to be able to get around on your own, but can you drive here? It's been a while since you were in the States."

"Of course I can drive! I am fully aware of the traffic laws of the State of Connecticut. Are you forgetting I drove here for many years before we moved overseas?"

"I'm sorry. You're right." I hadn't intended for my question to come out as an insult.

"Would you be able to drive me to the rental company this afternoon, then?"

"Yes, of course. How about after lunch?" At least I wouldn't have to worry about her being bored at home and rearranging more of my house if she could get out and amuse herself.

I had somehow envisioned Meredith choosing something sensible like a Nissan Sentra, but instead she drove away in a Race Red Mustang Convertible. She insisted she had always wanted to buy one when she and Phillip first got together, but he talked her out of it, claiming it was not only too expensive but too impractical. I didn't even try to keep up with her as she sped back to my house. I was discovering that there were a lot of things I never even guessed about my sister.

I found I was looking forward to getting back to work the next day. I missed seeing some of the patients I followed regularly. Judy was true to her word and only scheduled me for four visits on my first day, which would only take me until lunchtime. Afterward, I planned to stop over at Justin's and check on him and see how his physical therapy was going.

My first two patients of the day were ones I'd never met before, but after that, I was scheduled to see Sunny's father, Jim Moran, and then Mrs. Paine.

I was pleased to see Mr. Moran really had done a good job of getting his blood sugar under control and told him so.

"Yeah, well, Pauline has been all over making low-carb meals. Some of them aren't even too bad."

"You check out perfectly, and I'll contact your doctor, but I don't think I need to keep following you at this point. You're doing a great job," I said.

While I put away my stethoscope and BP cuff, Mr. Moran cleared his throat and said, "How is that boyfriend of yours doing? I heard what happened. Sunny says they are still looking for the culprits."

"Justin's improving nicely. I have every confidence the police will find the men involved. Has Sunny told you anything about what exactly they have found out so far? Any talk of possible suspects?" I didn't mention that I had done some of my own investigating and planned to update his daughter on what I found out.

"You know my daughter by now. I asked , but she just glared at me and reminded me I knew better than to question her about an ongoing investigation." He grinned. "But I tried." He walked me to the door. "Pauline is out shopping now, but she told me to give you her best, and we both hope we can see you again under nonmedical circumstances."

Mrs. Paine greeted me with a hug. "Oh, I was so upset to hear about your young man! I hope he is doing well now, though with you caring for him, I'm sure he can't help but get better."

She hobbled over to a seat in her easy chair using a knobby-looking cane. "As I said before, these criminals are out of control! If I could have at them, I'd give them a lesson!" She waved her cane in the air.

"I agree about the criminals, but what happened here?" I pointed to her ankle, which was encased in a soft brace.

"Oh! I twisted it coming down Ada Watkin's front stairs. I aggravated an old roller derby injury, I think. I told you about my roller derby days, didn't I?"

"Yes, you did, and I would have paid a great deal of money to have seen you in action! I'm sure rolling your ankle like that could be part of it, but according to the notes Dr. Scabbard sent, the X-rays show significant arthritis as well as tendonitis. Have you been taking the medication he gave you? Is that the brace he provided?"

"That brace is too hot to wear in this heat. This one is fine. The medication helps, but I suspect I'm just going to have to tolerate the arthritis for the most part." Her laugh always reminded me of tinkling bells. "The price of getting old."

"Maybe you should wear the sturdier brace here in the air conditioning and use the soft one when you are outside."

"All right. If you say so."

The way she said it made me sure she would do whatever she wanted to do. "How do you feel other than your ankle hurting?" I asked.

"Fine," She sat quietly while I examined her, then said, "Ada told me that they arrested the men who beat and robbed her. Do you suppose they could be the same people who attacked your boyfriend?"

I shook my head. "The police say they don't have any evidence to link them to the break-in at the veterinary practice."

"It does seem very frightening to think there are two such ruthless gangs targeting people. It may not be kind to say so, but when they are caught, they should receive the harshest sentence allowable."

I didn't respond, but I silently agreed with her.

Mrs. Paine started to stand. "I'm sorry, since my bum ankle was bothering me, I haven't done any baking for a couple of days. Would you like a glass of lemonade or iced tea before you go?"

"No, thank you. You just sit and rest. I can see myself out." I thought of one more question before I left, however. "I never asked, but does Mrs. Watkins have a dog by any chance?"

Mrs. Paine shook her head. "No. Poor Claude passed away a week or so before she was attacked. Ada was bereft. Not only was Claude her constant companion, but he had more blue ribbons than a country fair."

"Sorry to hear that. How awful she had to go through that attack in addition to losing her dog." I tucked that information away; it was a fragile connection to the other break-ins, but I could point out to Sunny Cody that Mrs. Watkins had a prize-winning dog prior to being burglarized. "Rest, take the medicine the doctor prescribed, and use your brace on that leg. All right?"

She smiled and said, "Of course, dear."

When I got to Justin's, Tyler, his physical therapist, was just leaving. "How did Justin do? I know he's determined to get back the full function in his hand and leg."

Tyler nodded. "Yes, he certainly is determined. I think he's doing great with his hand, though he needs to keep working on it to retain the strength and control he regained."

"But his leg?"

"It's better. He's frustrated because he wants to be able to walk and stand as he had before."

"Do you think he will ever walk normally again?" I knew Tyler wouldn't be able to answer, but I had to ask.

He shrugged. "Maybe, maybe not. He knows that, but he also knows it will never happen unless he keeps trying."

I thanked Tyler and went in to see for myself how Justin was doing. He was walking from one side of the living room to the other using his walker. I noticed he wasn't dragging his foot as much as he had been even the day before.

"Small improvements, right? My goal is to be able to walk with a cane by next week." He eased himself into an armchair, red-faced, sweaty, and slightly out of breath.

I bent to give him a quick kiss. "I bet you do it, too."

"I called Dr. Reddy and told him I think I can come back part-time by the end of next week."

"Really? Are you sure you aren't pushing yourself too hard?"

"No. I want to get back to work." Jasper bounded into the room and greeted me, then went to rest his head on Justin's lap. He looked down at the dog. "I know, you'll miss having me home all day," he stroked Jasper's ears, "but I have to get back into the old routine."

I thought about what I'd learned at his practice the previous day. "I didn't realize Stella Antonio was seeing someone. I saw him yesterday, well, kind of; he was leaving, and I caught a glimpse of him."

"Really? I don't remember if she ever mentioned having a boyfriend. I'm glad." He seemed to be genuinely pleased. That made me feel more secure that I had only been imagining any attraction between Stella and him.

He got quiet for a minute, then said, "I've been meaning to talk to you about something." I thought I saw a mischievous glint in his eyes.

His mother walked into the room just then. "Hi Melanie. Did he tell you he's been pacing back and forth all around the house all day long, determined to make that leg work better?" She gave Justin a worried look. "I know he needs to practice using it, but that much exercise can't be good either. He's wearing himself out!"

I didn't want to get into the middle of this. "I think as long as he takes breaks and doesn't tire himself out too much, he can exercise his leg as tolerated." I looked from one to the other of them and was satisfied that neither looked upset with my answer.

Mrs. McKenzie suggested we play a few hands of gin rummy, and the rest of the afternoon passed quickly. It wasn't until I was on the way home that I realized Justin had never told me what he wanted to talk to me about.

When I got home, I saw that Meredith had indeed gone grocery shopping; my refrigerator and cabinets hadn't looked so full in quite a while. I found her sitting out on the patio reading under a sun umbrella I had never seen before.

I pointed at the new umbrella. "I see you went out today. Thank you for doing the shopping. Did you do anything else interesting?"

She looked as if she was thinking, then shook her head. "No. Why do you ask?"

I smiled and said, "I just thought you'd take a little ride in your dream car, is all." By the look on her face, I knew that I was probably right. "You didn't get a speeding ticket or anything, did you?"

"No, of course not! How was your day?"

"Fine." I told her about Mrs. Paine, my feisty octogenarian patient, and how Justin was determined to get back to work soon. This made me think of her bookstore back in Bloomsbury, and I asked her about it.

She told me how much she enjoyed owning it, but trusted her manager, Millie, to run it in her absence. "Speaking of which, I'm nearly done with this mystery I'm reading, and I would love to finish it before dinner."

I took the hint and went in to call Lynn to see if she wanted to join us for dinner again.

She sounded apologetic. "I'd love to, but I have a class to teach at the Adult Ed Program tonight. Maybe tomorrow?"

"Of course. Have you heard from Brian? Any word when he'll be back from his business trip?" I asked.

"No. But I'm sure he must be busy with…business. Besides, as I said, I'm not sure we have progressed to that place in our relationship where he would call while he's away." I could hear a bit of disappointment in her voice.

"Okay. So, more time for the girls to get together!"

After dinner, I asked Meredith if she wanted to come to Hammonasset Beach State Park to walk Bruno with me.

"No. Thank you. I want to call Phillip, and then I'll just read for a while and go to bed. I'm really tired."

Somehow, I got the feeling she was avoiding me.

I took Bruno, and we walked our favorite path from Meigs Point to West Beach. The path was less crowded than usual for such a nice evening, and the sound of the waves lulled me as we strolled along. I forgot for a little while about the stress of the past few weeks. Something seemed off about the way Meredith was acting; it wasn't like her to keep anything back if something was bothering her, but I was able to put that out of my mind also. Bruno and I stayed at the beach, sitting on a bench and watching as the sun went down.

The next day at work wasn't as smooth as the previous one. First, I got a text from Lynn saying that she couldn't make it to have dinner with Meredith and me that night, and then there seemed to be issues with my first two patients of the day. Mrs. Leade was supposed to receive IV antibiotics via her central line, but was missing some of the supplies to maintain it. It took several phone calls to help her straighten out the problem, and when I left, I could tell she was still anxious about the situation. The next patient insisted she didn't need me to follow up with her and said she was going to call her physician and insist he cancel any further visits by my agency. The rest of my visits went well, but I was exhausted when I got home from work. I could hear Meredith out in the backyard playing with Bruno. I planned to change and grab a glass of iced tea before I joined them. I got a call from Sunny Cody just as I closed my bedroom door.

She got right to the point. "What were you thinking! I told you we spoke to the Brazen guy already! I can't keep covering for you grossly overstepping your bounds in my investigations. Mr. Brazen has threatened to sue the department for harassment now." I had never heard her so angry.

"I'm sorry, but I don't know what you are talking about. What happened with Mr. Brazen? Why is he upset?"

"Did you or did you not go to see him and interrogate him about the phone call made to Reddy Vet the night of the break-in? He said you strongly implied he was involved in setting up the crime." She had calmed down a bit, but not by much.

"No. I have never spoken to Calvin Brazen. Whoever contacted him, it wasn't me." I had a strong suspicion I knew who did, though. I was beginning to feel my own ire rising.

"He said it was a woman; I assumed it was you. If you know anything about who it was, you need to tell them to back off. This has added another complication to our investigation. Now we need to try to placate this crank. I must insist you stop poking into our investigation. I realize you have a stake in this, but from now on, you are forbidden to have anything to do with it."

I was getting angry at her also, now. "I've been giving you any information I get, and I've been conscientious about staying out of your way. As a matter of fact, I found out—"

"Stop. Just stop. I mean it." She ended the call.

I hurriedly changed and charged out to confront Meredith. "Did you go to speak to Calvin Brazen and harass him about making the phone call to Reddy Vet?" I didn't even try to hide how angry I was.

"I didn't 'harass' him. I only wanted to be sure that all the right questions were asked." She sounded indignant.

"The police already questioned him! I think they know what questions to ask! I just got a phone call from Sunny Cody, and she was livid. Mr. Brazen has filed a complaint. How did you even get his address?"

"I looked it up, of course. There's no need to get so upset. I'm sure the police deal with irate citizens all the time. In the end, there'll be no harm done."

I had to take a huge breath and then let it out before I could even respond. "Detective Cody *forbade* me to have anything to do with the investigation now."

She glared at me. "That won't stop you, however, will it? I mean, you seem to not like taking direction."

"*I* don't like taking direction! I've had to put up with your meddling and your unwanted advice through this entire visit. Not to mention you refusing to listen when I ask you to let me handle questioning people."

"I think I was being quite helpful."

"No, you weren't! You are trying to run everything as usual. I never even asked for your help!" I stormed back into the house, Bruno skittering in behind me, his little tail tucked between his legs. "I'm sorry, buddy. I didn't mean to upset you." I reached down to pet him. My hands were shaking. I went into the living room to sit and calm down. I had to admit, Meredith had been a *little* helpful, but then she ruined it by always trying to do things her way.

I heard the back door open and close, and then the door to Meredith's room slam. I felt like I needed to blow off more steam, so I took Bruno for a walk on Windy Reed Road. I hoped moving around might help me think, not only of a way to approach Sunny Cody with the information I'd gotten at Rita's Rescue, but of a way of handling the situation with Meredith. I was sorely tempted at that minute to tell her to leave, go back to New York to be with her husband. However, she was my sister. I didn't want to take a chance of permanently damaging our relationship.

When I got home, Meredith's door was still closed. I briefly considered knocking and apologizing for losing my temper, but then came to my senses. She was the one in the wrong, sneaking behind my back to talk to that man and putting any chance I could help find Justin's attacker in jeopardy. I fed Bruno, then made a shrimp casserole for dinner. Meredith still hadn't emerged from her room, though I thought the lovely aroma of the casserole would tempt even the most stubborn of people. I ate alone, then left some in a covered dish on the stove for Meredith.

After dinner, I called Lynn to make sure she was home, then I loaded Bruno into the car and we took a ride to her house. I told her about what happened with Meredith and Sunny calling to chew me out.

"Oh, brother. I like your sister, but I can see why you were apprehensive when you learned she was going to visit. I agree that she seems a tad—okay, more than a tad—controlling and opinionated. As far as Sunny Cody is concerned, she'll cool down. Especially since in the past you always have come up with valuable information for her."

"I suppose you're right." I realized I hadn't told her about Meredith and my trip to Rita's Rescue, and that it sounded like this Luc character could be involved in snatching and then selling pets. I filled her in on what we found out. "But Rita says she doesn't have any information on him, and no way to contact him. Justin said he will ask some of his colleagues in the area if they have had any dealings with Rita or know anyone named Luc."

"Have you notified Detective Cody of your suspicions?"

"Maybe I'll wait until I see if Justin finds out any more information I can give her. I have a feeling she is going to want hard facts before she follows up on any more of my tips. If she doesn't just outright arrest me for impeding a police investigation."

Lynn and I chatted for another hour or so, mostly about her art classes and the fact that she had two new clients who wanted paintings done. I was glad to get my mind off the upheaval in my own life. When I got home, Meredith still was nowhere to be seen, but the food was gone from where I left it, and the dish washed and put away. I didn't hear any noise coming from her room, so I assumed she was asleep. I was relieved because I was too tired to deal with the aftermath of our blow-up.

* * *

When I got up for work the next day, I passed Meredith carrying a cup of tea to her room. I said, "Good morning."

She just nodded and went into her room and closed the door.

I fumed for most of the morning. I had made the first overture, meager as it was. The least she could have done was return my greeting. It took a patient who had an infiltrated central line and needed to go to the emergency department to be treated to get my mind off my own problems. I volunteered to cover a few extra patients that day for a coworker who had to attend to a family emergency, so it was a bit later than I had originally planned when I got home.

I had gone over in my head what I wanted to say to Meredith. I would acknowledge that I had lost my temper and could have said things a bit more tactfully, but I would not admit that what I said was wrong. When I got home, her rental car was not in the driveway. I assumed she had decided to run a few errands or had decided to go to the beach. Dark clouds had started to roll in, so I hoped she would come home before the thunderstorm, though.

When Meredith hadn't returned by seven p.m., I decided to peek into her room. It looked like her suitcase was gone, as well as most of her toiletries. She must have gone back to New York to be with Phillip. She never even said goodbye. I checked my phone to see if I'd missed a text or a phone call from her. There were two calls marked "spam likely" and one number I didn't recognize, but nothing from Meredith. I scrolled to her phone number but then paused. No. I would wait. She should be the one to call me to let me know she was back in New York and what her plans were from there.

I sat out in the backyard with Bruno for a while, checking my phone every few minutes, when I was startled by the ringtone.

"Hi. It's me. I missed you today. Long day?" Justin asked.

"Yes." I told him about my fight with Meredith and that she took off back to New York without even letting me know or saying goodbye.

"That's too bad, I'm sorry. Give her a little time, though it sounds like you were right to be upset. However, from what you've told me of your sister, she has you beat in stubbornness, so you may have to be the one to finally start the conversation again."

I knew he was right, but I felt defensive. "But it has always been me who apologized when we had a disagreement. Even when I was little, our parents would make me say sorry first, telling me I should respect my older sister."

"Just think about it for a while. When are Meredith and Phillip going back to England?"

"I don't even know," I said.

"Anyway, the reason I called, besides to tell you how much I missed you today, was to let you know I finally heard back from two of my friends that are with practices in the area around Rita's Rescue. I got conflicting opinions about her and her operation."

I sat up straighter. "What did they say?"

"Bill Harrison said he has treated a couple of dogs from that rescue, strays that had been in bad shape when she got them. He thought Rita did a good job of caring for and getting homes for the animals. But Ricky Fulton said he had a feeling that something was fishy in his dealings with Rita. He couldn't say exactly what put his antenna up, but something just didn't seem right. From what I could tell, he was the one who saw her animals most recently."

"Why did she use two different vet practices, do you think?"

"Good question. I suppose it could have had to do with who could give her an appointment quicker," he said.

"Maybe. Did either of your associates mention knowing a volunteer from the rescue named Luc?"

"No, they said they always dealt with Rita or her daughter."

I remembered the teen we had seen at the front desk when Meredith and I first got to Rita's. "All right, thanks. I still don't think I have enough information that I can go to Sunny Cody with this. Especially since I am forbidden to even do more digging."

"Maybe you should remind her that it was your digging that helped get Walter back to his rightful owners," Justin said. "If you hadn't followed up on the tip from the groomer, who knows where Walter would have ended up."

It made me feel good to hear him praising me for getting involved in Sunny's investigation. In the past, we had butted heads over my getting involved in anything to do with the police. I smiled and said, "Thanks for saying that. Too bad the Dolans couldn't give the police any information on the man who returned their dog for the reward. It would seem like they would have something besides a vague description to give them." I had a thought. "I have another favor to ask," I said. "The Dolans promised when they offered the reward that there would be no questions asked of whoever returned the dog. I'm sure they didn't want to scare them off by getting the police involved. They might be willing to give any information they have to someone they trust, though. Would you consider calling the Dolans and talking to them yourself? Maybe they'll tell you something they didn't mention to the police."

Justin was quiet on the other end of the call for a moment, then said, "You could be right about them being willing to talk to someone not in law enforcement. I'll get their number from Traci at the front desk at work tomorrow and give it a try."

That night, I thought over again my argument with Meredith, but still felt determined to let her make the first move at reconciliation. I was sticking to my newfound resolve to stand up to her. Plus, I was hurt that she hadn't thought to tell me she planned to leave or even said a perfunctory "goodbye."

Chapter Twenty-Four

Justin called me at lunchtime the following day to let me know he had gotten in touch with the Dolans. "You were right. Mr. Dolan sounded a little hesitant at first when I asked if they had any information at all on the good Samaritan, but then I made up a story about Reddy Vet being grateful that their dog was returned to them. I said we wanted to give him some type of recognition. He said that, as promised in their reward offer, they didn't ask for a name or contact information, but the guy got a call while he was there. Mr. Dolan said whoever called was speaking loudly, and he thought he heard whoever it was call him 'Lou' when he answered."

I could feel my heart rate increase. "Or, it could have been 'Luc,' don't you think?"

"Yes, could have been." Justin sounded excited, too. "You're planning on taking that information to Detective Cody, aren't you? Promise me you won't try to find this Luc yourself, okay?"

"I won't. I'll let her know what I found out and let her take it from there. Now that it looks like he was the one who "found" the Dolans' dog, it might be enough for her to be willing to look for this Luc herself. I'll stop at the station after work today. Wish me luck."

I was nervous as I drove toward the police station that afternoon. I wasn't sure what kind of reception I was going to get when I showed up saying I had information for her. Sunny had told me before to stay out of her investigations, but this time Meredith's, and by extension, my meddling had caused her a problem. When I got to the station, the officer at the front desk was curt when I asked to speak to Detective Cody.

"She's not available right now, and I don't think she will be for the rest of the afternoon. Leave your name and—"

Just then, Sunny came out from the back of the station, followed by two officers. She scowled at me through the plexiglass in front of the front desk and then she strode out to talk to me. I was right, she didn't seem too pleased to see me. "What are you doing here? Wasn't I clear enough when I told you to stop interfering in our investigation?"

"Yes, very clear. However, I already found out something I think will help, but you ended the call before I could tell you what it was. I think I know who has been stealing people's pets. I suspect he could also be connected to the break-in at—"

She held up her hand. "Fine. Give your information to Officer Welton. We'll look into it when we get a chance. I'm involved in investigating a possible homicide right now, and that takes priority."

Officer Bridges approached Sunny. "They searched the water and shore area again, but still no ID found."

I was listening intently, but the desk officer noticed. "Please step back and wait in one of the chairs over there. Officer Welton will be out shortly to take your statement."

I watched as Sunny and her minions returned to the area at the back of the station. I gave the information I had on Rita's Rescue and Luc to Officer Welton, but she seemed to think it was scanty at best.

"So, you don't have any more information on this person other than he is named Lou or Luc, is shady looking, and seems to have good luck finding stray animals?" She sighed, "Okay, I'll make note of it, see if any more complaints come in about this individual. Right now, this doesn't give us much to go on." She thanked me for coming in, but I could see Luc and whatever he was involved in were sinking to the bottom of their list. When I left the station, it seemed like the place was in frantic motion, but none of it seemed connected to finding the person responsible for what happened to the Feldmans or Justin.

When I pulled into my driveway, I could see my neighbor Karen was out in her front yard talking to Hannah Foster, another neighbor. Karen waved me over.

"Did you hear? A family found a body late this morning at Hammonasset. It washed up on the other side of the jetty at Meigs Point."

That must be what Sunny was talking about. She made it sound like they were sure it was a homicide. "Did you hear anything else about it? Man or woman?" I knew they didn't have an ID yet, but I felt a quick lurch in my stomach. No. Meredith had gone back to New York City.

Hannah said, "I think I heard it was a man, but I'm not sure. The son of the woman who found it plays baseball with my son, but I don't want to bother her yet. I'm sure she is shaken up by it. We have a game tonight, and if she's there, I'll talk to her then."

"Okay. Thanks for telling me about it. It's so sad. If there was foul play, let's hope they find the murderer quickly," I said.

"There have been way too many violent crimes around here lately; the cops better get on the ball and find out who is responsible. I'm calling the town hall and demanding they light a fire under the police department." Karen looked from one to the other of us.

I said goodbye and went into the house. Hannah said she heard the body was that of a man, but I decided to call Meredith anyway. This silent treatment we were giving each other was ridiculous. My call went to voicemail. I left a message for her to call me, hoping it wasn't that she was ignoring me, just out at some function with Phillip.

I felt restless, not sure what I wanted to do next. I walked Bruno, then called Lynn to see if she was free to meet me for dinner somewhere, but she was teaching a class and then meeting a prospective client who wanted a portrait of her dog done. I made a quick sandwich for dinner and then turned on the television to catch the news. The lead story was that the Madison police were working with the Environmental Conservation State Police on investigating a possible homicide of a male found at Hammonasset Beach State Park. No ID had been determined, and anyone with information about the case should contact their local police department. At least it was confirmed that it was a man. I blew out a breath in relief.

Meredith did not return my call before bedtime, but at least now I was sure she was either busy or still sulking. However, I slept restlessly, causing poor Bruno to curl up in one corner at the foot of the bed.

Chapter Twenty-Five

I was off the next day, but got up early anyway, unsure of what to do. The police were obviously not going to act on the information I gave them any time soon. I could go back again to Rita's Rescue to see if I could speak to Rita's teenage daughter. She might have some information on Luc that her mother wasn't willing to share. The two young women volunteers might be there also. It's possible they neglected to call if Luc showed up again while they were there.

The more I thought about it, however, I was unsure whether it was a good idea to speak to someone at Rita's again about Luc. I would be breaking my word to Justin that I wouldn't look for him myself. Also, I'd reamed out Meredith for going off on her own to talk to Mr. Brazen when the police were handling it; wouldn't I be doing the same thing myself if I went back to Rita's? I felt restless, so I grabbed Bruno's leash from the hook by the door and took him for a walk, then when we got back, I started cleaning the house. I was clearing some of the interesting-looking shells I'd collected, some coins, and hair fasteners from the top of my dresser when I found the piece of metal I found at Dandyboy Farm. It was crusty with dirt and worn out where it must have rubbed against another dog tag or something. I tried rubbing away the dirt and reading what it said, but could only make out a few numbers and letters. My guess, based on the tags Bruno wore, was that it was an old rabies vaccination tag from one of Mr. Phelps's dogs. It could also be from one of the stolen dogs that the crooks were selling from there after Mr. Phelps died. Either way, it didn't offer up any clues as to who those people were or where they were now. I put the tag into the crystal dish on my dresser top, where I kept my souvenirs.

It was late morning by now, and I still hadn't heard back from my sister. I picked up my phone to call her again. Just as I was about to make the call, my phone rang in my hand.

"Hi. Are you busy?" It was Justin.

"No. I was about to try to reach Meredith again. I called her last night and left a message for her to call me back, but I haven't heard from her."

"So, you haven't spoken to her at all since she went back to New York?"

"No."

"I think you're right to reach out to her again, then. After that, it's up to her to respond." When I didn't reply, he went on, "I was wondering if you could do something for me. I need some forms for my medical insurance from my office at Reddy Vet. I called Traci and told her where to find them, and she'll have them at the front desk. Would you mind picking them up for me?"

"Of course. I'll go get them in a few minutes and bring them to you later." I remembered our interrupted conversation of a few days ago. "You never told me what you wanted to talk to me about the other day. What was it?"

He laughed and said, "I'll tell you later, in person."

"Thanks. Now I'm really curious what this is about."

He just laughed again in response.

I tried my sister after the call with Justin, but again it went to voicemail. If she hadn't called back by the time I got back from picking up the forms at Reddy Vet, I planned to call her husband, Phillip. I was sure he could talk some sense into her.

Bruno gave me his sad look as I prepared to leave for Reddy Vet. I had a few errands to run besides picking up the forms Justin needed, so I had to leave him home for the time being. "Sorry. You can come with me later when we go to see Justin and Jasper." He followed me to the door and sat quietly watching me as I left.

Just as I was about to pull out of my driveway, I got a call. Phillip's name came up on the display.

"Hello, Mel. I was wondering if you have spoken to Meredith today?" I always marveled at how deep and melodious my brother-in-law's voice was.

"No. Will you please tell her to call me? I've tried to call so we can work things out, but she hasn't returned my calls."

He was silent for a beat. "What do you mean, call you? Isn't she still staying with you?"

"No. I thought she went back to New York." I felt a sudden chill. "We had a disagreement two days ago, and I thought she left in a huff."

"She told me about the disagreement, but she didn't come here. She does have an old friend from her university years who lives not far from you. I suppose it's possible she went to stay with her for a few days." He was trying to sound reasonable, but I could hear the concern in his voice. "I can't remember her friend's name, however. Susan or Sarah, maybe?"

I had never heard her mention a Susan or a Sarah while she was here. I didn't want to alarm him, so I said, "You could be right and she's with an old friend, but I'll keep trying to get in touch with her. You try again, too, and let me know if you hear from her."

"Yes, will do."

As soon as I ended the call, I headed to the police station. It was the same officer as the last time I was there behind the desk. "I would like to report a missing person, please." My voice shook as I stated my reason for being there. "I'm a friend of Detective Cody. Is she available to take my statement?"

The officer looked sympathetic. "Sorry. She's tied up with a homicide case right now. I'll get someone else who can talk to you."

I paced as I waited. Meredith was stubborn, and she seemed really offended when I said she was not being helpful in finding the people responsible for what happened to Justin and Ernie Feldman. Maybe she was just licking her wounds at an old friend's house, but what if she had done something reckless? I quickly pushed away any thoughts of my own reckless behavior in the past year. Officer Weldon, the officer I spoke to the previous day, came out and led me into an interview room.

"What can we do for you today, Ms. Bass?" She seemed less than enthused to see me again.

I told her my sister was missing and gave her Meredith's description. I explained that she was staying with me while her husband was in New York on business, and that we had had a disagreement a couple of days ago, and that I thought she had gone back to be with her husband, but he hadn't seen her. "I'm very worried since Meredith hasn't returned calls from either her husband, Phillip, or me."

"Can I ask what your disagreement was about?"

I hesitated for a moment. "She thought she was helping by speaking to someone we thought was connected to the break-in at Reddy Vet. Detective Cody was less than pleased, and we got into an argument about what she did."

Officer Weldon gave me a cold stare. "I thought Detective Cody made it very clear to you and whoever was 'helping' you that you should stop interfering."

"She did. But I don't know if my sister took that directive to heart."

"I followed up on the information you gave me yesterday. I found nothing suspicious at Rita's Rescue, and Rita Mallard says she doesn't know much about this Luc you mentioned, and that he hasn't shown up to volunteer in a while."

"But..."

"Look, your sister is an adult. It could be she has a friend in the area you aren't aware of, or maybe she just wanted some alone time and is staying somewhere at the beach or gambling at one of the casinos."

The idea of my sister gambling was ridiculous, but then I'd never suspected she would be interested in crime-solving either. "She does have an old acquaintance in the area, but I don't have her name, and I don't think that is where she is, anyway. I'm afraid something terrible has happened to her."

Officer Weldon sighed. "Right now, all available officers are responding to a Silver Alert. Since you say your sister is an adult with no known impairments, we will look for her as soon as we can. In all likelihood, she will turn up on her own eventually. Try not to worry." She put away her note pad. "We'll be in touch if we have any information. Be sure to notify us if you finally hear from her. Have a good day." She rushed from the room.

In spite of Officer Weldon's reassurances, my feeling that Meredith had gotten into some kind of trouble intensified. I could believe she would be upset enough not to answer my calls, but not that she would ignore Phillip's. I tried to think of where Meredith would go if she was insistent on continuing our investigation of the crimes. The last place we got any information at all was at Rita's Rescue. It was a place to start. I could ask if Meredith had by chance been there to speak to them again. I had a feeling that Sunny had enough on her plate right now, so my 'interfering' as she called it wouldn't be her top priority. Besides, if she complained about me going to Rita's to ask questions again, I could explain I was just trying to find my sister.

When I got to the rescue, Rita was behind the desk. She immediately scowled as she recognized me. "If you're back to ask about Luc, you can just save your time. I haven't seen him, and don't want him back here anymore either. Also, I don't appreciate you going to the police and insinuating something illegal is going on here. I run a legit place!" She slammed down some papers she had been holding.

"I didn't come—"

"I don't care why you came. Leave." She headed toward the back of the building.

"Sorry. Mom's a bit on edge lately."

I jumped at the voice behind me. I hadn't heard anyone else come in. Rita's daughter walked around to stand behind the desk. "Like she said, we haven't seen that guy around here for a couple of days."

"I didn't come to ask about him. I was going to ask if there was a woman who may have come to ask about him, though. Forties, looks a little like me? You might remember her from when she was with me the other day." I was really hoping she had remembered both Meredith and me.

She started nodding even before I finished speaking. "Yeah. She came in the other day asking more questions about Luc. Lucky mom wasn't here because, as you can tell, he isn't exactly her favorite subject right now. I told her I didn't know that much about him, like my mom said before, and I told her we hadn't seen him lately. She seemed disappointed." The girl smiled then, "I thought I remembered her saying the first time she was here that she wanted to adopt a dog. I offered to show her the litter of cute puppies that just came in. She thanked me but said she was going to have to hold off on getting a dog right now."

I was at least right about her coming to talk to someone at Rita's Rescue again, but had no idea where to look next. "Thank you. If you see her again or Luc shows up, will you call me?" I gave her my number.

"Oh, yeah, one other weird thing. When the lady you were asking about was leaving, the vet who does some of our spay and neuters came in. They seemed to know each other. I couldn't hear what they were saying, but they talked for a few minutes."

I got an odd feeling. "What's this vet's name?"

"Dr. Anthony. She comes every once in a while. When she does, she doesn't charge us for the work."

"Do you mean Stella Antonio?"

"Yeah, her. After she talked to the other woman, Dr. Antonio got a call and left. She said she would come back another day, though."

I hurried to my car and headed toward Reddy Vet to speak to Stella. I prayed that Meredith had given her some idea of where she was headed next.

Chapter Twenty-Six

When I got to Reddy Vet, the parking lot was unusually full, and I noticed two people walking their dogs around different sections of the grounds. One woman kept looking eagerly toward the practice's entrance as if willing one of the receptionists to come out and call her in for her dog's appointment. I entered to find four more people waiting in the waiting room, one with a yowling cat in a carrier. Traci was on the phone, and the other receptionist, Andrea, was trying to help a client with a nervous-looking boxer mix who was making every effort to make a break for the door.

"Buster, no! Stay." The woman's voice was strained as she said to Andrea, "How much longer? We had an appointment with Dr. Antonio for over half an hour ago!"

"I'm so sorry. Dr. Reddy will see Buster next. Dr. Antonio is out of the office today."

Traci was making one phone call after another, and I overheard her asking clients if they could reschedule their appointments for later in the week. "Okay. Tomorrow at eleven a.m.. Thank you for understanding." She shook her head at me as she hung up the phone. "What a mess." She lowered her voice to a whisper, "Dr. Antonio never showed up this morning, and poor Dr. Reddy has been trying to handle the patient load all by himself. I've been able to reschedule several of her appointments, but it was too late to reach a lot of them. We're pretty backed up now. I even had to refer a few urgent cases to two veterinary practices in Branford."

"Did Stella Antonio call to say why she wasn't coming in?" I couldn't believe she would be so inconsiderate. Just as he promised, Justin was able to use a cane to walk now. He planned on coming in for two hours to see patients on a couple of days the following week, but if he knew what was going on today, he would want to rush in to help. I really didn't think he was ready for that.

"No. I tried calling her a couple of times, but the call goes right to voicemail."

That sounded concerning, but I still felt more annoyed than worried. I was especially upset because I was counting on her to give me any information she might have on where Meredith was off to after she saw her at Rita's Rescue.

Traci said, "Yesterday, I went into one of the exam rooms to tell Dr. Antonio that the supplies she ordered had arrived, and I overheard her on the phone. She told whoever it was she would be there in an hour. I asked her if she wanted me to go ahead and stock the supplies she ordered, but she said no, they were for a former long-time client of hers." Traci looked over at Andrea. "I know her seeing a patient like that is against our policy, but I didn't feel it was my place to remind her of that. Anyway, she took the box of supplies and left. She never mentioned not coming in today. Plus, she knows with Dr. McKenzie still out...anyway, I hope everything is all right."

"When you heard her on the phone, did you think she was talking to someone from her previous practice?" Why didn't she just have her former patient come to Reddy Vet if they wanted her to continue to follow their pet? "Where did she work before she came to work here?"

A very harried-looking Shauna came out to show Buster back into an exam room, and Traci asked, "Do you remember the name of the practice Stella Antonio came from?"

"I think she said it was Beckwith Animal Hospital, or something like that," Shauna said over her shoulder as she followed Buster and his mom down the hall.

That jogged my memory. The part of the name I could make out on the dog tag I found at Dandyboy Farm was "Be and it ended in "in' or "ih."

I took a wild stab, "You haven't seen Meredith, my sister, in the past couple of days, have you?"

The women looked at each other. "No. I don't think so."

It was a slim lead, but if I could talk to Stella, she might remember something, anything, to help me find Meredith.

I thanked Traci and Andrea and turned to leave.

"Oh. I almost forgot. Justin said to give these to you." Traci held out a manila folder toward me.

"Oh, yes, thanks." I had forgotten the forms he needed for insurance. Once I got into my car, I immediately googled Beckwith Animal Hospital, but got no matches. Alternate suggestions were Bounty Animals in Torrington, Bethany Animal Hospital in Bethany, and Breckwin Veterinary Clinic in Woodstock. That last could be the vet Mr. Phelps used to oversee the care of his dogs and verify the health status of the puppies to buyers. It sounded as if that was also the practice where Stella Antonio used to work. I took a chance and called the number listed for Breckwin Veterinary Clinic.

"Hi. My name is Melanie Bass. I bought my dog from a place called Dandyboy Farm a year ago. I'm ready to offer him for stud services, and I need his past medical records. My vet said he never received them. Am I correct that Mr. Phelps used one of your veterinarians, a Dr. Antonio?" I crossed my fingers.

"Dr. Antonio is no longer with us, but if you can give me the name and identification number on your bill of sale, I can look up his records and send them to your vet."

To cover my lie, I leaned on my horn and gasped. "Oh no! I'm sorry. I'm driving, and there's been an accident up ahead. I'll need to call you back with that info when I get home." I ended the call. Why hadn't Stella mentioned that she was familiar with Dandyboy Farm when Mrs. Graves said she bought Walter there?

I started my car and headed toward Woodstock. I would try Breckwin Vet first, see if there was a patient they knew of who Stella still cared for from her former practice, or if there was someone with whom she had developed a connection and might still be in contact with. I was a little worried now why Stella hadn't shown up for work. If she did have a connection with

Dandyboy Farm, what if she somehow stumbled upon the people who were involved in the break-in and they found out she worked at Reddy Vet now?

My thoughts were interrupted by the sound of an incoming call. It was Phillip again.

"Have you found out Meredith's whereabouts yet? I tried her again, and still no answer. I wonder if she has somehow lost her phone."

I was sure that even if she lost her phone, she would have found a way to contact Phillip. "No, I haven't found out where she is yet," I said. "But I spoke to someone who saw her after she left my house, and I'm following up with someone else who might know where she went from there." A bit of a leap, but I didn't see the point of panicking him yet. "Just to be safe, I did notify the police that we don't know where she is. They seemed confident she would show up on her own when she was ready."

"Notifying the police was a good plan. I'm sure she must be with her friend, though. Wish I could remember her blasted name." He paused. "If you do track her down, please call me right away."

When I got to Breckwin Vet, I was impressed with how large the practice appeared to be. I had expected a small one-story clinic, but the building had three wings, a tree-lined path for walking pets, and an awning-covered walkway to the front door. It certainly looked like an upscale practice that employed several veterinarians. Justin said Stella had only worked here for a little over a year and a half, and I wondered now why she had left such a prosperous-looking practice.

When I went inside, I was amazed at the size and setup of the waiting room. There were several small walled-off areas with a covered bench in each little cubicle so owners could keep their pets away from other clients if they wished. A very efficient looking practice, but certainly not as warm and welcoming as Reddy Vet. I had prepared a story to tell the people at the front desk, explaining why I needed to find Stella. There were three receptionists behind the large mahogany desk. I went over to the first one to call out, "May I help you?"

"Yes, I believe Dr. Stella Antonio used to work here. I'm from Reddy Vet, where she practices now, and I have some supplies she asked me to bring to her. She said she was seeing a client she used to treat when she practiced here, but I'm afraid the service is poor, and her phone cut out when she gave me the address. I haven't been able to get her again. I was hoping you might know the name and address of the client she is seeing."

The woman behind the desk gave me an exasperated look. "I'm sorry, but I can't help you. If Dr. Antonio continued to see a patient after she left, I have no idea who it might be."

The receptionist sitting next to her piped in, "The only client I ever remember Stella consistently following was Andy Phelps's kennel." She looked up at me. "Poor Mr. Phelps passed away several months ago, and Dr. Antonio left the practice shortly afterward. I don't remember anyone else asking specifically for her since then."

"Thank you. I guess I'll just keep trying to reach her to find out where I'm to meet her." So, Stella had a strong connection to Dandyboy Farm. I was beginning to get a strange feeling about the association. I decided to take a ride to the kennel again. I thought about the last time I had been there with Lynn. As if she could read my thoughts, just then I got a call from her.

"Hi. Any word from Meredith yet?"

"No. I don't know where she is, either."

"What do you mean? I thought she went back to New York."

I fought to keep my voice from breaking, "Phillip called this morning. She's not with him, and he doesn't know where she is. He thought she was still staying with me. I've notified the police, but they said she's an adult and will return when she's ready. I don't have a good feeling, though. I'm worried she's in trouble!'

"What are you going to do? Where are you now? I can meet you, and we can figure something out."

I told her about my hunch that she went back to Rita's Rescue to find Luc, and that while she was there, she ran into Stella Antonio. "I found out Stella used to be the vet Andy Phelps used for Dandyboy Farm."

"No way!"

I explained that Stella said she was going to treat a former client yesterday, and how she never showed up for work today. "She's the last person I know who spoke to Meredith before she disappeared. I need to find Stella and ask if Meredith told her anything about where she was going. Also, maybe Stella told Meredith something that could help me figure out where to find her. I'm going to check out Dandyboy Farm now to see if Stella is there and has been using the place to see former clients."

"Wait for me! You can't go alone. I'm only about a half hour away. I wa…meeting…a cl…"

As if to bear out my lie about the poor phone reception, Lynn's call started to break up. "What? I can't hear you." My phone went dead. Lynn had a valid point, but I wouldn't be alone. If I was correct, I'd find Stella at Dandyboy and get some answers from her about what she and Meredith spoke about. Also, I had questions about why if she was familiar with Dandyboy Farm, she failed to mention it when we connected Walter the labradoodle to the place. Also, why was she seeing an old client there? Even if it was a dog bought from Phelps, why not go to the owner's home or have them come to Reddy Vet to see her? I thought again about the possibility that if Stella had gone to see her client there, she could have found the criminals instead.

When Lynn and I went to Dandyboy Farm, it looked like if the criminals who broke into Reddy Vet were using it, they had since left. The State Police came to the same conclusion. But what was to say they hadn't come back again? I was only minutes away from Dandyboy. I could just do as the mysterious car did when we were there—drive up to see if it looked like Stella might be there, then leave if I didn't see her car or if something looked suspicious. I gripped the wheel tightly as I drove up the rutted driveway. I wasn't sure if I wanted to find another vehicle there or not.

Chapter Twenty-Seven

I let out my breath as I reached the barn/kennel. It didn't look as if anyone was here after all. I drove past the farmhouse and didn't see anything there either at first. Then I noticed the front end of a black car that was pulled behind the house. Stella drove a black BMW. I had seen it parked in the practice's lot many times. I stopped my car and got out to get a better look. My first impression was wrong. There were two cars. There was a tarp thrown over one of them, but a red fender peeked out from under one corner. I pulled back the tarp to get a better look. It was a red Mustang convertible. Meredith's Dooney and Bourke handbag, her sunglasses, and a cell phone were on the rear seat. I ran up the steps to the house and banged on the door. "Meredith? Are you in there? Stella!" There was no answer, and the door was locked. I couldn't come up with any reason why Meredith should be with Stella, but I was equally relieved to find her, and angry that she had worried us so.

I walked toward the building holding what looked to me like newer kennels than the ones I remembered seeing in the converted barn, and called out again, "Meredith? It's me, Melanie. Where are you?"

As I approached the kennels, I thought I heard a noise coming from inside the building. The door was unlocked, and I opened it cautiously. Part of the building was comprised of a long, narrow room with a window on either end. It was dim inside and stuffy. I noticed a window air conditioner that looked like it hadn't been in use since Dandyboy closed down. There were ten inside/outside dog enclosures jutting from the inside room, and I heard mumbling and thumping coming from the two enclosures at the far end.

I followed the noise and found Meredith sitting on the floor of one of the enclosures with a gag in her mouth. Her hands and feet were tied, and she was secured by a leash wrapped around her neck and attached to a hook on the side wall of the cubicle. There was an empty water bottle and a few granola bar wrappers scattered around her. Next to her in the end enclosure was Stella, also bound and gagged. I yanked open the door to Meredith's enclosure first and pulled the gag from her mouth. "Meredith! Are you all right? What happened?"

"Thank heaven you found us. Get me loose!" I undid her bindings, and Meredith struggled to get to her feet. I moved on to free Stella.

As soon as I pulled the gag from Stella's mouth, she said, "Hurry up! We need to get out of here before they get back!"

It took me a moment to get over the shock of finding them like that. "What are you doing here? Who did this to you?"

Stella answered, "Some people you don't want to mess with. They'll be back soon, so we need to get out of here." She looked genuinely frightened. "Come on!" She ran toward the door.

As we followed her, Meredith said to Stella, "Who was that man? The one who made me drive here? Do you know him?"

I chimed in, "Yes, why *are* you here?"

"I don't have time to explain." Stella felt the pocket of her jeans. "Damn, they took my keys." She looked at Meredith.

I could hear my sister's voice shaking. "He made me drive, but took my keys when we got here. He had a gun."

"We'll take my car," I said.

We had just taken a few steps toward the farmhouse where our cars were parked when I saw a dust cloud and heard the approach of a car racing up the driveway.

"Quick. This way." Stella veered toward the barn. We had just ducked inside when it sounded like the car drove a short distance past us and stopped. "They'll probably go into the house first, then send someone to check on us in the kennel," she whispered.

I looked around the barn for a place we could hide. They would eventually find us if we tried to hide in any one of the kennels here, which were converted horse stalls with half doors. The grooming area had no door at all.

"Come on. There's a small storeroom on the left at the back where Phelps kept supplies and dog food." Stella motioned us to follow her.

I took out my cell phone to see if I had any service yet. I had half a bar. I had just managed to punch in "9" When a voice behind me said, "Drop the phone. Turn around. All of you."

The guy standing in the doorway was huge, and he had a gun. He looked from Stella to Meredith, then at me. "Who is this now? This is getting to be quite a party." He spoke with a slight Slavic accent. He pointed his gun at me. "What are you doing here?" Then he said to Stella, "Did you tell her about this place?"

"No. I found—" I was interrupted as two more men came into the barn. One of them looked familiar, but I wasn't sure where I'd seen him before.

Stella suddenly seemed more angry than afraid. "Gregor, thank God you're here. That idiot Trent tied me up and left me here." She glared at one of the men behind Gregor. "You think they weren't going to miss me when I didn't show up at work today?" She returned her attention to Gregor. "I'd like to know what's going on. Why did you ask me to meet you here anyway?" She craned her neck as if to look behind the three men standing there. "And who's this other guy? Where's my brother? What happened to Luc?"

I gasped and looked at her. Luc was her brother?

Stella started to move toward Gregor, but he aimed the gun at her, motioning her to move back to stand with us.

He shrugged. "Luc's been replaced." He tipped his head toward the man who I was sure I'd seen somewhere before. "He really wasn't a very strong swimmer. Though, I admit, it is hard to swim with a bullet in your chest."

I thought I saw a flicker of surprise in the eyes of Luc's replacement, but he quickly recovered his unreadable expression.

Stella burst into tears. "No!" She started toward him again, but the second man also pulled a gun, stepped in front of her, and pushed her back to stand with us again. "Why?"

Gregor sighed. "He was getting sloppy. Leading people a bit too close to the operation." He motioned toward Meredith and me. Then he turned his attention back to Stella. "As you may have guessed, you also are no longer needed. Much of this is your fault, anyway. Trent called about his poor, sick dog as instructed. Things would have gone smoothly if you had been where you were supposed to be, if you had followed the plan."

"I tried. I told you, the answering service was supposed to notify me the night of the break-in. I didn't hear from them, so I thought plans had changed."

The one I assumed was Trent had been standing silently up until now. "Gregor, I'm gonna go look outside again. See if there is anyone else we didn't expect to find here." He wiped his forehead with the back of one hand. "Besides, it's hot in here. I need some air."

I noticed the hand he wiped away the perspiration with was bandaged, and he looked a little pale, as if he wasn't feeling well. After he left, Gregor said, "All of you, go sit over there." He motioned toward one of the dog pens. He turned to his cohort. "Look in that cupboard in the back there and see if there is some kind of rope."

Stella started to whimper. "No. Please. I won't—"

He pointed the gun at her again. "Quiet!"

The other man, whose name I never got, said, "I think I saw some rope on the front porch of the house. I'll check on Trent, too, while I'm out there."

Gregor just grunted and herded us toward one of the kennels. Once we were seated, Gregor closed the wooden half gate and stood guard with the gun in one hand and his phone in the other. He took occasional glances down at the screen as if he was waiting for a call or a text.

I tried to gauge how long he looked away each time. There were three of us, if we rushed him all at once before either of the other men returned…but then he had a gun, and at least one of us would get hurt, and I was afraid it wouldn't be him.

My thoughts were interrupted when Stella whispered to me, "I'm sorry about Justin. No one was supposed to get hurt that night. I was supposed to be there and let them in."

I glared at her. "Sorry isn't going to help us now. And it doesn't make up for what happened to Justin, either."

Meredith hissed at Stella, "You! I felt sorry for you! I trusted you!"

Stella whispered, "Never mind that. We have to find a way to—"

"Stop whispering!" Gregor slammed his hand against the top of the kennel door. Then, he yelled over his shoulder. "Hey! What's taking so long?"

His partner rushed into the barn again, out of breath and waving a coil of rope. "Trent says he just needs another minute."

Gregor motioned toward us. "Start tying—hands first—then feet. Trent can help you when he comes back in."

New guy started with Stella, and while he was working, I started feeling the floor behind me for something I could use as a weapon. I nudged Meredith, and nodding slightly, indicated she should do the same. The kennel we were in was one of the ones that hadn't been used for a while, and it had a lot of debris scattered around. My hand landed on bits of chewed toys, a rock, and a nail. I palmed the nail and then hid it under my butt.

I noticed that even with Gregor yelling at him to hurry up, the guy was taking his own sweet time. Also, I was pretty sure, while he was hunching over Stella, securing her hands behind her back, he was blocking Gregor's view of me for a few minutes. I reached as far back as I could to where the wall of the barn was separated by a half inch or so from the wooden floor. I felt something sharp and longish that I prayed was a pair of scissors that had been used for grooming. I wrenched it free and shoved it under my butt, also, as he moved to tie up Meredith. My sister turned to look at me and mouthed, "What now?"

I swallowed as I realized this was my moment to decide whether I should use the scissors to stab the man before he tied me up. Frightened as I was, I wasn't sure I could actually stab him, let alone stab him before he pulled the gun tucked into the back of his pants. Even if I disabled him, I had no doubt Gregor wouldn't hesitate to shoot me. I was spared any decision about whether to try to use the scissors when Trent burst back through the door, pushing someone in front of him.

"Look what I found!" He shoved Lynn forward, and she stumbled and fell.

The man tying up Meredith bolted upright, a look of shock on his face. He quickly recovered, however, and rushed over and grabbed Lynn by the wrist before she could even cry out. "Over here." As he shoved her down next to me, I heard him whisper, "Quiet. Don't say a word."

Lynn's expression quickly went from disbelief to anger, but she didn't say anything.

Trent called out, "Everything all right, Brian? You know her?"

Brian went back to stand with the other two men. "Naw. I thought maybe I did."

Lynn hissed, "I thought I knew you, too!"

Gregor said, "Hurry up and finish tying them up. Trent, help him. Too many people are showing up; we've got to get out of here."

"What are we going to do with them?" asked Trent.

Gregor looked around the old barn. "This is an old building, abandoned for a while. It wouldn't be impossible that vagrants were camping out here and accidentally set it on fire."

Stella started to cry again, but I felt both Meredith and Lynn stiffen on either side of me. All the fear and indecision I'd felt turned to a cold knot of resolve. Better to at least try to fight back before we were incinerated. I inched out the nail I had hidden, nudged Lynn, and passed it to her. I gripped the handle of the scissors, which were shorter than I thought, but very sharp. Trent bent over me to tie my hands, and I plunged the scissors into his midsection; at the same time, Meredith used her bound feet to kick him hard in the side. He screamed, grabbing his stomach as he rolled away. I heard an "owww!" from Brian as he reared back from Lynn, grabbing his cheek. All this was followed by a loud bang. The wood over my head splintered as Gregor shot.

After that, all hell broke loose. Brian pivoted away from Lynn and fired at Gregor. As Gregor went down, there was the sound of more people bursting into the barn. "Hands up! Police."

I was relieved to see five officers, all heavily armed. Trent rolled around on the floor, the scissors still embedded in his midsection and blood soaking the front of his shirt. One of the officers stood over him, her weapon trained on him. Another officer went to check on Gregor and radioed for two ambulances. Brian said to one of the armed officers, "Help me untie the women, but that one is going in for questioning." He motioned toward Stella.

The officer looked at the blood on Brian's face and said, "Sure. You injured Detective Clemson?"

Brian shook his head, wiping his cheek with his sleeve. "No, I'll be fine."

I didn't wait for the officer to untie Meredith, but did it myself. Then I embraced her and said, "I was so scared."

"I was, too. We did fight back, though, didn't we?" I could feel her trembling.

Blood still oozing from his cheek, Brian approached Lynn, "I'm sorry. I promise I'll explain later." Then he was called away by the officer who seemed to be in charge.

Lynn just stared at him and nodded. I noticed she had taken a couple of steps backward as he approached her.

Lynn, Meredith, and I all hurried to leave the barn and stood off to the side, still too dazed by the events of the past hour to even begin to discuss it. Apparently, Gregor's wound wasn't fatal, at least not yet, as ambulances took both him and Trevor away. Stella continued to sob as she was led away in handcuffs and loaded into one of the police cars.

Finally, one of the officers came over to us. "We'll need all of you to come to the police barracks and make a statement. Would you be able to do that now, while it's all fresh in your memories?"

I didn't think any of what had happened would fade from our memories anytime soon, but we all agreed. I offered to drive both Lynn and Meredith, eager to hear Meredith's explanation of how she ended up at Dandyboy Farm.

"How did you end up here? And why?" I asked her as soon as we got in the car.

She took a few minutes, as if to organize her thoughts. "My feelings were hurt when you claimed I wasn't a help in finding who was responsible for the break-ins. I planned to go back to New York, but as I was packing, I got a call from one of those young women we met when we went to Rita's Rescue.

She said she tried to reach you, but you didn't answer her call."

I suddenly thought of the unknown number who'd called when I was waiting to hear from Meredith.

"She said her friend was looking through her photos on her phone and noticed one she took of one of the dogs that were up for adoption. She noticed Luc was in the background on one of them. She said I had to hurry if I wanted to see it, though, because her friend had to get home soon. I asked if she could send it to me, but her friend said no, she was worried about even getting involved in whatever we were doing. I thought maybe if I could catch her before she left, I could convince her to send the photo to my phone. I thought it would help if we could find out what he looked like. When I got there, the young woman I spoke to said her friend had gotten a phone call from her mother and had to leave. As I was preparing to leave also, I met Stella Antonio, and I told her why I was there. I let her know we thought this Luc might be involved with the people who broke into Reddy Vet. I told her what we had heard about him and that we had gone to the police. She seemed upset. She said she had seen Luc at the rescue and couldn't believe he would do that."

Meredith took a deep breath. "What a fool I was. She made a phone call, then said she would walk out with me. She told me she had an emergency to attend to. Some emergency! As soon as I got to my car, Trent grabbed me and made me drive here at gunpoint." Her voice was choking up. I reached over to rub her shoulder. "I yelled for Stella to call for help when he grabbed me, but now I'm sure she never did. A day or so later, Trent showed up again and shoved her into the kennel next to me."

Lynn piped up. "I want to know exactly how she fits into this whole thing. So, you think this Luc you were looking for was her brother?"

"It sounds like it. He must be the guy who came to see her at work, and Traci and Shauna assumed was her boyfriend." I was also sure, after what Gregor said, that Luc's was the body that washed up on shore at Hammonasset. "There is still a lot I don't understand, though."

Lynn blew out a big breath. "Me too."

* * *

When we arrived at the police barracks, we were shown one by one into an interview room to make our statements about what had happened. Meredith went first, and I told Lynn about finding Stella's and Meredith's cars and then finding them tied up in the newer kennel building. "We didn't have time to get to our cars before the men came back. Stella led us to the barn to hide, but before we could, Gregor and his crew found us." I paused as the memory of Gregor pointing his gun at us washed over me. "Thank you for coming to help me, though I'm sorry you got swept up in this."

Lynn waved away my apology. "Of course I was going to come to find you. I only wish I could have been more help."

"You were pretty handy with that nail," I said.

She laughed. "Speaking of which—" she motioned toward Brian, who was approaching us, a bandage over the left side of his jaw.

He came over to sit next to Lynn. "Once again, I'm sorry. I can't tell you everything, but I owe you some sort of explanation. First, my name isn't Brian, it's Brendan Clemson, and I don't work in finance."

Lynn snorted, "Yeah, I figured that out."

"Gregor Kaminski is behind a growing crime ring in this part of the state. It's taken us a while to infiltrate them, but we were able to get a lead after we arrested some guys involved in another robbery in the area. I'm sorry I couldn't be up front with you when we met and let you know I'm a police officer." He looked over at me. "Thanks to all of you, we're able to get Gregor on several charges now that will keep him locked up for a long time."

Still too shaken to say more, I just nodded and said, "Good."

Lynn didn't give any response to what Brian/Brendan was saying.

After a minute of awkward silence, he stood, and looking at Lynn said, "I hope you'll give me a chance to make it up to you for the deception. Would it be alright if once we get these creeps charged, I call you?"

Lynn hesitated for a few minutes, then said, "You can call. I'll have to think about if I'll answer, though."

He nodded. "That's fair."

Before he walked away, I asked, "What about Stella Antonio? How was she involved?"

He shook his head. "We're still working on that."

I motioned to his bandaged cheek. "I'd check that I'm up to date with my tetanus shot if I was you."

Meredith came out of the room, and Lynn went in next. Meredith looked exhausted after her interview. "Are you all right?" I asked as she sank down in the chair next to me.

"Yes. I feel better having told the police about the ordeal." She reached for my hand, and we sat quietly until it was my turn to be interviewed.

I found myself being a bit defensive at first when questioned about why I got involved in a police investigation, but when I explained that my fiancé had been seriously injured in the break-in at Reddy Vet, and then that my sister was missing and I was looking for her, the officer interviewing me just nodded and continued to take down my statement. I thought of Justin then. How was I going to explain getting myself and both Lynn and Meredith in such dire circumstances?

Before I left the room, I asked again about how Stella was involved and what would happen to her. I was told the investigation was still ongoing. So, basically, no comment.

After we retrieved the cars left at Dandyboy Farm, Meredith followed me back to my house, but Lynn begged off and went straight home to recover. I promised to call her later.

Chapter Twenty-Eight

When we got home, I sat for a while with Bruno in my lap, trying to digest all that had happened and what we had learned. I was beginning to wonder if we would ever get the whole story, though. Meredith went right to her room to call Phillip, and I could hear her voice raised a couple of times in what I took to be a heated explanation.

Gregor had tossed my phone into one of the other kennels after he ordered me to drop it, and it wasn't until I got permission from the police to retrieve it that I saw I had two missed calls and a text from Justin. I really needed to call him and explain what had happened.

I was trying to frame how I was going to break the news to him when he called me.

"What happened? When you didn't come over this afternoon, I tried calling, but you didn't pick up. I called Traci at work, and she said that you had been there and that she had given you the insurance forms. She also told me Stella Antonio never showed up for work today and that you were asking all kinds of questions about her. She said you seemed upset about something. What's going on?"

I realized I hadn't spoken to him since before I found out Meredith was missing. This was a story best told in person, so despite feeling both physically and emotionally drained, I said, "Why don't I come over and I'll explain everything."

"I'm not sure I like what that implies. Are you all right? Did something bad happen?"

"I'll tell you all about it when I get there."

Justin looked me over thoroughly when he answered the door. "You look rung out. Come sit. Do you want a cup of tea?"

"No, thank you." I just wanted to get the retelling of the day's events over and prayed he would have some understanding of how I could get into such a dangerous situation.

I started out by telling him about Phillip's call just as I was leaving to get the forms he wanted, and how it led to Rita's Rescue, then trying to track down Stella to see if she knew where Meredith had gone. "Before you say anything, I did go to the police first. It turns out they were working on finding someone else, an elderly person, and said they would look for Meredith as soon as that person was located. The officer took all Meredith's information, and was sympathetic, but when I mentioned her husband told me she might be with a friend, I think she saw the situation as less urgent. The officer said that I shouldn't worry, that Meredith would turn up on her own."

He mumbled something that sounded like an obscenity, something he rarely did. "I can't believe they wouldn't do something right away when you told them how worried you were. I only wish you had called me. I don't know if there was any way I could have helped, but at least I would have known what was going on."

"I'm sorry, you're right." I took a deep breath, then I told him what happened when I finally found both Meredith and Stella. He didn't respond at first, so I said, "Lucky for us, one of Gregor's henchmen turned out to be an undercover police officer." I couldn't help but give a nervous chuckle, though I was still shaking at the memory, "We put up a pretty good fight on our own, too."

His voice was husky when he finally spoke. "Melanie...I don't know what to say. What if...I don't want to think about what if." He cleared his throat. "Was Meredith all right when you found her? And you weren't injured?"

"No. We are both fine, and so is Lynn. I swear I never would have gone to that place again unless I was looking for my sister. I just felt so helpless when the police wouldn't look for her, and I felt like I had to do something." I fought down a sob. "I know you must be tired of me getting into these situations, but I was both worried and angry at the thought of something happening to Meredith." I began to cry in earnest now, hoping he would forgive my recklessness once again.

Justin put his arms around me, making soothing sounds. When I got myself under control, he held me away so he could look at me. "I don't remember too much about the night I was beaten up at the vet practice, but some things are coming back to me in fragments. I remember I headed toward the rear door when I heard them breaking in. Someone yelled what I thought was 'hello,' but now, from what you've told me, he might have been saying 'Stella.' The first guy I saw was the short one. He was wearing a balaclava, but I could see by his eyes that he looked surprised to see me. He hesitated for just a few beats before he and the others jumped me, but it was enough time that I could have run for the front door and tried to escape. Except, when I saw them, I felt such anger, such a sense of violation that they would force themselves in and were obviously up to no good, that I didn't take that moment to run. I kept rushing toward them. In retrospect, it was a very foolish move. So, I think I understand."

I pulled him into a hug. "Thank you. I guess we both were lucky to survive." We sat quietly for a few minutes, my head on his shoulder. Any last scraps of energy I had were drained away after relating the day's events. I tried to stifle a huge yawn.

"I think I'd better go now, I need to check in with Meredith. She was calling her husband, Phillip, when I left, and I want to hear how that went." I told him I would let myself out and left him with a lingering kiss and a promise to come back the next day.

When I got home, Meredith was in the kitchen. "I've put the kettle on for tea. But if you'd like something stronger, I wouldn't object to joining you."

I shook my head. "No. Tea would be wonderful."

She took another mug down from the cabinet. "I'm going to finish packing and go back to New York for a while to be with Phillip. I'm afraid he didn't take it well when he found out where I was, and what happened."

"I'm worried now he's going to think I'm a bad influence and will forbid you to visit me again." I was joking, but realized it might actually be true.

"He would never! Plus, I know I have to claim the blame for the last bit that happened. You warned me to stop poking my nose into the investigation. I was trying to prove I could be of some help after all, but unfortunately, it didn't work out that way."

"You ended up leading us to the criminals, so in spite of everything that happened, I think you were a great help." I smiled at her, "Plus that kick was professional soccer worthy and really helped disable Trent."

"I have to admit it felt good, too."

As we drank our tea, Meredith told me she planned to come back to see me again once Phillip settled down. "If you don't mind, of course. I bet we can find something to do that won't end in gunfire."

"I'm sure you're right." I laughed again.

I followed Meredith the following day to return her rental car, then took her to the train station. She waved as she got out of my car. "I'll call you."

* * *

The next day's news confirmed that the body found washed ashore at Hammonasset Beach State Park was that of Lucas Nowak.

Even though I had given my statement to the State Police after the incident at Dandyboy Farm, Sunny Cody asked me if I would mind coming in to tell my story to her. She said she still had a few questions. Since I hoped she'd answer a few questions of my own, I was glad to agree.

When I asked her what they had found out about the people involved in the break-in, she warned, "I can only tell you things that are or will soon be public knowledge. Stella Antonio verified that Luc was her brother."

Since their last names were different, I assumed Antonio must be Stella's ex-husband's name.

"Doctor Antonio has been released on bail but will be charged in connection to the break-in at Reddy Vet. She denies, however, having anything to do with the break-in at the Feldmans' or the other burglaries in the area, and currently there is no evidence to connect her to them."

"What about Gregor and Trent? They were involved, weren't they?"

"Yes. I can confirm that there is a long list of charges being brought against them." She cleared her throat. "Now, I have some questions about Rita's Rescue. Could you tell me what you saw when you were there and repeat any information you may have gotten from Rita or the volunteers about Lucas Nowak and the people he was working with?"

I told her what little I knew, and when I asked if they were going to investigate the place regarding the other crimes, Sunny told me she wasn't at liberty to discuss it.

When I went to Justin's the next day, he said he had some information that would interest me. He told me Stella had asked to meet with both him and Martin Reddy to apologize for her part in setting up the break-in at the clinic and for what happened to Justin. He said it was a difficult conversation, but that he ended up feeling a little sorry for her. "She insisted on explaining to Martin and me how she got involved with the break-in. She said that years ago, she and her brother made a practice of finding lost pets and rescuing abandoned ones. However, a few years ago, Luc found out it could be quite lucrative to 'rescue' and resell certain pets. She tried to persuade him to stop, but instead, he got mixed up with people who stole more than dogs and cats. He also got into quite a bit of gambling debt, and that is how he got involved with Gregor."

"She just let him continue on that road?" I asked. "And how did she end up helping him?"

Justin shook his head, "I don't know. She claimed Luc was in big trouble with the people he owed money to and begged her to help him. She agreed, but once she started tipping him off about valuable animals and covering for him, she was in too deep. Gregor threatened both her and Luc if she refused to help. She said she didn't want to go to the police because her part in what Luc and his cronies had been doing would be revealed, and she would lose her license."

"But why break into her own practice?"

"I asked her the same thing. She said again, no one was supposed to get hurt, that they were just supposed to make it look like they broke in, tied her up, and made off with the drugs and any money in the safe. She said Luc was improvising when he took the dogs. I think she thought insurance would cover our losses, so no harm done."

"So, she made sure it happened on a night when the burglar alarm wasn't working, and she would be on call. Except the answering service called the wrong person." I was angry at her all over again. She acted so concerned when Justin got injured, but in fact, it was in large part, her fault. "What happens now? With the practice, I mean?"

I could feel Justin shifting a bit as he tried to get his left leg into a more comfortable position. "Obviously, Stella won't be back. I'm going to start working three four-hour shifts per week until I get all my strength back. We have already put out feelers for two additional vets to join the practice. I think Bill Hobbs might be interested in coming on board permanently."

"Two vets?" I asked.

"Yes. Martin says he really wants to go into full retirement now. He's going to stay to help get whoever we hire settled and into the routine, but then he's done." Justin smiled, "That's one thing I wanted to talk to you about. Martin asked me if I wanted to take over the practice, buy him out. What do you think?"

I considered it for a minute. "I think it's a great idea. You used to have your own practice before you joined his. Reddy Vet is a wonderful veterinary practice, and I know you'll make it even better. Thank you for asking my opinion, but it really is your decision."

He shifted again so he could look directly at me. I could see a mischievous look in his eyes again. "I was hoping the decision would be partly yours. I know I suffered a head injury, and things have been a little foggy for a while, but I swear I keep hearing everyone referring to you as my fiancée."

I could feel I was blushing. "I…well…when you got hurt and—"

"Will you? Marry me? "

I could feel my heart pounding. "Even though I keep getting myself into risky situations?"

"Especially since you keep getting into risky situations. I want you where I can keep an eye on you." He waved at his left leg. "Please don't make me go down on bended knee—I really don't think I can get up again."

I laughed. "Then, yes, I will marry you."

Justin had thought to buy a lovely bottle of champagne, but after our initial toast, the bottle sat neglected as we spent the remainder of the afternoon celebrating our new commitment in other ways.

Chapter Twenty-Nine

After I told Bruno, the first person I called to announce Justin's and my engagement was Lynn.

"I'm coming right over! Break out the champagne or at least open a bottle of wine!" True to her word, she was at my house in fifteen minutes. "Let me see the ring!"

"Justin wants me to pick it out myself. We're going to look on my next day off." After I told her all about how he had proposed, I updated her on what he had said about Stella and how she was involved in the break-in. I was hesitant to ask at first, but said, "Have you spoken to Brian, I mean Brendan, again since the arrest?"

"I refused to take his calls at first, but then I was curious about how a few things went down that day. I asked him how the police were notified, since it wasn't me who called before I got to Dandyboy—something I deeply regret. He said he went out to get some rope to restrain the three of you before I got there, and that gave him the opportunity to call for backup. I asked him what he would have done if the cops hadn't gotten there in time."

"What did he say?" I asked.

"Improvise. And somehow I don't think he was kidding."

I was quiet for a moment. "Do you think you're going to start seeing him again?"

"At first, I wasn't sure I wanted to be involved with someone who would need to keep secrets from me, but then he assured me he wasn't going undercover again anytime soon. I really like him, and he said he genuinely was interested in art and felt we had really formed a connection before all this happened. I decided this time to take a page from your playbook and agree to go out with him again, but we would need to really take it slow."

"I think that's a good idea. I liked him, too. Well, except for when he was pretending to help hold us hostage."

She laughed. "Yes, there is that. I apologized for raking his face with that nail, but he said he knew he totally deserved it."

As we finished our wine, Lynn asked, "What did Meredith say when you told her about your engagement?"

"I haven't told her yet. She's coming to stay with me again for a few days before Phillip's work finishes here and they need to go back to London. I want to tell her in person."

* * *

I wasn't sure why Malcolm asked me to meet him at his place after work a few days later. All I could think of was that he had heard about Justin's and my engagement. But I knew he liked Justin, so I was sure he wasn't going to try to talk me out of marrying him.

When he opened the door, he had a huge smile on his face, and a chunky brown and white form rushed to lick my legs.

"Daphne! How...?" I was grinning as I followed them inside.

"I got a call from the Wrights. They said that things hadn't gone well when they tried to breed Daphne." He reached down to rub her ears. "She didn't seem to enjoy the whole process, and when it finally was...um...successful, she couldn't seem to get pregnant. They decided to sell her and try again with a bitch they saw for sale at a local dog show."

"Poor dog. I mean the one they plan to buy. Daphne is very, very lucky!" I bent to pet her as she came to sit by my feet.

"I'm the lucky one. Anyway, they thought of me right away. I would have paid any amount to get her back, but they said they would sell her to me at a discount since I had taken such good care of her before."

"How *kind* of them," I said. "I can't tell you how glad I am it worked out this way, though."

"Yes, and I'll be contacting that boyfriend—I mean fiancé—of yours to set up an appointment to have her spayed. No more thoughts of ever breeding her again."

***

Meredith called me after my last appointment the following day. "I'm coming tomorrow to stay with you for a couple of days. Phillip will still be in New York for another two weeks or so, but I need to fly home. I heard from Timothy that he and Lena have broken up. He's devastated. I want to be there to support him."

"I'm sorry about Timothy, though I know you didn't approve of his relationship with Lena. I can't wait to see you, however. I have something to show you."

I had decided on an engagement ring very different from the ring Artie gave me when he proposed. It was a small emerald surrounded by tiny diamonds. Meredith noticed the ring as soon as I arrived to pick her up.

"What? Oh my goodness! Wonderful news!"

I was unable to get a word in edgewise for the rest of the afternoon.

"Have you started planning the wedding yet? I think the spring would be a good time; winter in New England is so uncertain. I will need time to settle things at home, then I can fly back, and we can book a place for the reception. Maybe an off-white gown, even though most brides wear white no matter the circumstances these days. Sit down dinner or just hors d'oeuvres and cake? Well, we'll have to talk about it."

I let her ramble on; there was plenty of time for me to let her know I would stand firm on my own ideas about the wedding. For now, I was just glad we were both safe and still speaking.

Acknowledgments

I would like to thank Annette Pompano for providing the spark of an idea for this book. We were discussing having rescue dogs, and she wondered if some rescues weren't really rescues after all. While this is not something either of us really believe, still....

Thank you to my dear friends and writing group partners, Roberta Isleib (Lucy Burdette) and Ang Pompano, for their never-ending patience and wonderful suggestions. You both know the right questions to ask! I also want to thank our morning write-in group: Eileen Doyle, Lisa Hardracker, Louise Talotta, and Ang Pompano for their always informative conversation, support, and encouragement. It is a wonderful way to start a writing session.

I am grateful for having had much experience as a sibling—I am the eldest of eight children. I might just have used a bit of that understanding in writing Melanie and Meredith.

Finally, thank you and much love to my family, especially those in my household—Laura, Josh, Jeffrey, and Rich for their understanding and support.

About the Author

Christine Falcone is the author of the Melanie Bass Mystery series. She has also previously published short stories in publications such as *Imagine, Lancrom Review,* and *Deadfall: Crime Stories by New England Writers.* She is a member of Sisters in Crime and Mystery Writers of America.

Prior to her retirement, she worked for nearly forty years as an RN in a Neonatal Intensive Care Unit. She lives on the Connecticut Shoreline with her family and her dog Toby, who is not nearly as well-behaved as Bruno, the canine in her mystery series. (But he is just as loved!)

AUTHOR WEBSITE:
   www.christinefalcone.com

SOCIAL MEDIA HANDLE:
   Facebook: Christine Falcone

Also by Christine Falcone

Ex'd Out

Borrowed Trouble

Cutting Remarks